ONE OF THE BOYS

ALSO BY JAYNE COWIE

Curfew

ONE OF THE BOYS

JAYNE COWIE

BERKLEY
NEW YORK

BERKLEY

An imprint of Penguin Random House LLC

penguinrandomhouse.com

Copyright © 2023 by Jayne Cowie

Readers Guide copyright © 2023 by Jayne Cowie

BERKLEY and the BERKLEY & B colophon are registered trademarks of
Penguin Random House LLC.

Library of Congress Cataloging-in-Publication Data

Names: Cowie, Jayne, author.
Title: One of the boys / Jayne Cowie.
Description: First edition. | New York : Berkley, 2023.
Identifiers: LCCN 2022051571 (print) | LCCN 2022051572 (ebook) |
ISBN 9780593336809 (trade paperback) | ISBN 9780593336816 (ebook)
Classification: LCC PR6103.O97134 O64 2023 (print) |
LCC PR6103.O97134 (ebook) | DDC 823/.92—dc23
LC record available at https://lccn.loc.gov/2022051571
LC ebook record available at https://lccn.loc.gov/2022051572

First Edition: July 2023

Printed in the United States of America
1st Printing

Book design by Tiffany Estreicher

For all the mothers of boys

Today saw the release of a new documentary, The Violence Gene, which follows a team of scientists in Stockholm who have spent the last ten years studying the genetic makeup of the male prison population. Psychologists have long suspected that there is something different about men who end up in prison, particularly those who commit violent crimes. Difficult childhoods, poverty, and a lack of education have all been blamed. But is that the whole story? Is the problem not in the environment but inside the very DNA of these men? That's something Professor Helmi Nordlund and her team have been trying to find out. Since 1994, they have been tracking the distribution of one particular gene, which they call the M gene, and which can be found in ninety-seven percent of men in prison for violent crime compared to nine percent of the general population.

"It is an exciting discovery," Professor Nordlund says in the trailer for the documentary. "By the time a man is in prison, it is too late. A crime has already been committed. He has ruined his life and, quite often, the lives of many others. But the discovery of the M gene could allow us to identify these men before they go that far, perhaps even in childhood. If we can do that, we could change the future, not just for the men themselves but for all of us."

ONE OF THE BOYS

All she'd ever wanted was to protect her son. That was it. To do her job as his mother and do it well. The first time she had held him in her arms, she had promised she would always take care of him. She would never let anyone hurt him. She would keep him safe from the world, a world that hated boys, that tested them at birth, and that punished them for crimes they might never even commit.

Failure had been inevitable in hindsight. All the signs had been there. His birth, for example, had been a complete disaster. The early months of exhaustion and struggle and fear that she would never be able to love him the way she wanted to. And as he'd grown older, all the poor decisions she'd made and the lies she'd told everyone, including herself.

But none of it came even close to what the woman opposite her had done.

They were separated by the breadth of the table and a sheet of Perspex made cloudy by too much cleaning, and it felt like she was looking at her through water. In a strange way, it helped. It made the woman seem farther away and not quite real. "Why did you do it?"

"I didn't have a choice," she replied. That familiar voice, once so brash and full of life, took up hardly any room at all.

"Of course you had a choice!" Her nose was running, a sure sign that she was on the cusp of bursting into tears. She hadn't brought tissues. She didn't have anything apart from the sleeve of her white cotton blouse. She'd been forced to leave her bag in a locker by the entrance. "You didn't have to be a coward. You could've faced up to the truth a long time ago. This is what the test is for. Identifying dangerous boys before they hurt anyone. If you'd just . . ."

"Just what?" Lank strands of hair hung lifelessly around the woman's cheeks. She'd lost even more weight over the past month, her cheeks sinking back into her skull, and when she shifted in her seat, she seemed entirely concave, as if her body was folding in on itself. "Labeled him as dangerous from birth? Let the world treat him badly when he'd done nothing to deserve it?"

"At least then we would have known. We could have helped him."

For the first time, the other woman looked at her properly. Her eyes were flat. A ghost of a smile played across her mouth. "I did help him."

"No, you didn't. You hid from the truth. You decided that it didn't matter." She didn't know why she was so upset by it. Given the circumstances, it was the least of her problems, but it felt like the end of the world. Even now, after everything that had happened. So much pain had been caused. So many lives destroyed. "You always thought you were a better mother than me. But you're in here and I'm not."

"You should be." She leaned forward, her nose almost pressing against the screen, her mouth twisted in fury. "You're hardly an innocent party in all this."

"I would never have done what you did! Never!"

The anger vanished. The woman sat back, folded her arms, and laughed. It was a cruel, unpleasant sound. "Keep telling yourself that," she said. "But we both know the truth. You'd have done it in a heartbeat if you'd thought it would help him."

She couldn't stand it any longer. She got to her feet and hurried to the door, legs trembling. It was only as she reached it that she stopped, took a breath, turned. "Commit murder, you mean? I don't think so."

Not until she was outside did she realize she was crying. Because she knew, deep down, that it was true.

CHAPTER ONE

‖‖‖ BEA

Eighteen years ago

> GSK has announced today that they have developed a new
> noninvasive test for the M gene, which requires only a cheek
> swab and gives a result in forty-eight hours. Current testing
> requires a blood sample and can take several weeks, with a
> second test often being needed due to inconclusive results. It
> is thought that the NHS will begin offering the swab test to
> parents of newborn boys by the end of the year.

Like many things in her life, motherhood came as something of a shock to Bea Mitchell. She hadn't planned it,
she wasn't prepared for it, and it was obvious from the start
that she had no idea what she was doing. She was twenty-
three, unmarried, and hadn't even realized she might be
pregnant until she was almost four months gone and her
jeans wouldn't fit anymore, and even then she'd spent almost
a week thinking it was the cream doughnuts she couldn't
seem to stop stuffing in her face. And now, nine months

gone, peeing every five minutes, and barely able to dress herself, it seemed she still hadn't figured it out.

"You've come too early," the midwife said. "We can't admit you until you're in established labor, and that could
take hours. Go home."

The woman walked off, stiff-backed, before Bea could
say anything else. Bea could feel her brain slowing down.
Her thoughts wouldn't come together. The air inside the
building was too heavy, too hot. She turned and waddled
back outside into the cold. It had started to rain, huge chilly
droplets bouncing off the pavement, the road, her head. She
wasn't wearing a coat because the one she had wouldn't fasten over her belly, and the only shoes she could still get on
were her flip-flops.

Her boyfriend, Alfie, stood beside her and sparked up a
cigarette with a trembling hand. He'd stopped smoking
when she'd found out that she was pregnant. She hadn't even
known that he had cigarettes on him. "What should we do?"

Bea pressed her hand flat against the wall and leaned all
her weight on it, digging her nails into the gritty stone as
she breathed her way through a particularly sharp contrac-
tion. "I don't know."

"We should probably go home," Alfie said. "Right? There's
no point hanging around here when you're not actually in labor yet. You heard what that midwife said. We can always
come back later." He looked even paler than usual, head buried inside the hood of his parka, two days' worth of stubble
darkening his chin. The end of the cigarette glowed as he
sucked on it.

"Right," Bea said. They walked around to the front of the hospital and had the bus stop in sight before Bea knew that she couldn't make it. It didn't matter that she wasn't in labor yet, that it might be hours before she was. She couldn't get on the bus, sit on the hard, cramped seat, leaning into the corners, bouncing over potholes. She just couldn't.

"You go on," she said to him. "I'll stay here. I'll phone you if anything happens."

"Are you sure? I don't want to leave you on your own." He dropped the cigarette butt to the ground and put his foot on it.

"I'm sure. Go on."

"Has your phone got enough charge?"

"It's got enough," she said. "Give me my bag."

He held out her backpack, and when she didn't take it, needing instead to breathe through another wave of pain, he set it gently at her feet. She wasn't entirely sorry to see him go. Her sister and brother-in-law had both warned her that Alfie would not make a good birthing partner. It didn't matter, she told herself. Women had been giving birth for millions of years. She could do this without him. Wasn't it always a solo effort anyway, in the end? Announcing "We're pregnant!" didn't stop the woman from doing all of it: the sickness, the exhaustion, the food cravings and the aversions, the skin that stretched until it bled, and the feet that swelled, and the body that felt like it belonged to someone else—because it did. The man got to go to the pub and brag to his mates about his virility.

And then there was this. The part she'd read about over

and over and now knew she was totally unprepared for. Her legs and back were on fire as she shuffled into the emergency room, found a quiet spot where the receptionist couldn't see her, and sat there for the next forty minutes, the other people in the room reduced to little more than blurry shapes. She pulled off her hoodie and found her T-shirt drenched with sweat. If this was only the beginning, she didn't know how she would make it to the end. How could it possibly get worse than this? How could anyone be expected to survive it?

She held in the noises she so desperately wanted to make, and when she couldn't hold them in anymore, she somehow got to her feet and staggered over to the bathroom and locked herself in.

She sank to the floor, resting her forehead against the cold steel of the toilet rim. Time seemed to dissolve around her. She closed her eyes. Looking at things seemed like too much effort. She took a breath, and then another, and her body started to push, and it did it even though she didn't want to, the midwife had said it was too early, and the book she'd read had said it was bad to push too early, but she couldn't stop herself. She felt her baby start to move down, huge and hard and impossible. She cried for her mother, something she would later feel ashamed of, because her mother had died two years before. Somehow, her hands found the waistband of her leggings and got them down.

She caught her baby as he emerged, slowly and then all at once, with a gush of hot liquid, crying out with relief as the pain, which had been overwhelming, suddenly stopped.

He was slippery, but his little body had places in it where her hands could fit, like his armpits and under his bottom, as if he had been designed for exactly this, to be caught by his mother as he made the transition from the warm, safe world inside her body to the cold, cruel world outside it.

She lifted him to her chest, his little hands leaving smears of blood on her T-shirt. "I thought you were going to kill me," she said. She would remember always that those had been the first words he had heard, though she would never tell him. When he grew older and asked her to tell this story, which she would, many times, she would lie about that part.

But not about all of it.

She looked around, saw the long red cord of the emergency alarm, managed to reach it, managed to pull it. There was noise outside the door, someone knocking, someone shouting, "Are you all right in there?"

"I had my baby," Bea called, but she didn't know if her voice was loud enough to carry. She didn't have any more voice to give, anyway. Whoever was outside managed to unlock the door, it was yanked open, and she caught a glimpse of the waiting room, everyone turning to try and see what had happened, the drama in the bathroom far more interesting than their bellyache (or infected toenail or unfortunate accident with a kitchen knife).

"You should have told us you were about to deliver!" the man in scrubs said crossly, as if this was all somehow her fault.

"I had my baby," Bea said again, but she was no longer looking at the man in the doorway, because her baby had just realized that he had been born. He opened his eyes and blinked up at her, obviously shocked, and then he opened his mouth and started to cry, tongue wobbling against toothless gums. She felt that sound right inside the marrow of her bones.

Things became a blur after that. She remembered a wheelchair and sheets and blankets, and being wheeled through the waiting room, feeling all those eyes sit heavy on her, not wanting to meet any of them. There were hands hidden in latex gloves and people in white coats, and the baby was taken from her even though she hadn't given permission for anyone else to touch him, and he was given back to her with his face wiped and his wrist tagged, wrapped in a white cloth with a dark blue edge that made him look like Mother Teresa.

A few hours later, she was given a bed in a postnatal ward, where a pink plastic curtain that didn't close properly and stopped several inches from the floor was deemed sufficient to give her privacy. Alfie came tiptoeing in with a paper bag from McDonald's in his hand.

"I brought you this," he said, holding it out. He peered at the baby in his little plastic box. "He's very small, isn't he?"

"Nine pounds," Bea said. *Not small at all. I've got seventeen stitches to prove it.* "You can pick him up."

"Are you sure? He's asleep. I don't want to wake him." There was an empty chair next to the bed, but Alfie didn't sit in it. He looked like he wanted to bolt. "Have you told your sister yet?"

"Not yet," she said.

"Don't you think you should? You know what she's like.

We'll never hear the end of it if she thinks she wasn't your number one priority."

Bea glanced at her phone, saw the ten percent charge remaining, and reluctantly called Antonia. She kept it short. Yes, everything was fine. A boy. Nine pounds. Yes, that was big. She was tired. She had to go. Yes, she would send a picture. (She didn't.)

Bea was more surprised than she should have been when, half an hour later, her brother-in-law tweaked back the curtain and stuck his head round. "Mind if I come in?"

That was Owen, always perfectly polite. He smiled at Bea, nodded at Alfie. Bea had finally managed to get Alfie to sit down, but he hadn't taken his coat off, and there was a smear of yellow mustard on his chin. When she looked at Owen in his shirt and tie and white doctor's coat, she felt a pang of shame.

"I heard you had a rough time," he said as he stood next to the plastic box that they called a cot and looked down at her son, who was asleep, still in his Mother Teresa getup. One hand had managed to escape, and he was sucking his thumb, tiny fingers splayed across his face like a starfish.

"Do you mind if I . . ." Owen began, but he was already unwrapping the baby, so she didn't bother to answer. What was the point? She watched as Owen examined him, touching his hands, his feet, his round little tummy with the blue stump of his surprisingly juicy umbilical cord in the middle of it, and she gritted her teeth as her son howled out his disapproval. Her gaze flicked to Alfie, and she realized that he, too, was watching. She wondered how he felt, seeing the ease with which Owen touched his son when he'd been too afraid to even pick him up.

"He seems healthy enough," Owen said, wrapping him back up again. "You were lucky that nothing went wrong. Giving birth alone can be very dangerous."

"I didn't do it on purpose!"

"At least you were in the right place," Owen said, continuing as if she hadn't said anything. "Quite the drama. It's all anyone downstairs can talk about."

He stroked the baby's cheek and then, finally, he turned his attention to Bea. Her bed was next to the window, and the light outside was fading. What remained bathed Owen in soft shadow. Bea pulled the sheet up to her chin, a shield against him. All of a sudden, she felt very vulnerable and leaky and sore and afraid. Everyone knew in theory that you were allowed to tell a doctor you didn't want them to touch you, but to actually do it was something else entirely. She didn't want Owen to touch her, especially not in front of Alfie. She didn't want him to put her in the position of having to stop him.

"Congratulations," he said. "He's a lovely little boy. Have you got a name for him yet?"

"Simon," Alfie said. "After my dad."

Bea looked at Alfie in disbelief. That hadn't been on their list. He'd never even mentioned wanting to use it. And anyway, shouldn't it be her decision, given that she was the one who'd done all the work? She opened her mouth to reply, but Owen got in there first.

He looked at Bea. "Are you going to have him tested?"

"Tested for what?" Alfie replied, although Bea knew that the question had been directed at her.

"For the M gene. It's simple, completely painless."

"I don't know," Alfie said, turning to Bea, looking for the answer.

Bea ignored him. "Why?" she asked Owen.

"Why what?"

"Why should I have him tested?"

"It's important to know what you're dealing with," Owen said.

"I'm dealing with a baby," Bea said, and she turned her face to the window, away from Owen, away from Alfie, away from her son. She hadn't had any of the other tests while she was pregnant, and she had no intention of having this one. She didn't understand why anyone did. The idea that you would want to classify a baby as right or wrong, good or bad, perfect or imperfect, was abhorrent to her. As far as she was concerned, you got what you were given and you made the best of it.

"What is that supposed to mean?" Alfie asked. "Are you saying there's something wrong with him?"

"I'm not saying anything of the sort," Owen told him. "I'm merely making you aware of your options." Bea sensed more than heard the pause in his breathing, the moment of careful consideration, and she looked at his reflection in the window and realized that he was watching her. "Antonia is pregnant, by the way. It's still early days, so we aren't telling everyone yet. Risk of miscarriage and all that. But I thought you should know."

"Congratulations," she said. She felt suddenly, unexpectedly, that she wanted to cry, and it struck her as odd that this should be the moment when the tears came after everything that had happened in the past few hours.

"Yeah, congrats," Alfie said, echoing her words as the baby started to howl. The noise was enough to have both men making their excuses and leaving, but it wasn't until they had gone that Bea leaned over and snatched the baby up from his crib. She held him close to her body, her breasts pulsing in time with his cries, Owen's words echoing in her ears.

"There's nothing wrong with you," she whispered to him. "I won't let anyone say otherwise. You're perfect, you hear me? Perfect. And we are not calling you Simon!"

||| ANTONIA

Now

Antonia sat in the driver's seat of her beautiful white Mercedes, French manicured hands on the steering wheel, tapping impatiently as she waited for the old man in front to finally commit and join the flow of traffic on the roundabout. She was late. She hated being late. Especially for Jack.

When she got to the school, she dumped the car in an empty disabled space close to the door and sprinted in, not an easy feat in heels, her red Gucci bag tucked under her arm. She was in the auditorium with two minutes to spare. She pressed a hand against her chest as she fought to catch her breath, feeling the thump of her heart against her palm as Lily waved at her from the other side of the auditorium and gestured to the empty seat next to her.

Antonia quickly made her way over. Lily greeted her with an air-kiss next to each cheek. "I wasn't sure you were going to make it!"

"Neither was I. My lunchtime appointment ran over." Antonia opened her bag, took out her compact, and checked her face. Her nose was shiny, and she patted at it with the little sponge, moving the mirror around to check her hair. It fell perfectly into place with a few flicks of her fingers, justifying the price she paid at the salon she went to every other week.

"Was there a problem?" Lily asked. Her hair was longer and darker than Antonia's, tied up with a satin band, and she was wearing a deep green dress with an ankle-length skirt and high collar. Antonia didn't particularly like the Victorian waif look, but the two of them were friends first and foremost because they and their husbands co-owned a clinic that treated M+ boys, not because they had the same taste in clothes.

Owen and Paul were both pediatricians and took care of the medical side of things. Lily worked part-time as the office manager, answering the phone and emails, sending out letters, running the website, and doing all the general admin needed to keep the place running.

As for Antonia, she dealt with the parents. She held their hands when the stress of having an M+ son got to be too much, taught them tried-and-tested parenting strategies, and helped them accept that it wasn't something they could walk away from.

"Nothing I couldn't handle," she said, snapping the compact shut and slipping it back into her bag. "Just what you might call a slight difference of opinion."

Lily laughed. "You mean they're refusing to follow the program properly and then wondering why it isn't working?"

"As I recall, their exact words were 'We cut the tablets down to three days a week because we're worried about giving medication to someone so young,'" Antonia said as the head teacher walked out into the middle of the floor. He was a tall, thin man in a navy blue suit with a careful comb-over. The kids called him Lurch.

He clapped his hands together several times, signaling to the parents to stop talking and pay attention, then launched into the usual speech. Antonia didn't listen. Her attention was drawn to the doorway at the side, where she could see Jack waiting. Her beautiful son. Her heart sighed a little at the sight of him. Puberty wasn't always kind. She saw that at the clinic on a daily basis. It was obvious here, too, if you looked at the other boys in the line, even though all the ones here were M—. They wouldn't be at this school otherwise.

But her son seemed to be the exception. His skin had remained smooth and beautiful, his blue-black hair as glossy as a raven's wing, and he'd kept the long eyelashes he'd had as a little boy. His pants were too short again, though.

Antonia took her phone out of her bag and ordered some new ones. She took another look at him and ordered a bundle of shirts as well. There had been a time when it had felt like he would be small forever. She still didn't know what to make of this new adult-sized version. Not that he was an adult, not even close, despite the fact that he'd be eighteen on his next birthday, and not long after that, he'd leave home and head off to college.

Antonia didn't like to think about that. She couldn't imagine not being able to see him every day, not being able to hear his voice, to touch him, to mother him. She still picked him up from school whenever she could, something that drove Owen up the wall. "You have to stop babying him," he'd said to her over breakfast just that morning. "We bought him a car. Let him use it! He needs to learn some independence, Antonia."

"He will," she'd replied. "He *is*."

But there really wasn't any rush, was there?

The head teacher finished his speech, and then the kids paraded in. Lily lifted her arm to wave at her daughter Ginny. Antonia waved, too, discreetly, just enough to catch Jack's eye and let him know she was there. He flashed her a quick half smile, and she got a glimpse of the man he would be five or ten years from now, and then it was gone, and he was just seventeen again. Antonia knew just how lucky she was to have an M– son. She thanked her lucky stars for it every single day.

Not all mothers were so fortunate. Some women found themselves with sons who were awful. Loud and aggressive and, occasionally, downright dangerous. But at least those who weren't normal could be identified early now, long before they caused any trouble, and no one made excuses for them anymore. No one said "boys will be boys." It wasn't acceptable to shrug and laugh and pretend that nothing could be done, that acceptance was the only way, that it was the responsibility of girls to move up and move aside and bend themselves to fit around their male peers. The test had changed that.

Not that everyone was on board with it. Some people

genuinely believed that it was wrong to acknowledge that the problem lay with men and try to get ahead of it. Not that it was all men, of course, but it was a significant minority. What they had in common was their maleness and the M gene. It had been found in girls, too, but it didn't seem to have the same impact on behavior. Girls who tested positive were a little bossy, perhaps a little pushy, but they weren't dangerous. There was no need to test or medicate them.

Not like boys.

Not like Lily's stepson.

Or Antonia's nephew.

Antonia stopped herself before she could go any further down that path. She forced herself to focus on the here and now, on her son. He was all that mattered. It took almost half an hour for the head teacher to hand out the prizes and shake all the hands. Antonia thought she might burst with pride when Jack was given not one but two awards for his violin playing. He glanced up and caught her eye, and she gave him a double thumbs-up.

"He's done well," Lily said. Her daughter Ginny had received her own prize for clarinet, flushing as red as her hair as it was handed over and scurrying away like a little mouse afterward.

"Yes," Antonia said. "He's earned it, though." All those hours of lessons and practice, working at Mozart and Bach until she heard the music in her sleep. But Jack loved it. It had given him a sense of purpose and confidence that his failure to do well at sports could have so easily knocked.

Aggressive male behavior might be less acceptable now, but traditional views of masculinity hadn't shifted that far. It still wasn't easy to be a gentle boy who didn't play rugby or soccer.

She said her goodbyes to Lily, then went back to the car to wait for Jack, using the time to check her phone. She told herself that she was looking for messages from patients at the clinic, and that was true, but she quickly found herself tapping her sister's name into Google. She didn't do it often. But now and then, the urge would get the better of her. She would always feel grubby afterward and hastily delete her search history and tell herself she wasn't going to do it again.

Bea Mitchell

She stared down at the screen, then closed the page without tapping search. She tucked her phone back inside her bag and busied her hands with a lipstick instead. A quick touch-up in the rearview mirror made her feel better. She was just putting her sunglasses on when Jack appeared. He dumped his bag and violin case in the trunk before clambering into the passenger seat and slamming the door, bringing with him the smell of a hot teenage boy. "Where's Dad?" he asked as he reached for his seat belt.

"He couldn't make it," Antonia said. "He asked me to tell you he's sorry."

"He always says that. Sometimes I think he cares more about his job than he does about me."

Antonia started the car. "That's hardly fair," she told him.

"You know how important the clinic is. The things we're doing . . . there are a lot of M-positive boys in desperate need of help. Their families need us, Jack. They don't have the things you do. They don't have the same opportunities. They won't get to go off to a fantastic school, and they definitely won't be going to one with girls."

Out of the corner of her eye, she saw her son flush. *Ah*, she thought to herself. *Gotcha*. Until recently, she hadn't even been sure that Jack had realized that he had a crush on Ginny, although it had been obvious to Antonia for months. It had been a bittersweet moment. She was amused but, at the same time, sad that he had to grow up.

"That's hardly my fault!" he said hotly.

"No, it's not," she said. She felt calmer now, on firmer ground, and focused on the road as she drove them out of the parking lot. "But you got a negative M test. Just think about what life would be like if you were positive."

"I don't need to think about that," Jack said. "Because I'm not. I just wish that I didn't have to share him with everyone else. He's *my* dad."

"I know," she said. "He does his best, though. And you have me. Don't forget that."

"You work there, too," Jack grumbled.

"You're my priority and always will be."

Not that her job wasn't important to her. It gave her a great deal of pleasure to put on a tailored suit and silk blouse each morning, to arm herself with matching bag and heels, to walk into her beautiful office with its soft gray carpet and pretty artwork, and to check her schedule and see it full. She

liked what she and Owen had built. What they were doing.
They were good at it. They were doing something that *mattered*.

Though none of it mattered as much as Jack, of course. He
was her baby. Her only child. She'd worked too hard to have
him to not put him first. But, she reminded herself, she was
working at the clinic for Jack as much as for herself. A school
like his wasn't cheap, and medical school wouldn't be, either.
She'd recently starting looking at apartments close to the
two colleges he was interested in so that she'd be ready to
buy once he had his place. She wanted to make sure that he
had decent accommodation and not grungy student digs.

Their house was a twenty-minute drive from the school.
Jack put the radio on and sang along with it. It made Antonia smile. His voice was not his best instrument. When
they got to their wide tree-lined street, she dropped down a
gear and kept her speed low. The trash cans had been emptied that morning, and the ones that belonged to the elderly
gentleman who lived opposite were still on the pavement.
Antonia made a mental note to put them away for him before she went in the house. She kept an eye out for next
door's silver tabby, too, because it seemed to have a death
wish and liked to run out into the road whenever it saw a
car coming.

But this time, it wasn't the cat that stopped her but something else completely unexpected.

She slammed on the brakes.

"Whoa!" Jack said loudly, flinging out a hand to brace
himself against the dash. "Mom!"

Antonia gripped the wheel, staring at the battered Audi parked on the street outside the house. It was a car she knew, and yet it wasn't. The bumper had been caved in as if it had been backed into a concrete post, and the license plate was held on with thick silver tape. The rear windshield wiper was missing, as was the left side mirror. It was so dirty that she could barely see the paint underneath, though she knew it to be a pale silver-blue.

"Oh my god," Jack said quietly. "That looks like our old car."

Antonia forced herself to take a breath and pulled into the drive, barely missing the gatepost. Then she got out of the car and walked back out onto the road. The door of the other car was pushed slowly open. A foot emerged, shod in a scruffy white tennis shoe, then a leg encased in battered denim, and then the rest of the body.

The world seemed to shift under her feet. "Bea?" she said faintly.

"Hello, Antonia," her sister said, one hand on the edge of the door, as if she, too, needed to hold herself steady, though the Bea that Antonia remembered had never wobbled at anything.

All the familiar pieces were there: the eyes, the shape of the chin, the defiant line of the shoulders. But Bea hadn't always looked so tired or so worn. Her hair hadn't been streaked with gray. She hadn't dressed like she was homeless.

Then the passenger door opened and another figure got out, this one taller than her sister, with close-cropped dark hair and a massive black eye, and Antonia thought for a moment that she was going to pass out. The last time she had seen her nephew, he had still been a little boy.

Not anymore.

Jack was out of the car before she could stop him. "Simon!" he shouted, his excitement obvious. "Oh my god!" He slammed the car door and rushed over to where his cousin stood. The two boys moved close as if preparing to dance and then threw their arms around each other. The hug was fierce. Best friends reunited. It made Antonia's eyes sting. She had to look away.

She had to look at her sister. "What are you doing here?"

Unlike her son, she couldn't bring herself to move closer. She didn't like the way Bea's car looked outside her house, or the suddenness of her reappearance, or the wave of sheer terror that rose up inside her when she thought about what had happened the last time their sons had been together.

All those years apart, swept aside in a moment. She could almost smell the salt in the air. Out of the corner of her eye, she saw Jack unlock the front door and let his cousin into her house, and she wanted to scream at him not to.

"Can we talk inside?" Bea said. "It's been a long drive."

And just like that, Bea did the thing she'd always been able to do. She made Antonia feel small when, if anything, it should be the other way around. Antonia wanted to say, *No, go away, this is my house, my life, and you aren't part of it. I don't want you to be part of it. I remember what happened when you were.*

But she didn't because Bea was family, and you didn't do that to family. "Of course." She pasted on a smile. "How rude of me! Please, go in, go in. You must be tired." *You certainly look it*, she thought as she followed her sister into the house. Close up, Bea smelled unwashed, and her skin was so pale it was almost gray, as if she'd been spending a lot of time indoors.

Something had clearly gone very, very wrong.

"Can I use the bathroom?" Bea replied, her hand already on the door.

"Of course!"

Bea went in, closing and locking the door behind her. The smell lingered in the hallway. Antonia grimaced. She'd have to disinfect everything and change the hand towels before Owen got home. There was no sign of the boys, but she could hear movement at the top of the stairs. The thought of the two of them up there alone made her nervous. The thought of going up there to check on them was worse.

She needed a drink. She went into the kitchen to get one. The cleaner had come that morning and the place was pristine, the marble spotless and gleaming, something which would normally fill Antonia with joy. It went unnoticed as she took a wineglass down from the cupboard. She was jittery with shock. She took a bottle of chardonnay from the fridge, split the cork in her haste to get it out, and was in the middle of filling the glass when Bea walked back in.

"What are you doing here, Bea?" she asked as she picked up the glass and took a long drink from it. The wine spread sharply over her tongue, and she let it sit there for a second before swallowing, afraid she might choke.

"I'm sorry to have just turned up out of the blue," Bea said. "It's good to see you, though. You look well."

"Thank you." She didn't return the compliment. It wasn't in her nature to lie, and she'd already done more than enough of that for her sister over the years. When Bea had left on that awful day five years before, when Antonia had given her the keys for the car that currently sat rotting outside the house, she had promised herself that it was the last time. That she would never fix one of Bea's messes again. *Go,* she had said. *I'll deal with things here.*

Bea had hugged her, tears wet against her cheek, and then she had gotten behind the wheel of that car and driven off. She hadn't looked back. There had been cards at Christmas and on Antonia's birthday for a while, but then those had stopped, and Bea had become a ghost. Antonia had no idea where she was and no way of contacting her. It had hurt more than she'd expected.

But her life had slowly flowed into the gap created by Bea and Simon's absence, and she'd moved on. The clinic was busier than ever. She and Owen were in a good place in their marriage. And Jack had calmed down a lot without his cousin around. Before Bea had left, Antonia hadn't really been aware that having her sister in her life was like having a piece of grit in her shoe, one she had grown so used to that she barely noticed the discomfort anymore. It wasn't until Bea had gone and she felt her absence that she realized just how difficult it had been.

Now Bea was back. Had she known that at some point her sister would turn up on her doorstep? Yes. Yes, of course she had. She had known that since the day Bea had left. "Are you in trouble?"

"No, we're not in trouble," Bea said. She laughed. "Honestly, Antonia, you always think the worst. I just wanted to see you. That's all."

I just wanted to see you. Antonia felt an odd pain in her chest. For years, she'd longed to hear those words from her sister. To have Bea give her some sign that their relationship wasn't all one-way, that despite their differences, Bea loved her in return. "Do you want to stay for dinner?" she asked, surprising herself. Owen wouldn't like it, but surely one meal together as a family would be okay.

"Actually, I was hoping to stay a bit longer than that," Bea said. She moved restlessly, shifting her weight from one foot to the other, scratching at her forearm as she did so, leaving dry white lines on her skin. She'd added a tattoo of a heart near her wrist at some point. It didn't look good.

"How long?"

"A couple of days," Bea said. "If that's all right with you?"

For five years, Antonia had wondered if she'd made the right choice on that awful day. She'd wondered if she should have made Bea stay and face up to what Simon had done. If it had been anyone but Bea, she would have. But Bea was her baby sister. It had always been Antonia's job to protect her. And old habits died hard. Whatever mess Bea was in, Antonia knew she would help her get out of it, because that's what sisters did.

"Of course," she said, forcing a smile. "You're welcome to stay as long as you want."

CHAPTER THREE

‖‖ ANTONIA

Seventeen years ago

If Simon's birth was primitive, Jack's was the opposite. There was no lonely shock on the cold floor of a public bathroom for Antonia. Instead, there was something far, far worse. She had already been trying for a year when Bea got herself knocked up by that idiot she lived with. She had barely been able to look at Bea for weeks afterward, would lock herself in the bathroom and cry after every visit as Bea's stomach became more and more prominent. When Owen suggested that they try IVF, she had agreed immediately.

Here, at last, had been people who understood. The process had been incredibly unpleasant, bordering on cruel sometimes, but it had worked, and Antonia felt that it had given her a far deeper understanding of just how special and precious a child was than Bea ever would have. She had already stopped working, at Owen's suggestion, and spent her days going swimming, doing yoga, having her feet pedicured, and taking carefully posed photos for a collage she intended to put together after the birth, wanting to document this special time, determined not to forget any of it. She was strict with her diet. No caffeine, no raw eggs, no blue cheese, no alcohol. She had regular ultrasound scans at a private clinic, and that helped her anxiety, but even so, she woke up every morning convinced that this was the day when something would go wrong, and six weeks before her baby was due, it did. A sensation like a balloon popping somewhere inside her, a wet patch on the back of her maternity jeans, a panicked rush to the hospital to be told that her water had broken early. The worst phone calls she'd ever made in her life—to Owen, to Bea, to her mother and in-laws. Steroid injections in her backside to help mature lungs that weren't ready for the outside world yet. Twenty-four hours of monitoring, and then an emergency Cesarean. She was allowed to hold her baby until he started to breathe like a pug on a hot afternoon, and a doctor came and took him away.

When Owen told her not to worry, that it was merely a precaution, that their son would be fine, she wanted to physically hurt him. She felt like her heart was breaking. After all she had been through, to then have to deal with this . . . It wasn't right. It wasn't *fair*. She had done everything she was supposed to, and things had gone wrong anyway.

She spent four days in the hospital recovering, her bedside table crammed with flowers and cards, the nurses calm and attentive. Nothing was too much trouble. Jack was returned to her two days after he'd been taken away. He was nothing like Bea's baby; he didn't have eyelashes or fingernails, and his skin appeared to be two sizes too big. There was so much thick white hair on his upper back and arms that he looked like a tiny werewolf. He was so fragile and small compared to Simon.

"We should have him tested for the M gene before we take him home," Owen said as he sat in the comfortable armchair next to her bed, Jack cradled in his arms. He stroked Jack's tiny face. "It's just a cheek swab, a cotton bud in his mouth. Nothing to worry about. It won't hurt him, I promise you." He stood up, and when she held her arms out for the baby, he passed him over. "I'll tell the midwife. You can hold him while it's done."

"Right," Antonia said as she looked down at her dear little boy. There wasn't a single trace of aggression in him. She didn't need the test to tell her that. But it was important to Owen, and so it was important to her, too. She wasn't like Bea. She didn't take motherhood lightly. "Yes, of course we'll have it done."

"Good," Owen said. He went to find the midwife, returning a few minutes later with the woman in tow, young and in blue scrubs, with the kit in her hand.

Antonia watched closely as the woman stroked Jack's cheek with a gloved finger, making him root for what his newborn instinct told him was food. His mouth opened. The cotton buds were in and out in a flash, and that was it. Easy. The easiest part of all of it, in fact, and certainly easier than the car seat they both struggled to strap him into before they finally went home.

But when Antonia posted on her blog that he'd had his M test, she got some unexpected backlash.

> What are you going to do if your precious baby gets a
> positive result?

> If you really loved your son, you wouldn't put him
> through that.

> Why don't you admit that you wanted a designer baby?

> Waste of money.

> You don't deserve to be a mother.

Antonia pushed her keyboard away as if it had burned her, and she cried. She had thought these people were her friends. Why were they being so cruel? She deleted all the comments immediately and took the post down. It was three days before she was able to bring herself to post again. She was more careful after that. When Jack's M test result came through, she didn't share it online. She rang Owen and told him straightaway. "I knew it would be negative," he said. He sounded pleased. It made her feel better.

"Yes," Antonia told him. "Me too."

"I can't say it's not a relief to have it confirmed, though," he said. "Have you told Bea?"

"Not yet," she said. "Do you think I should?"

"Yes," he said. "If she knows that Jack is negative, it might help persuade her to have Simon tested, too." There was the sound of someone else talking in the background. "I have to go. I love you."

"I love you, too," Antonia told him. Then she sent Bea a text inviting her over for lunch, but Bea said she couldn't make it because she was working. She made excuses the next day and the day after that, too, and Antonia cried again, this time with frustration. In the end, she texted Bea back to tell her that Jack had tested negative for the M gene and left it at that. She was recovering from major surgery, after all. She didn't need Bea's drama on top.

That Friday, she got a taxi to the hospital and introduced Jack to Owen's colleagues. She watched carefully as Owen showed Jack off, as people admired his tiny features and dusting of soft hair. "Owen tells me you got a negative M test," one of them said, another doctor called Paul. "Congratulations."

"Thank you," Antonia said.

"It's going to be a big deal in a few years. I don't think

people have really grasped that yet. They still seem to think that if they make enough noise online, they can make it go away. But it isn't going anywhere. It's the future, it really is. Identifying M-positive boys means we can help them. Now that we know that male violence has an underlying genetic cause, that it's a medical problem, we can treat it."

Jack started to whimper at that point, and Paul smiled sympathetically and moved away. She knew that he had a little boy of his own, a bit older than Jack, but someone pressed tea and homemade carrot cake on her and she soon forgot to ask about him. Owen let her use his office so she could feed Jack in private, and she went home tired but relieved that it had all gone so well.

Not that Jack was easy most of the time. Antonia understood why, and she didn't resent him for it. He had come into the world too soon, and that made everything difficult for him. The days blurred into weeks. All of a sudden, Jack was three months old. Antonia felt like she'd aged thirty years in that time, and yet it seemed to have passed in the blink of an eye. That was when she realized that she hadn't seen her sister since Jack was born. They'd exchanged text messages, but there hadn't been any real contact. It felt . . . it felt almost as if Bea was avoiding her, and that wouldn't do.

She had a haircut and a manicure, swelling with pride as the women at the salon cooed over Jack, and then she picked up an assortment of cookies and fruit and a bunch of flowers and set off for Bea's house. There was no point phoning ahead. It would only give Bea the chance to make some excuse.

When she got to Bea's street, she parked as close to the house as she could. Then she picked up the gifts and Jack, who was still asleep in his car seat, and knocked on the door. "Be home," she muttered as she waited, shifting her weight from one foot to the other. "Please be home."

She was in luck.

The door opened and there was Bea, hair pulled back, wearing ancient jeans and a T-shirt several sizes too big, with a blood-soaked tissue held against her nose. She blinked when she saw Antonia, and then she sighed.

"What happened?" Antonia asked, horrified.

Bea looked away. "I suppose you want to come in." She stood back, making room for Antonia to get past.

Inside, the house was cool and smelled faintly of lemon floor cleaner. The television was on, showing some noisy kids' TV show.

"Do you want tea?" Bea called over her shoulder as she headed back into the kitchen. Antonia followed her, gripping the handle of Jack's car seat tightly. Every muscle seemed to have gone stiff.

"No, I don't want tea," she said as soon as they reached the kitchen and Bea had nowhere else to run. "I want you to tell me what happened to your face!"

"A toddler with a very hard head happened," Bea said dryly.

Antonia put the bag of fruit and cookies on the table but didn't put Jack down. She felt the sudden need to be able to make a quick exit. "Simon did it?"

"Yes, Simon," Bea said, as if that had been a stupid question.

"On purpose?"

As if he had heard her, Simon appeared in the doorway. The sound caught Antonia's attention. She turned to look at him and blinked in surprise. "He's crawling?"

"That is what they do at this age."

Simon grinned up at her, revealing several little white teeth. His hair, white-blond, curled around his ears. He looked like a grubby-faced cherub. Perhaps he was.

But her sister's face told another story.

||| JACK

Now

Jack flopped back on his bed, trying to act casual as he greedily drank in every detail of his cousin, though inside, his heart was racing, and he could feel sweat seeping into the collar of his shirt. Simon was here. He was really here. "I wasn't sure you were going to turn up."

"Neither was I," Simon replied. "Took some work to get my mom to agree. She isn't happy about it." He rubbed the back of his neck and yawned. "I didn't sleep at all last night. I'm exhausted."

"You look it," Jack told him. He crossed his legs at the ankle, his gaze falling on Simon's face, more specifically on his left eye, which was the color of blackberry jam. "I've never seen a bruise as bad as that before. Does it . . . does it hurt?"

Simon gestured to his face. "This? Course it fucking hurts. Did you get the appointment?"

"Tomorrow morning," Jack told him. "It's at the hospital. I'll take a sick day, and we can get an Uber there. Mom's got CCTV all over the outside of the house, and she'll get weird if she sees my car is gone."

Simon nodded. "All right. Good." Then he looked around. "Nice room. Wasn't everything Star Wars last time I was here?"

Jack laughed. He sat up, started pulling at his striped school tie, loosening the knot so that he could take it off. "Got rid of all that ages ago."

When they'd come back from their last vacation together, in fact. By the time his dad had picked them up and driven them home, Jack wasn't the same person who had sat in the back of the car with his cousin on the way there, playing on his Switch and drinking warm lemonade from a can. What had happened had changed everything, including him.

He tossed his tie onto the end of the bed, took off his blazer, and wondered if Simon still thought about that day or the things that had followed it.

"Bit better than what I've been living with," Simon said. He stood in the middle of the room with his hands buried in the pockets of his ratty cargo shorts, like he'd been invited into Aladdin's cave and told not to touch anything.

Jack wished he would relax. "I saw the photo. Looked like a dump." He shifted position a little so that he could pull his phone out of his back pocket and check the screen. He'd sent Ginny a video of a cat on a Roomba. She'd sent him a smiley face in return. He was half tempted to tell her that Simon was here. No. It was a stupid idea. The fewer people who knew, the better.

Simon strolled over to the window and looked out at the

road. "It was," he said. "You wouldn't have lasted five minutes in it, fancy boy."

"Very funny," Jack said.

"I wasn't joking. Got any painkillers?"

Jack leaned over and opened his bedside drawer, which was crammed with new and half-empty packets of all the various things his mother made him take: vitamins and supplements and painkillers for his migraines. He rummaged around, found what he was looking for, and tossed it to Simon.

Simon popped a couple of pills from their packaging and swallowed them dry. "Thanks," he said.

"You shouldn't have let him land one."

"I didn't do it on purpose. Anyway, I'd have liked to see you stop him. You look just as spoiled and soft as you always did. Are you allowed to wipe your own ass yet, or is Aunt Antonia still doing it for you?"

Jack rolled his eyes. "Fuck off."

"She is!" Simon shook his head. "You're such a prince."

"She's not as bad as she was."

Simon snickered. "I remember when she used to make you drink warm milk at every bedtime and tell you to grow up big and strong."

Jack flexed his arm. "Didn't work, did it?"

He kicked the drawer shut as Simon moved away from the window and over to his shelf of music awards. There were plenty of them: certificates from all the exams he'd taken, most of them passed with distinction, trophies from a couple of competitions, some he'd won at school. He hadn't put the ones he'd gotten today on the shelf yet, as they were still in the car, but there was a space for them at the end.

"Impressive," Simon said, pointing at them. Then he explored Jack's desk, his fingers drifting over the laptop, the iPad, the pens and pencils in their steel pot, the neat row of Warhammer figures. His hands were a mess, too, the knuckles scabbed.

Jack hadn't realized that the damage would be quite so visible, and it worried him. "What are you going to tell my parents happened to your face?" And they would ask; he was sure of it. Simon was a mess. This wasn't the minor bumps and bruises that Jack had expected. It was scary.

"I'll say I fell off my bike or something."

His mom would probably buy that, though Jack wasn't sure about his dad. But it was a bit late to worry about that now. "I can't believe you dropped out of school," he said, feeling the need to change the subject.

Simon shrugged. "Didn't have much choice."

"I guess not." It felt so adult, so far beyond what Jack was doing, and he couldn't quite believe it. Simon was clever. He was the sort of person who could do amazing feats of mental arithmetic without even trying. "What about college?"

He knew the question was stupid even before he asked it. A boy like Simon, with his history and no money, wouldn't be going to college.

"What about it?" Simon replied. "I assume you're going."

"Dad still wants me to do medicine. He's got it all planned. He's even got me doing work experience at the clinic."

"Hanging out with the M-positive boys? That explains a lot. What about you? What do you want to do?"

"I don't know," Jack said. "I haven't really thought about it." It hadn't occurred to him that there was anything to think about. He'd known since he was little that he was going to go down the same route as his dad.

"Can I use your shower?" Simon asked.

"Yeah, sure," Jack said. He waved Simon in the direction of the en suite. "Towels are in the cupboard."

He ran a finger around the inside of his collar, wishing he'd thought to shower. He didn't usually sweat like this. He felt jittery and strange, Christmas Eve excited, but at the same time, a bit sick and afraid. Seeing Simon again was more overwhelming than he'd anticipated.

Both of them had grown, it was true, but he sensed that Simon had grown differently somehow. There was a lean strength to his body that Jack knew didn't exist in his own. But then, Simon had always been different.

For months after the vacation, whenever he thought about what had happened, about the slippery seaweed on the rocks, the barnacles that cut your feet if you weren't careful, about the salt in the air and the swirl of blood in the water, he'd wanted to talk to Simon. But he hadn't known what to say, and Simon had never mentioned it in any of his messages, either.

Eventually, the events of that week in Cornwall became a distant memory. The girl had been forgotten, too, though Jack kept track of the social media accounts of her younger sister and would look at them late at night when he was bored.

Did Simon do that?

The sound of water thundering against the shower floor cut into the silence, and Jack knew he wasn't going to get an answer to that—not for a while, anyway—so he went downstairs to see if there was anything to eat. He found the remains of an apple crumble in the fridge and ate it straight from the bowl with the fridge door open, the cold air stroking his face.

They'd gotten past the first hurdle. Antonia had let Bea and Simon into the house. Jack had been prepared to have to put up a fight to get her to agree, but she'd surprised him with how quickly she'd welcomed them. He had no idea what was going to happen or what his dad was going to say when he got home from work, though. But he knew one thing. His dad wasn't nearly as soft as Antonia, and he wasn't going to be happy about it.

He scraped up the last bite of crumble, then dumped the empty bowl in the sink and was about to go back upstairs when scratching at the door of the utility room caught his attention. He opened the door to find their dog, Flash, right behind it. Flash pushed his way past Jack and almost knocked him over in his rush to get to the back door. When Jack looked in the utility room, he saw that Flash's bed and water bowl were in there, too, and he felt a prickle of irritation. The cleaner had promised that she'd stop locking Flash in there.

He opened the back door and had just stepped outside, Flash at his heels, when he heard his mother's voice. He stopped where he was, hooking his fingers around the dog's collar. The dog responded by squatting and doing his business right there on the patio.

". . . I just can't believe how much Simon has grown," Antonia was saying. She was drunk. She tried to hide it, but he could always tell. Her voice took on this weird tone after the first glass.

"I feel the same about Jack," said Bea. "Our boys are almost men. Hard to believe, isn't it?"

Jack had mixed feelings about Bea. Most of the time, she'd ignored him, which had been fine by him. But she'd also been strict in ways that he didn't like. You couldn't take stuff from her fridge without asking, you couldn't watch what you wanted on TV, you couldn't use your phone without her glaring at you and telling you to put it away. She wouldn't even let Simon have a day off school when he was ill. *If you're not dead, you're well enough to go to school*, she'd always said. Jack didn't understand it. Surely it was better to take a sick day when you needed one. His mother had never had a problem with that.

"What happened to Simon's face?" he heard Antonia ask.

Jack tightened his grip on Flash's collar. He felt his pulse speed up a little, and he could hear the subtle swoosh of blood in his ears.

"Rugby injury," Bea said. "You know what teenage boys are like. Don't know their own strength."

Jack held his breath, waiting to see if his mother would swallow the lie.

Antonia laughed. "Yes," she said. "Makes me glad Jack is into music rather than sports."

Jack exhaled. He went quietly back into the house, Flash at his side, and met Simon coming down the stairs as he was heading back up them. The two of them stopped, almost eye to eye, and Jack was suddenly overwhelmed with pleasure at the sight of his cousin here in his house. He couldn't hold back his grin. "Glad you're here, mate," he said.

"Me too." Simon grinned back, and then his gaze dropped to Flash. "Yours?"

"Well, a family dog, really. My dad wanted a Labrador but my mum said they're too silly, so we got a German shepherd instead. To be honest I think she wanted him as a guard dog in case some pissed-off kid from the clinic finds out where we live and tries to break in."

"Big bastard, isn't he?"

"And in need of a walk. Want to come with me?"

Simon looked down at Flash again. "Sure," he said.

The dog was well trained enough not to need a leash, and he trotted at Jack's heels, hot breath touching the backs of his knees. Simon strolled alongside them. His shoes were a mess as well as his shorts, and his socks didn't match.

But somehow none of that seemed to matter. Because he was here. He was back. It was the two of them together again, and they had a plan. They were going to fix things. There would be no more running away after this. Lost in these thoughts, Jack forgot to tell Simon what Bea had said about his injuries being from rugby.

Simon's untested status had been a big deal when they were kids. Jack could still remember all the times his mother had tried to persuade Bea to have him tested. She'd never succeeded. Bea had made up her mind, and getting her to change it was like trying to persuade the captain of the *Titanic* to turn back.

But Simon wasn't going to be untested for much longer.

Simon ran a hand over his head. His hair was cut military short, showing off the shape of his skull, and there was a bruise on his arm that Jack hadn't noticed before, gray-blue and deep under the skin. It looked painful.

"Thanks, Jack," he said. "For doing this."

"We're family," Jack said. "Why wouldn't I?"

||| BEA

Fourteen years ago

M Gene Testing Extended to All Boys Seven and Under

As of today, all parents of a boy age seven or under will be able to have their sons tested for the M gene by their GP. The test, which involves swabbing the inside of the cheek and then sending the sample for analysis, identifies boys who have a particular version of the so-called M gene that has been linked to violent behavior. So far, it has only been carried out in newborns. Minister for Health Yvonne Barnes said, "Supporting families has always been at the heart of this government, and we know that there are many parents who want to access the test but who have been unable to because their sons are too old. We believe that to be unfair." The test will be voluntary, and the information will remain a confidential part of a child's medical record.

Birthday parties were a big deal; Bea knew that. Not so much for her or for Simon. For his last birthday, he got a squashed chocolate cake from the reduced shelf at the supermarket, one toy, and one book. Fortunately, given his age, he hadn't yet figured out that most kids would consider this to be a pretty poor show. But for Antonia, birthdays were a major production, and Jack's third birthday was no exception.

Planning had started weeks in advance. Bea had tried her best to avoid her sister during this time, but she was like a buzzing fly: noisy, and skilled at dodging attempts to swat it. Bea had learned early in life that it was best to let Antonia make a lot of fuss and claim all the attention when she was in this sort of mood.

She went to the party as instructed on the card that Antonia had dropped off at her house. (The instructions had also been repeated via email and text message.) She rolled her eyes at the dress code (smart casual) and turned up in her usual jeans and a T-shirt she'd nicked from an old boyfriend that said SAVE WATER, DRINK BEER on the front. Simon wore his favorite outfit, a Spider-Man costume that she'd found in a charity shop. Alfie was working and couldn't make it. Bea wasn't sorry. They'd argued over who had drunk the last of the milk that morning, and she didn't want to look at his stupid face anytime soon.

She misjudged the timing, perhaps a little on purpose, and they finally arrived thirty minutes after they were supposed to. By then, the driveway and street were full of BMWs and Range Rovers that took up half the sidewalk as well as half the road, and Bea was forced to park her old Volkswagen on the next street.

As she walked up the driveway with Simon, she could hear excited squeals mingled with a flat background hum. She had no idea what was causing it until they went around to the back of the house and saw the massive bouncy castle that had been positioned at one end of the garden. The staffing cost alone would probably have paid Bea's rent for a month. It was hard not to feel pissy about it.

She'd realized a long time ago that she and Antonia were very different people headed in different directions. And she'd done nothing to try and stop it. If anything, she was honest enough with herself to admit that she often made decisions on the basis that they were the opposite of what Antonia would do, sometimes to her own detriment.

Simon pulled free from her grip and went straight for the bouncy castle. "Shoes!" Bea yelled after him, and he stopped just long enough to kick them off in the middle of the grass. She wandered over and picked them up, tucking them inside her bag, then went inside the house. There seemed to be adults everywhere, women with vacation tans and pretty jewelry probably bought for them by the assortment of men who all seemed to be wearing casual blue shirts.

She felt their eyes on her, and her skin prickled.

"Hello?" said one of them, a woman in a pink plaid dress. She made it sound like a question rather than a friendly greeting. Bea didn't recognize her, although that wasn't surprising. Antonia didn't usually let her mix with her posh friends. "Can I help you with something?"

"No, thanks," Bea said cheerily. There was a pile of presents on the table in the dining room, and she added hers to it, tucking it at the bottom so that it was hidden out of sight. The book was new and carefully chosen, but some of the boxes looked big enough to hold a microwave, and she had no chance of competing with that. She reminded herself that there would be free food and went into the kitchen to find some. Unfortunately, she ran into Owen before she got there.

"Bea," he said.

"Hello, Owen."

Just like the others, he was wearing a blue shirt, his pale and open at the collar. His gaze seemed to jump all over her body, as if he couldn't decide which part of it to look at, before settling on the three silver hoops in her left ear. "There's food in the kitchen, sandwiches and the like, and drinks are on a table in the garden. Please, help yourself."

Always so polite. "Right," she said. "Having a good time?"

"Yes," he said. "Of course."

When he and Antonia had first started going out, Bea had been intimidated by his good job, his superior level of education, his firm confidence. Antonia wanted a "good" husband and made no secret of the fact that by *good* she meant six feet tall and earning a hefty salary, preferably doing something she could use to make other women feel jealous, and Bea's only defense against it was pretending she hadn't noticed and didn't care.

But Bea knew a few things about Owen that he'd rather she didn't, and there was something delicious in that. *Yes,* she wanted to say. *I'm here. No, I didn't have anything else to wear, and, no, I won't apologize for myself or for my son, and if you have a problem with us, we could always talk about that thing I know you don't want to talk about.*

"You'll have to excuse me, Bea. I've just got to . . ."

He eased his way past her. His shoulder bumped against hers. She could have moved out of the way, given him enough room to get past, but it felt better to stand her ground. Owen never seemed to know what to do with her. It hadn't always been like this. For a long time, she'd been Antonia's younger sister and nothing more, barely registering on his radar. She'd been the figure at the end of the row in their wedding photograph, wearing a dress the color of old mushrooms that made her look dead. Then there had been that afternoon when he had turned up at her flat, redeyed and smelling of whiskey. She still didn't know why she'd let him in that day, or any of the others that had followed it.

Still, free food. She found the table in the kitchen, got a plate, and overloaded it with tiny sandwiches and hummus and carrot sticks, then went out into the garden. Most of the children were on or around the bouncy castle, apart from a couple of timid ones who clung to their mothers' skirts, thumbs plugged firmly in their mouths. There were chairs dotted around. Bea found an empty pair under the plum tree and sat on one of them. The branches were heavy with fruit, and every so often some would fall off and hit the ground with a thud and a splat of red juice. That was probably why everyone else had avoided those seats. Too

worried about a direct hit ruining their dry-clean-only out-
fits. Bea didn't have such concerns. If you couldn't throw it
in the washing machine along with everything else, she
didn't buy it.

She pulled a carrier bag out of her back pocket and shook
it open. She grabbed a couple of the fallen fruits and tossed
them into the bag, positioning it between her feet, discreetly
watching the other guests as she did so.

The group gathered close to the drink table had to be
the people Owen worked with at the hospital. And the
women on the picnic blankets—the ones in brightly colored
wrap dresses and flip-flops trying to hide their post-baby
tummies—they had to be from some sort of toddler group.
They had that look about them: tired but defensive, ready to
declare that mothering was a full-time job and a valuable
one at that.

Bea didn't dispute it. It was just that in her case, she didn't
get to choose mothering or work, she had to do both, often
at the same time. She couldn't afford childcare, and she
couldn't afford not to work, so she did shifts for an agency
that supplied domestic cleaners and took Simon with her.
She wasn't supposed to, but she figured it was fine as long as
she didn't get caught. He was probably the only four-year-
old here who knew how to work a vacuum cleaner.

And he was probably the only untested boy, she thought
as another plum fell from the tree and she picked it up and
threw it into the bag. Over the past year, the test had taken
off in a way that Bea had not expected. It had gone from being something niche, discussed only by doctors and parents

of newborn boys, to something that even random people on the street seemed to be aware of.

At least she wasn't the only woman who didn't fit in. There was someone else who didn't seem to have received the colorful dress memo, having opted instead for black pants and a sleeveless top in the same color. The woman was tall and lean, and she stood on her own, watching the action on the bouncy castle, ropy arms folded tightly across her narrow middle.

She turned and caught Bea's gaze, and Bea immediately looked away, feeling like she'd been caught doing something wrong. She stuffed a sandwich into her mouth and started to chew. She was only halfway through it when a shadow moved across the grass in front of her, and then the woman sat down on the empty chair.

"Hi," she said. "I'm Zara."

She held out a hand, a confident gesture that Bea reciprocated only because there seemed no other option. "Bea."

"You're the sister."

"That's right," Bea said, surprised.

"I thought so. Your two boys are very alike, aren't they? Could almost be brothers."

"You're not the first person to say that," Bea replied, taking a bite of a second sandwich. "I guess we've got strong genes in our family. How do you know Antonia?"

"My husband works with Owen," Zara said.

"He's a doctor?"

"Yes. I used to be a lawyer, before I had our son."

Another wealthy housewife, Bea thought to herself. *Oh, joy.*

Zara turned her head and stared at the bouncy castle, presumably because her son was on it. "I hear you didn't have yours tested."

"No, I didn't," Bea said, shaking her head. She paused. *Oh, what the hell?* Might as well say it before she was asked. "I think it's cruel."

"I wish I hadn't." Zara reached up, tightened her ponytail. "But then, I never in a million years thought that we'd get a positive result."

"Your son is M-positive?"

It was the first time that Bea had met someone willing to admit to it. She'd met plenty, like her sister, who announced their negative status with undeniable pride. But having an M+ son was a bit like having a child who wet the bed or wasn't very bright. You kept it to yourself.

"Yes," Zara replied. She stared straight ahead. "Malcolm's fine; honestly he is. I don't want you to think . . ."

"I didn't think anything," Bea interrupted her. "I judge people by how they behave, not on the basis of some stupid test."

She was about to get up and go back into the kitchen for more food when a scream came from the direction of the bouncy castle. It was high-pitched and furious and quickly morphed into a howl that made her wince. Zara was on her feet and moving before Bea had even put her plate down. She scrambled up onto the bouncy castle and wobbled her way forward as everyone else in the garden fell silent. Several parents rushed over to see what had happened.

It only took a few seconds before Zara reappeared with a

small floppy-haired boy under one arm. She had to be seriously strong, Bea thought, because he was fighting her every step of the way.

No one moved. No one said a word. Bea could only watch as Zara staggered to the edge of the bouncy castle and slithered down onto the grass. Her chin was pressed into her chest, her face flaming red, her gaze fixed on the ground. Her son was screaming like he was being murdered. The sound made Bea want to cover her ears.

Only when two other little boys crawled to the edge of the bouncy castle did anyone else move. One of them was Simon, his face pale, his eyes wide and worried. The other was Jack, and he was red-faced and sobbing.

Antonia shot across the lawn like a bullet. She snatched up her son and wrapped her arms around him. He buried his face in her neck as she stroked his hair and asked him in a high-pitched, crooning voice if he was all right. Then she marched straight over to Zara.

"You need to control your son," Antonia raged. "And if you won't, don't take him to a birthday party." It was said with such venom that Bea could feel it pressing against her skin. She didn't think that she had ever seen her sister so angry.

"We were invited," Zara said as she gave up and put her struggling son down. He immediately made a run for it but was quickly caught by a man who Bea assumed was his father. They had the same distinctive aquiline nose.

"Not by me," Antonia hissed back. She was leaning forward slightly, and her face had taken on a hard, pointy look.

There was no reasoning with her when she got like this. The only thing you could do was to get out of her way.

"Time to go, little buddy," Bea said to Simon, leaning down so she could whisper it close to his ear. She took his hand and carefully picked her way between the other adults, who were watching Antonia and Zara with poorly disguised glee. None of them took any notice as she went back into the house, grabbed a bottle of orange juice and some butter from the fridge, and then left via the front door. She didn't want to wait around for someone to remember that, whatever had happened, Simon had been in the middle of it, too.

She hadn't really wanted to go to the party anyway. Next time she would listen to her gut rather than let Antonia bulldoze her into stuff she wasn't sure about. She had just crossed the street when she heard footsteps behind her and turned to see Zara and her husband rushing out of the house. He was carrying their little boy, arms wrapped tightly around him so that he couldn't struggle. The child was roughly loaded into the back seat of a Range Rover. Bea could still hear him screaming even after the car door had been closed.

Zara took a packet of cigarettes out of her pocket, lit one with a shaking hand, and then took a long drag. Her husband put his arms around her. She shook him off. His face turned dark.

Feeling like she was intruding on a private scene, Bea held on to Simon's hand a little tighter and gave a tug, prompting him to walk faster. She had meant what she'd said when she'd told Zara she thought that testing children was cruel.

You got what you were given, and you had to make the best of it.

She knew she was the odd one out in feeling that way. Sometimes it seemed like everyone felt entitled to know everything about their children even before they were born. Is it pink or blue? Does it have any genetic diseases that I might want to opt out of dealing with? Does it have the correct number of fingers and toes? Is it perfect? Or do I want to reject this one and see if I get a better one next time?

As she glanced back at Zara, she knew she'd made the right choice when she'd refused to have Simon tested. She'd seen the way Antonia and the other parents at the party had reacted, and she'd just watched the miserable fallout from that play out right in front of her.

Her life was already difficult enough. She was broke, she had no real career prospects, and she was living with a man who thought mixing pasta with a tin of soup constituted cooking.

She didn't need to make it worse.

||| BEA

Now

Bea sat alone in the enormous backyard of her sister's enormous house with only a jug of ice water and a small bowl of olives for company. Antonia had made some excuse about needing to make dinner. Bea didn't mind. It was quiet out here. The rosebushes were in full bloom, and there was a dove cooing in an apple tree. With her back to the house, she could pretend that she was sitting in a lovely park somewhere and that everything wasn't falling apart.

It had been so hard to look at her sister.

Antonia's hair swung around her ears in a Vidal Sassoon bob as glossy as honey. Her French manicure was perfect, setting off the large solitaire in her engagement ring, and her clothes subtly whispered *Money, money, money* every time she moved. She didn't seem to have aged at all.

Bea didn't need to look in a mirror to know that the same wasn't true of herself. She'd always been so proud of her lack of vanity, had worn it like a badge of honor in the face of

Antonia's beauty treatments and obsessive gym schedule. Now it just made her feel stupid.

The kitchen window was open, letting out the sound of cupboards being opened and closed, the clatter of pans, the sizzle of onions and olive oil. And then, expected but unwanted, the sound of her brother-in-law's voice. Bea stiffened in her seat, holding her breath as she strained to listen, trying to make out the words.

"Darling!" Antonia said. "I'm so glad you're home!"

"What is that car doing outside our house?"

"I know you're not going to believe this, but . . ."

There was no mistaking the wobble in her sister's voice. Bea sighed, got to her feet, and walked over to the French doors that led into the kitchen. She didn't let herself hesitate before opening one side and walking in. "Hello, Owen," she said from the doorway, and she saw the color drain from his face and then surge back into it almost as quickly.

"Bea?" he said as if he couldn't believe it. "What are you doing here?"

"I thought it was time I paid you a visit," she replied. "You look well."

"Glass of wine, anyone?" Antonia said brightly, opening the fridge and reaching for a bottle.

"Not for me, thanks." Bea shook her head.

"It's been a long time," Owen said as Antonia hastily filled a glass and held it out to him. King of the castle as always, Antonia his fussing little servant, the perfect doctor's wife.

Bea made herself meet his gaze and look straight into his

eyes. (Hazel green. She'd forgotten that.) "Five years," she confirmed.

"And Simon's here, too?"

"Yes," she said. She tucked her hands into the pockets of her jeans. "Is that a problem?"

There was a chilly pause. "No," Owen said. "I was merely curious. He's what, eighteen now?"

"Three months ago," Bea said. She could sense Antonia hovering nearby. She had forgotten how uncomfortable she found being in a room with both of them at the same time. But she also found herself able to acknowledge it and then ignore it. It didn't seem to matter anymore. Bigger mistakes had been made since then, the type that made the poor decisions of her youth seem exactly that.

"Ah," Owen replied. "And he's well, I take it? You both are?"

"We're doing all right," Bea said. She was hardly going to tell him the truth. "How's life at the clinic?"

"I can't complain," Owen said, a brittle smile pulling at the edges of his mouth. "Are you working?"

"Of course," Bea said. She smiled, too, forgetting for a moment that her teeth were bad. She remembered when she saw him recoil. "Wasn't I always?"

"Well, if you'll excuse me," he said, "I need to shower and change."

He slipped past Antonia and out of the kitchen, leaving Bea once again alone with her sister. She hadn't realized until that moment that she'd been expecting him to throw her out of the house. When Antonia turned back to stir the food, Bea found that she was shaking, and she couldn't tell how she felt about it. Had she *wanted* Owen to kick her and Simon out? She didn't know. Simon had been so desperate to come here, and she'd agreed because there didn't seem to be any other option.

"Can I help with anything?" she asked. She needed something to do. Something to stop her from thinking so hard.

"You could set the table," Antonia told her. She didn't have to tell Bea where anything was. The layout of the kitchen hadn't changed in the last five years, although the kitchen itself was new, the cabinets glossy black instead of the oak she remembered. Bea gathered cutlery and napkins, and quickly and silently laid five neat places as Antonia muttered something about salt and noisily rummaged in the spice drawer.

Seeing her chance, Bea slipped upstairs, her feet gentle as she went. She wanted to talk to her son before he saw Owen. She knew how to move quietly when she needed to, and the physical work she'd been doing had put strength into her legs and her back. She paused outside Jack's bedroom. There was no sound. She pushed the door open slowly, only to find the room empty. She lingered there for a moment, looking at Jack's lovely room and all the things that could have been Simon's had she made different choices.

There wasn't anger. That had burned itself out long ago. There was only acceptance and perhaps a little regret. It wasn't an easy life, the one she had made for herself and for Simon.

She didn't hear Owen come up behind her, and when she felt his touch on her shoulder, she spun, fists up, ready to defend herself. "Fucking hell, Owen," she said, breathless. "You scared me."

He stared down at her. She slowly lowered her hands. It was harder than it should have been. "What are you really doing here, Bea?" he asked. "What do you want? Is it money? Because if it is . . ."

"No, I don't want your effing money," she said, although she couldn't deny that she was tempted. It would solve a lot of her problems. But she had learned the hard way that once you started running away from them, you couldn't stop. And she wanted to stop. "I'm here to see my sister. Isn't that enough?"

"I don't believe you."

"Believe what you like," she said flippantly.

"She's happy, Bea," he said. "It took a long time for her to feel that way. And I won't let you take it away from her again."

"I don't want to take anything away from her," she told him. "I never have. If I did, I could have taken *everything*. Or have you forgotten that?"

||| ANTONIA

Fourteen years ago

British Medical Journal #379 (Published 14 July 2013)

ARE DRUG THERAPIES A SUITABLE METHOD OF BEHAVIOR MANAGEMENT IN BOYS IDENTIFIED AS CARRIERS OF THE M GENE?

M. Scott, J. Hardisen, and M. S. Ali, University of Oxford

It has been suggested by several studies that there may be some benefit in offering medication to boys who have tested positively for the M gene in order to manage their aggressive tendencies. It has already been shown that antipsychotic medications can be used with patients who are prone to violent outbursts in psychiatric settings, and it is believed that a similar effect may be achieved in the pediatric population with dosages appropriately reduced. In this study, eighteen boys ages four to seven, all with confirmed positive tests, were given medication for six weeks, and its effectiveness

*evaluated via questionnaires and parental interviews. Fif-
teen out of eighteen boys showed signs of improvement, but
side effects were considered to outweigh the benefits. However, this has demonstrated the potential for drug treatments
and the willingness of parents to use them if appropriate
medications can be identified.*

For Antonia, that birthday party was a catalyst for change.
It remained a topic of discussion among her friends
for several weeks afterward as they replayed and dissected
everything that had happened and every word that had been
said. Zara was swiftly cut off. No one wanted their children
to be around a boy like Malcolm.

Once Zara was completely out of Antonia's social circle,
she was forgotten. They moved on to other things: who
was pregnant or wanted to be, who had gained weight,
who was getting a divorce.

But Antonia couldn't move on. She couldn't seem to let it
go, no matter how hard she tried. She read medical papers
online, read and reread articles in psychology journals—
something she hadn't done since she'd left college. She dis-
covered that several hospitals had begun drug trials, and the
early findings seemed to suggest that antidepressants and
sedatives might help the boys control the mood swings and
rages associated with the M gene, while treatments commonly used for attention deficit disorder seemed to make
them worse.

She mentioned it to Owen one morning as he was getting ready for work.

"It's an area of interest, definitely," he said as he buttoned his pristine white shirt. "The ER department is talking to the parents of older boys who present with injuries, especially those caused by reckless behavior or fighting, and I've got funding to test them. The boys who are positive are being invited to take part in a drug trial the university is running. But it's likely to be several years before we have solid data, and it could take even longer before any treatment is approved nationwide."

"But it's different for private patients, right?"

"Oh, yes," he said, warming to the subject. "Completely different. I can prescribe more freely, and parents would cover the cost of the testing and medication themselves."

Antonia ran a brush through her hair as she mulled that over. An idea was starting to take shape. Owen spent most of his time working at the hospital, but they'd talked about his desire to go into private practice one day. Perhaps this was the opportunity they had been waiting for. "Is that something you'd be interested in?"

He paused in the middle of knotting his tie. "I've been thinking about it," he said. "But it's a big step, Antonia. It would take a lot of work."

"It would be worth it," she said. "The NHS is marvelous, but it moves so slowly. You and I both know that. What's the point in having the test if bureaucracy prevents you from helping boys who are positive?"

"I agree. And I love how passionate you are about it." He wrapped his arms around her. "If I'm going to do this, I need you to be fully on board with it."

"I am," she said. "And I think you should open your own clinic. Start seeing boys now. Not everyone would be able to afford it, I know that, but some people would, and that's better than nothing."

"I'd need to bring in a partner."

"Have you got anyone in mind?"

"As a matter of fact, I do," he said. "Do you remember Paul? He came to Jack's birthday party. We've been talking about the possibility of setting something up together. He's got some good ideas."

Antonia felt herself stiffen, and she could tell that Owen felt it, too, because he abruptly let go of her. "What?" he asked.

"Paul?" she asked quietly. "Zara's husband? Their son is positive, Owen."

"Yes," Owen said, a crease forming between his brows, his voice suddenly sharp. "But that's a good thing. Parents who come to us will know that we understand what they're going through."

"Of course," she said. He was right, she told herself. It would make a difference. And there was no reason why their families should mix. She wouldn't have to spend any time with that boy, or his mother. She moved back into his arms, pretending that his snappish tone hadn't upset her. "I hadn't considered that."

Owen left while Jack was still in bed. Antonia went downstairs and made herself a coffee and got Jack's breakfast things ready. She heard his door open only a couple of minutes after she'd sat down with her mug, followed by the thump of his little feet on the stairs, and she greeted him with a hug and a smile.

As Jack chewed his way through an almond croissant doused in honey, she texted Bea to ask for the address of the house she would be cleaning that morning, intending to go over there for a couple of hours so that the two boys could play together. It was difficult for Bea, who had to work and couldn't afford childcare, and Antonia liked to help out whenever she could. And she worried about her sister. Not knowing Simon's status might be okay now, while he was small, but what about when he got bigger?

Not a good time, Bea texted back.

It was never a good time as far as Bea was concerned. Antonia didn't understand why her sister was so determined to make life hard for herself. She scrolled back through the messages until she found the address of the house that Bea had cleaned on previous Thursdays. "Shall we go and see Simon?" she asked Jack.

"Yes!" he said eagerly, and so it was decided. He watched television as Antonia updated her blog again, adding photos of the new handbag and earrings she'd bought the previous day, as well as a couple of photos of Jack and a comment about how cute he looked with bed hair. She'd started to get a bit of a following, and she didn't like to let her readers down.

She loaded the dishwasher, then the two of them got in the car. He wanted to sit in the front, so she had to unstrap and move his seat, but eventually he was settled, and she gave him his iPad with his favorite game already loaded. He touched her face with the palm of his hand. The hot contact made her smile. He was such a lovely boy.

The house was a beautiful detached redbrick affair with a semicircular drive and wisteria growing up the front, and dominating the front lawn was a fountain with half-nude nymphs frolicking in it. It had been ugly the first time Antonia had seen it, and didn't improve upon second viewing. Where did they think they were living, Versailles? Antonia parked and knocked on the huge front door using the lion's head knocker. When she tried the door, it was open, so she walked straight in. "Bea?" she called out. "Bea, we're here!"

Jack, who was used to these visits to stranger's houses, rushed straight past her and went in search of his cousin, his shoes squeaking on the polished parquet floor. Bea emerged from a room off the hallway, yellow rubber gloves on, cloth in hand. She wiped her forehead with the hem of her T-shirt. "I told you it wasn't a good time," she said crossly.

"But we're here now!"

"I can see that. It'll have to be a short visit. The house has been put up for sale, and I've got to be in and out in an hour because someone is coming to view it."

"Oh!" Antonia said, surprised and a little disappointed. "I didn't realize. Why didn't you say?"

"I did," Bea said. "You didn't listen. Can you go and find Jack, please?"

But Antonia followed her back into the room she'd just been cleaning instead, watching from the doorway as Bea climbed up into the window and quickly polished each tiny pane. Her jeans had a rip in the bottom and her purple cotton panties were on show. It was not a good look.

"I'm busy, Antonia," she said.

There was obvious impatience in her tone, and it stung. "I wouldn't have bothered coming if I'd known you were going to be like this."

"Sorry," Bea said, pausing midwipe. She sighed. "It's just been a difficult morning. Alfie's sick, and I was expecting to get a full day's pay today, which I obviously won't now that I've only got an hour here."

"Do you need money?"

She started polishing again, even faster this time. "No."

You always were a terrible liar, Antonia thought to herself as she took a couple of steps forward into the room. It had been dressed for show, with sweet-smelling pink roses in a vase on the mantelpiece and copies of *Vogue* and *GQ* on the coffee table. She took out her phone and snapped a picture of the flowers for her blog. "Has Simon said anything about Jack's birthday party?"

"Nope," Bea said.

"Jack's still pretty shaken up by it. He's having trouble sleeping, can't stand it if I leave him alone for more than a couple of minutes. Honestly, Bea, if I'd known what that child was going to do, I'd never have let Owen invite him. The whole point of the test is to help us make decisions about what's best for our children, and that includes choosing who to let them spend time with."

"Stop it," Bea said, jumping down from the window and

pulling off the gloves. "I know what you're trying to do, and it won't work."

"What's that supposed to mean?"

"It doesn't mean anything." She pushed the hair back from her face, took out her phone, and checked the time. "I really am busy, Antonia. I'm sorry that Jack is having a hard time, but I don't know what you expect me to do about it."

"I don't expect you to do anything! I just thought you might understand, that's all. You know how difficult his birthday was for me. All I wanted was for him to have a nice party. I don't think that was too much to ask."

"I understand that Zara must be having an incredibly hard time," Bea said, "with people treating her son like a leper."

Antonia stared at her in disbelief. "*She's* having a hard time? My son was born prematurely, Bea. They took him away from me when he was less than an hour old. He spent his first few days being poked and prodded by strangers, and I wasn't even allowed to be there with him. I can't even enjoy his birthday because all I can think about is what went wrong."

Bea walked over and gently touched her arm. "All right, all right," she said. "For god's sake, calm down. Yes, I know that Jack's birthday is always hard for you. But he's okay now. He's healthy; he passed his M test. He had a tricky start, but he got through it—you both did. And there are a lot of people who have it worse. That's all I was trying to say."

Antonia could feel her face heating. She didn't understand why Bea always tried to minimize what had happened to Jack. But then, Bea had strange ideas about a lot of things. Look at her refusal to have Simon tested. Look at her defending Zara and her M+ son. "Yes, well," she said. "Soon there'll be no excuse for boys like Malcolm if they behave badly."

"What do you mean?"

"You must have seen the news reports about drug treatments!"

"I don't really watch the news," Bea said. She tucked the cloth into the waistband of her jeans and looked around the room, as if she were trying to find something else to clean, though from what Antonia could see, it was spotless. She couldn't fault her sister's work.

"Honestly, Bea! Don't you care about what's happening in the world?"

"I care that I've still got three bedrooms to do," Bea replied, and eased past her toward the stairs.

Antonia followed her.

"If you're coming upstairs, you're cleaning a toilet," Bea called back to her.

Antonia was not deterred. "Owen is setting up a private clinic for M-positive boys." She was rewarded with the slightest pause in her sister's stride, but nothing more, and she wanted more. "Don't you think it's a brilliant idea? He'll be able to offer support to their parents and provide medications that can help them manage their symptoms. It could be life-changing. As long as it's caught early enough, it will be treatable."

Bea stopped at the top of the stairs and turned to face her. "Can you hear yourself? You're talking about medicating children who aren't ill, and history tells us that never ends well."

"It's not like that at all. Please, Bea. Just think about it. There's help for these boys, which means that there's no reason not to have Simon tested."

"Antonia," Bea said in the way that she had when they'd been little and Antonia had crossed some invisible line. She didn't say anything else. She didn't have to.

Antonia heard the warning loud and clear. When Bea disappeared into one of the bedrooms, she left her to it. Antonia knew she had to choose which battles to fight.

She went to find the boys instead. They were in the playroom at the back of the house. Simon had a box of Legos and was beavering away, building something that might have been a car or might have been a robot. He was wearing a faded T-shirt and needed a haircut, very much the poor cousin in comparison to Jack, in his new jeans and little leather boots.

Antonia settled herself on the sofa, quietly fuming. Although her gaze was automatically drawn to her son, she made herself focus on Simon instead, watching as he noisily sifted through the Legos. Jack sat next to him, grabbing pieces at random and offering them to Simon. She loved watching the two of them play together. Their bond was obvious, even at this early age.

It was unlikely that Jack would have a sibling. She wasn't sure that she could go through all that again. Simon was the closest he was going to get, and she desperately wanted to protect their relationship, to give it room to grow. It would be good for Simon, too, to spend time with a boy like Jack.

If only she knew what Simon *was*. But once Bea had made

up her mind about something, she was immovable. Antonia could still remember the time when she had refused to wear a hat for a whole winter. She'd said that she didn't like the feel of the wool, that it was itchy, and that she'd rather be cold. It had driven Antonia up the wall. This business with the test was no different.

The obvious solution was to cut ties with her sister. She had plenty of other friends, and Jack wasn't short of playmates. But he had a special bond with Simon, and she didn't know if she could take that away from him.

She loved Bea.

But sometimes she hated her, too.

||| SIMON

Now

Simon's face hurt. He'd found it difficult to sleep, because every time that he rolled over, he would press the bruise against the pillow and wake himself up, floundering in the few seconds it took for his brain to remember that he was at Jack's house and not in the damp trailer that he had slept in for the past four months.

He peered at the clock at the side of the bed. Five in the morning. Might as well get up. His brain wouldn't let him go back to sleep anyway. He went to the bathroom and splashed some cold water on his face, then pulled on shorts and a T-shirt and went downstairs in search of something to eat.

Being back in this house was weird. The previous evening had been weird, too. He'd sat through an awkward family dinner where Antonia had done most of the talking. No one had said anything about the bruises on his face. He got the impression that they'd all been trying very hard not to. That was fine by him.

At least the food had been good. He'd focused on that, ignoring his uncle Owen, who he could feel watching him from the other end of the table. Simon didn't like Owen. He couldn't put his finger on why exactly. It was just a feeling he had whenever Owen was around, a tightness in the pit of his stomach, a sense that he needed to watch his back. He knew why Owen didn't like him. It was obvious. Owen believed in the test, and Simon hadn't had it. He didn't follow Owen's particular brand of religion, the one that said all boys should face judgment at birth, their futures as angels or demons decided before they'd even developed bladder control.

Fuck that.

But Simon was also a realist. He knew the world he lived in, and he knew that he couldn't change it. It was time to stop fighting the inevitable.

A quick survey of the downstairs told him that everyone else was still in bed, so he crept into the kitchen. He took orange juice from the fridge and drank it straight from the bottle, all of it. Folded a slice of bread in half and stuffed it in his mouth in one go. Plucked a handful of grapes from the bunch in the fancy fruit bowl. He was looking in the fridge again when Owen walked in and caught him.

Simon refused to feel ashamed. He was hungry, there was more than enough food in this kitchen for the three people who lived here, and no one had told him he couldn't.

"You're up early," Owen said.

"Force of habit," Simon replied. He took out a large tub of strawberry yogurt, watching his uncle out of the corner of his eye. Bea had told him not to tell his aunt and uncle where they'd been living or what they'd been doing, but it was difficult not to. He wanted to tell Owen just to see the shock on his face.

But he didn't. Instead, he peeled the lid from the tub, took a spoon out of the drawer, and started to eat it in quick, greedy mouthfuls.

Owen set about playing with the fancy coffee machine. "Would you like one?"

No. "Yes. Please." He didn't realize, until it was too late, that this was Owen's way of keeping him in the room a little longer. If he'd known, he would have refused. But it smelled so good, and he had lived with so little for so long.

"What happened to your eye?" Owen asked him as he put a mug in position and pressed a button.

"I . . . I had an accident." It was sort of true. He hadn't intended to let the other boy punch him in the face.

Owen let the silence stretch before he responded. "I see. What sort of accident?"

"Fell over." Also true. He had fallen. When his legs had given out.

"Your mother said you were injured playing rugby."

Shit. "Yes. A rugby accident. The other boy . . . he didn't mean to knock me over. That's what I meant when I said it was an accident." He spooned more yogurt into his mouth before he could say anything else and make it worse.

Owen handed him a mug of coffee. It was a proper mug with a thick handle that had yellow flowers painted on it. It was nothing like the chipped enamel one he often used.

ONE OF THE BOYS

That one was buried somewhere in the trunk of the car, thrown in unwashed, along with everything else. At least, he thought it was. There hadn't been time to check. All that had mattered, afterward, was getting out of there and then persuading Bea to bring him here.

"Did you get medical attention?" Owen asked him.

"No," Simon said.

Owen pushed forward a jug of milk. Simon added a generous helping to his coffee, although there was cream in the fridge, and he would have preferred that and would have taken some if Owen weren't there. But he felt suddenly self-conscious and all too aware that this was Owen's house, that he was a visitor, and an unwelcome one at that.

"Why not?"

"Didn't need it. I'm fine. It's just a black eye. It's not going to kill me."

"Would you mind if I had a look at you?"

Simon carefully set the cup down on the kitchen counter. The hair had suddenly stood up on the back of his neck, a sure sign that he needed to be careful. "What for?"

"You've had a nasty knock to the face. I'd like to check that your eye is okay, that you don't have a fractured cheekbone. It would probably be a good idea to have your teeth looked at, too, and to check for a concussion."

"I'm fine."

"You don't look it," Owen told him. "Come on. It will only take a minute."

Simon wanted to say no, but he couldn't see any way around it. What if he refused and Owen made them leave?

So he submitted and let Owen touch his face and shine a light in his eye. He didn't tell him about the older bruises on his ribs and his back, about the fact that it hurt if he laughed. His uncle didn't need to know about that. Even Jack didn't know about that.

"Are you still untested?" Owen asked him when the examination was finally over.

"Do you honestly think my mom would let me have it?"

"You're eighteen now," Owen replied. "It's no longer her decision." A pause. The sound of their breathing. The smell of Owen's aftershave, grassy and expensive. "It would make your life a lot easier, you know."

"Not if it came back positive," Simon said. He knew how much his aunt and uncle charged for treatment at their fancy clinic, and he couldn't afford it. He'd also met plenty of boys from good families who'd ended up at the farm because they'd been pushed out of everywhere else. He wouldn't go as far as to say that the treatment was snake oil, but it wasn't a magic wand, either.

Owen leaned back against the countertop and looked at him thoughtfully, thumb rubbing against his chin. "Do you think it might?"

"I don't know," Simon said, pissed that Owen was asking him all these questions, pissed that he'd been stupid enough to give him the opportunity. Simon had long ago accepted that he was probably positive. He only had to look at some of the things that he'd done to know that. But if he was going to be tested, he was going to do it his way, and that was none of his uncle's business.

"Do you think you have problems with impulse control? Violent urges?"

What was he supposed to say to that? *Yes, in fact I'm feeling them now?* Owen would never understand anyway, living in this big house, living his perfect life with his M– son. Simon liked his cousin, but sometimes he wanted to scream at the unfairness of it all. "No more than anyone else, I guess."

"Well, that's good," Owen said. "Your eye should be fine. You're young and healthy, and it will heal. But there's a limit to how much abuse a body can take, even a young body like yours. Do you understand what I'm saying?"

Simon nodded. "Stop playing rugby and take up knitting."

Owen chuckled. "Something like that."

He made it sound so easy, but it wasn't. "Is it all right if I take the dog for a walk?" Simon asked. He needed to be outside. He couldn't breathe in here.

"Sure," Owen said after a moment. "He's well trained, obeys the usual commands. Sit, heel, down. But you'll have to pick up after him. Bags are in the utility room, next to the dog food."

"Thanks," Simon said. He downed the rest of his coffee in one go. Flash was sprawled in his basket in the utility room, but he jumped up as soon as he saw Simon, tongue out, ears pricked. Jack had said the dog belonged to Antonia. Simon couldn't see it, personally, but what did he know. There was a leash coiled up next to the bags, so he picked it up and hooked it onto Flash's collar.

The dog looked at him. *Is that really necessary?* he seemed to be saying.

Simon tugged on the leash. The dog didn't resist, which made Simon feel a little better. By the time he led the dog out into the kitchen, Owen had disappeared. The two of them headed out the front door. It was already bright outside, the birds hard at work flirting with each other, the sky cloudless. Simon could tell it was going to be a hot one.

Normally, he'd already have been at work for an hour, loading endless squashed plastic bottles into the grinder that would turn them into pellets, ready to be made into something else. It had been thankless and mind-numbing, and it had made his feet and arms and back hurt. And then there had been the after-work activities, the ones that had caused all the trouble.

Next to that, walking a dog was a piece of piss.

He took Flash across the fields, a route that he remembered quickly once he was back here. Nothing outside of his cousin's house had changed. But inside it? The last time he'd seen his uncle, he'd been twelve and much shorter. It felt strange to find the two of them eye to eye. He felt strange around Jack, too. He hadn't forgotten what had happened the last time the two of them had been together. Had Jack? Without warning, he felt the coffee heave in his stomach.

The sickness that came when he thought about that night in Cornwall was the one thing that had made Simon hope that there was still a chance he was M−. He could, if he worked at it, talk himself into believing that it was circumstance that had made him do what he'd done at the farm rather than some innate flaw. He wasn't broken; he was living in a broken society. He could cope with that. What he couldn't cope with anymore was living in the gray in-between as an untested boy, an unknown.

Because when people didn't know, they assumed you were bad.

At least the dog didn't ask him any difficult questions. Flash was huge, with big scary teeth and shits that looked like a bear had done them. He didn't bark much or pull on the leash, so Simon took it off, though he had a moment of panic when a silly little mutt with curly white fur and a high-pitched yap came rushing up to them. But Flash simply growled at it, and it ran away. Maybe that was the point. Antonia had always treated Jack like he was made of glass. Maybe the dog was added protection.

The fields gave way to a park. Simon put on a burst of speed, the dog following, then slowed down and jogged over to the swings. He sat on one of them. Flash wandered off to sniff at the bushes. Simon pressed his heels against the rubber matting and gently moved himself to and fro. He'd come here for breathing room, to give himself space to think, but he realized now that was the last thing he needed. He just wanted today to be over.

"Jack?"

It was a female voice, relatively young, if he was any judge. He grabbed the chains, twisted around to look at her. She stood a few meters away. Black leggings, tennis shoes, one of those tops that showed her belly button. Her hair was pulled up into a high ponytail, and she had her phone strapped to her arm. A ripple of what felt like electricity moved through his body.

"No," he said. "I'm Simon."

"Oh." She blushed. "I thought . . . That is Jack's dog, right?" She pointed at Flash, who had one leg cocked against a nearby tree.

"Yeah," Simon said. "That's Flash. I'm Jack's cousin. We're staying with him for a few days."

"Oh," she said again. She finally looked at him properly and blinked. "Wait, did you say *Simon*? I'm Ginny."

Ginny? He stared at her. "Ginny Rabbino?"

"That's me. Well, Ginny Sloan now, officially. I changed my name to my stepdad's ages ago. You didn't recognize me, did you?"

"Oh my god," he said, otherwise speechless. He felt suddenly horribly embarrassed by his hair and his clothes, and when her gaze lingered on his injured face, he wanted the ground to open up and swallow him. She had gone to school with Jack, and he hadn't known her that well, but their paths had crossed a few times. Jack had some photos of her on his Instagram. Simon had spent longer than he should have looking at them. "Last time I saw you, you were . . ." He stopped himself before he could say anything bad.

"Eleven and chubby," she said, puffing out her cheeks and making her face round. "Yes, I remember. I didn't know you were back."

"I'm not, really," Simon said, feeling immediately stupid. "Only for a few days. We're just visiting." There was an awkward silence, and he sensed she was waiting for him to say something more. He fumbled for words. "Do you want me to pass on a message? To Jack?"

"No," she said. "It's fine. It was nice to see you, Simon." And with that, she set off at a run, giving Flash a wide berth.

Ginny Rabbino.

He swallowed the saliva that had filled his mouth and told himself not to be so stupid. She would never be interested in a boy like him.

But after he got tested?

Maybe.

CHAPTER NINE

BEA

Fourteen years ago

Bea didn't see much of Antonia over the next few months. She was invited for dinner a couple of times, but when it came to it, she just couldn't face it. She told Antonia that Simon was sick, knowing how protective her sister was of Jack. The last thing she wanted was to spend an evening listening to Owen drone on about the test and how amazing all this modern science was.

Amazing for you, she thought, *with all the money you'll be making. Not for the rest of us.* As far as she was concerned, it was just something else that middle-class parents could do to show off their good parenting credentials, like organic vegetables and private schooling.

She had bigger problems, anyway. Real-world problems. Alfie had gotten a job working as a gardener for the local council, which meant that he and Bea could no longer split the childcare during the week. Bea had managed when she only had Simon three days a week, but five was too much.

She was going to have to put Simon in day care and somehow find a way to make the money work. She tried half a dozen before she found one that had a space. When she visited, it was lovely, with a beautiful outdoor play area and a library full of books. The children were all wearing green-and-red T-shirts that made Bea think of Christmas elves. Simon kept a tight grip on her hand, but she could sense his desire to join in.

The woman who ran the place talked quickly and nonstop with the softly undulating tone that made Bea feel like she was back in grade school. "I assume your son has had all his vaccinations?" she asked.

"Yes, of course," Bea said, though she was only half listening. She was busy doing a few mental sums. The day care was more expensive than she'd budgeted for, but now that she'd seen it, she wanted him to come here. She wanted to give him this.

"And he's tested?"

She caught herself before she could reply. "Excuse me?"

"I asked if he's been tested."

"Are you allowed to ask that?"

The woman turned a funny color and coughed, then checked her watch. "Oh!" she said. "Look at the time! I'm terribly sorry. It's snack time, and we don't allow visitors to be here for that."

Bea found herself being quickly ushered back to the front door, which was unlocked and held open for her. "It was lovely to see you!" the woman said. "We'll be in touch soon to let you know if we have a place!" Then the door was closed firmly behind them, and Bea heard the sound of the lock turning, a sharp snick.

It took her a moment to gather herself.

"Mommy?" Simon asked.

She picked him up. She didn't know what to say. All of a sudden, the building, which had seemed so inviting, seemed closed off and unwelcoming, its shiny exterior nothing more than a facade. It reminded her of visiting Santa's village when she was a child. It seemed magical and beautiful at first, and then after you'd been in and opened the gift you'd been given and found that it was a nasty plastic doll with a badly painted face and a weird smell, you realized that it wasn't magical at all.

She tried another four preschools. Three of them wouldn't even arrange a visit when she refused to answer their question about the test. That evening she spent an hour on the internet desperately trying to find out if preschools were legally allowed to exclude boys who hadn't been tested, but the information on the government website was so confusing that she was left none the wiser.

"We should sue them," Alfie said.

"We're not suing them," Bea said. "That's ridiculous. How would we pay for an attorney?"

"Well, it shouldn't be allowed!"

"I'll find somewhere," she promised him.

And she did.

Unlike the others, this one didn't ask for much more than his date of birth and address. "He gets two days a week for free," the woman said briskly over the phone. "If you want more than that, you'll have to pay. We charge for lunches. Milk is also extra; otherwise, they get water and one piece of fruit a day. We promote healthy eating here."

"Right," Bea said. The information had been fired at her like bullets. She felt like she should have questions, but she couldn't think of any. She was sent some forms, which she filled in and returned. They didn't say anything about the test. She felt a little better. When they got there for Simon's first morning, no one seemed to have any idea who she was, and the building, with its crumbling Victorian brickwork and rusting cast-iron drainpipes, made her think of a workhouse, and she felt a lot worse. The view from the window was of a main road. There were swings in the playground, but a seat was missing from one, the chains hanging like a pair of thin arms.

Not for the first time, Bea wobbled. But there was no other choice. She let Simon go in and then went online and looked at test appointments. The first one she could get was a month away. She booked it. She didn't tell Alfie.

But, to her surprise, the first couple of weeks of day care were fine, probably more traumatic for her than for Simon.

It was quickly obvious to her that he needed the company of other children, and she felt bad for having deprived him of it. Things quickly got easier. It became routine. His vocabulary exploded. She canceled the appointment.

Then, on the third week, Bea noticed a woman standing apart from the group at pickup time. There was something familiar about her. She didn't look like she belonged with the other mothers, with her sharply tailored pants and gorgeous quilted leather bag. At first, Bea thought she might live in one of the houses she cleaned, though she couldn't imagine any of the women who lived in them using this day care.

The woman turned her head, as if she could feel Bea's stare on the back of her neck, and it was then that Bea knew where she'd seen her before. It had been at Jack's birthday party. She was the mother of the M+ boy who had caused all the trouble. She looked steadily at Bea, her gaze unwavering. Bea's instinct was to run, but she had nowhere to run to, and she could hardly leave Simon.

"Hello," the woman said. "Do we know each other?"

"I think you might know my sister, Antonia?"

The woman narrowed her eyes. "The birthday party," she said.

Bea felt her mouth go dry. "I'm afraid so."

The woman shook her head, a wry grin curving her lips. "Gosh, this is awkward," she said. "I'm Zara, by the way. I'm sorry to say I can't remember your name. It all got a bit lost in the . . . drama."

"I'm Bea." She tucked a loose strand of hair behind her ear. "How are you?"

"I'm . . . not so good, to be honest. My husband and I split up a couple of weeks after the party."

Bea was shocked. "Oh my god. I'm so sorry."

"Don't be," Zara said. She tried to smile. "It's probably for the best. We weren't getting along, and it was only making the situation with Malcolm worse." She opened her bag and fished inside it, then took out her phone. The screen was cracked. Up close, the bag had a split in the leather, and the pants had seen better days, too. "Can I have your number? Perhaps we could meet up sometime."

"Sure," Bea said, because it would be rude not to.

Zara tapped the number into her phone, then dropped it back into her bag as the doors were opened and the children were brought out one by one. Usually Bea arrived right at the end of pickup, when most of the other children had gone, but she'd arrived early today. It was the first time that she noticed how few girls there were, an odd fact that she acknowledged but didn't really consider further, the thought slipping easily from her mind as Simon came running out.

She dropped to her knees, opening her arms for her son to run into, and she hugged him tightly, touching his face, smelling his hot little boy smell. Although she was finding life much easier now that he was at day care, she still missed him terribly.

Then Zara's son was brought out. He trudged over to Zara with a sullen look on his face. She didn't hug him. He had lank pale hair, a red jacket, and a scab on his top lip. He was—although Bea would never have said it out loud—a pasty and unattractive child.

"I'll call you soon," Zara said to Bea.

She hadn't acknowledged her son. It seemed to Bea that she was deliberately choosing not to look at him, and that made Bea not like the other woman very much. But she pushed the feeling back. She always made a concerted effort not to judge other people. You never really knew what was going on in their lives. And Zara was having a difficult time. That was obvious.

"Great!" Bea replied, injecting the word with false cheer. She took Simon's hand as Zara turned on her heel and marched back toward the road, her little boy trailing along behind her.

It caused a quick little pain in the vicinity of Bea's heart, but it was soon forgotten as she was consumed by Simon's chatter, letting it fill up the space left by his absence. She didn't spare Zara another thought until she called her later that evening and invited her for coffee.

It wasn't really something that Bea had time for, but she found the offer of female company too tempting to turn down. It was hard to admit that Alfie wasn't enough for her, but the bottom line was that she was an overworked mother, constantly worrying about money, about time, about everything, and Alfie couldn't understand a lot of how she felt. He hadn't been the one who had given birth in a bathroom. His body wasn't damaged in ways that he had no choice but to accept. He parented only when he wanted to, took on only the good bits, and left the rest to her. Although Antonia was exhausting, she understood in her own way, which was why Bea held on to that relationship, even though her sister's obsession with the test made it so damn difficult sometimes. It was funny, she thought. Jack's test was negative, so Antonia should have been able to move on and forget about it, but instead, it had become her whole life. Obviously, Owen was mostly to blame for that, but Antonia didn't need to be quite so happy about it.

"Do you see much of your sister?" Zara asked almost as soon as they'd sat down with their coffees, black for her, latte for Bea.

"Not really," Bea replied truthfully. "She's . . . we're very different people." That seemed the politest way of putting it.

"Oh," Zara replied. "Well, my ex is in the process of becoming a partner in the clinic that Owen is setting up. I thought she might have mentioned it."

Bea couldn't help but wonder how Antonia managed to square that circle, given the way she'd behaved toward Zara at the party. Though in her experience, her sister had always been far more forgiving of men than women. "Not to me," she said. "But I'm sure she'll find a way to rub her success in my face soon enough."

Zara laughed, and soon Bea did, too. It felt good. It loosened a little knot of tension inside her, something that had been there since she'd first realized that she was pregnant. She'd been alone for a long time. Yes, she had Alfie, but that was as much about convenience as it was about love, for her at least. They didn't really talk, not properly, not about things that mattered. She couldn't tell him her secrets. She couldn't tell Antonia, either. She didn't know if she could

tell Zara yet. But at least she could laugh. That was something.

"You should come to dinner," Zara said. "Malcolm is going to Paul's for the weekend, and I'll have the place to
myself. It would be nice to have company."

"I'd love to," Bea said, and so it was arranged for that Saturday. Alfie said he would take Simon to his mother's, but
at the last minute he came down with a cold (how convenient), so Bea took him with her. She told herself that she
didn't mind. She didn't have to shop, cook, or wash up, and
she had a bag of crayons and coloring books to keep Simon
amused. Zara's house was just across the street from one
that she cleaned regularly, which made it easy to find.

To her surprise, Malcolm answered the door. He was
wearing a T-shirt and underpants, and as he looked up at
Bea, she felt a shiver run down her spine, as if someone had
touched her with cold fingers. There was something about
him that set her teeth on edge, even as she told herself that he
was just a normal little boy, just like any other little boy, just
like Simon. The M test didn't matter. It didn't mean anything
in a child this young.

"Hello," she said, forcing herself to smile at him. "Is your
mom in?"

He ignored her and looked at Simon, one hand wrapped
around the edge of the door. His nails were chewed to the
quick. "I've got a goldfish. Do you want to see it?"

Simon looked up at Bea, his eyes wide. "Can I?"

Bea knew there was no chance of saying no to that. Simon was obsessed with animals, and was constantly nag-

ging for a pet. "If Malcolm's mommy says it's okay," she told
him, wishing Zara would appear.

But Malcolm grabbed Simon's arm, and the two boys disappeared into the house before that could happen. Bea followed.
As soon as she stepped inside, she heard adult voices coming
from upstairs, one male and one female, and it was clear from
the tone of those voices that they were having a fight.

Shit, she thought to herself. *What do I do?*

She couldn't just sneak back out again, not without Simon. She walked quietly forward into the house, checking
each room as she passed it, but there was no sign of him,
and sweat began to gather under her arms. "Damn you, Simon," she muttered. In the kitchen, onions and tomatoes
sat on the cutting board next to a large knife, evidence that
the promised meal wasn't even close to being ready.

She went back to the hallway, trying to summon up the
courage to venture upstairs, only to find a man coming
down them. He was wearing casual pants and a striped shirt
unbuttoned at the collar. He was tanned and lean and reminded her of Owen. They both had the same healthy, mon-
eyed look about them—arrogance combined with vanity.

He stopped when he saw her, and she felt his gaze snap
across her body, taking her in, assessing her, dismissing her
as a woman of potential sexual interest. She didn't think he
even knew that he'd done it. If they'd met in a public place,
he would have barreled straight past her, probably straight
through her, without even breaking stride.

"Hello," he said. "You must be Bea. I'm Paul."

He was a handshaker, but he kept it brief, and if he was

concerned that Bea might have overheard the two of them arguing, he showed no sign of it.

"Zara will be down in a minute," he said.

Bea wondered if she should mention that she knew they had split up. She shifted her weight from foot to foot. God, this was awkward. "Malcolm took Simon to look at his fish," she said.

"Right," Paul said. He leaned back and shouted up the stairs. "Zara! You need to check what your son is doing!"

Then he turned his attention back to Bea. "I understand that you're Owen's sister-in-law," he said.

"That's right."

"Your son isn't tested, is he?"

Not this again. "No," Bea replied, trying to see past him. She was starting to feel a little worried. She'd rather know where Simon was and what he was doing than stand here and discuss her parenting choices.

"You should seriously consider it. We're doing some brilliant stuff for M-positive boys now. The research is moving at a rapid pace. The hope is that with the right treatment, they'll be able to live full, normal lives."

"You make it sound like a disease."

"It is a disease," Paul said. His eyes narrowed a little, as if her response had irritated him. "How else would you describe it?"

"I thought the M gene was a predisposition. It's not a guarantee of anything. Surely with the right parenting . . ." She trailed off. Why was she bothering? He wouldn't agree with her. He ran a clinic that existed only because of the test. It went without saying that he'd support it.

"Lovely in theory," he said. "But we live in the real world, and most children don't get the right parenting. And even when they do, it's not always enough. M-positive boys can be extremely challenging. Trust me. I know that better than anyone."

Zara chose that exact moment to come down the stairs. She was dressed casually in skinny jeans and a black T-shirt; her cheeks were pink, and Bea could tell that she'd been crying.

"Hi," she said to Bea. She rubbed at her face with her sleeve and tried to smile. The attempt was not successful.

"It was nice to meet you, Bea," Paul said, moving past her.

"Where are you going?" Zara asked him. "What about Malcolm?"

"He isn't ready," he said. "I told you to have him ready, and you didn't. What do you expect me to do? I can't wait around all evening. I've got plans."

"You mean *she's* got plans, and you've decided they're more important than your son," Zara said.

"Her name is Lily."

He glanced at Bea as if expecting her to show him some support. Bea wished the ground would open up and swallow her. He'd already moved on? Really? No wonder Zara was pissed off.

"Fine," Zara said. "Leave Malcolm here. Go running off to your perfect new family. But don't expect me to be reasonable in the divorce. I'm going to *ruin* you. See how interested she is then, when you're broke."

Suddenly, she jerked around and thundered back up the stairs as if she'd heard something. Bea hesitated, but only for a moment, before following her. There was a sudden sick feeling in her stomach, a heaviness, an overwhelming sense that something was wrong.

Simon stood at the top of the stairs, biting his thumb, one foot pressed on top of the other in the way that he did when he was anxious. He was watching something in a room farther down the hall. He looked up as Bea approached.

"What did you do?" she asked him.

"I wanted to hold the fish," he said. "But it jumped out of my hand, and then Malcolm said we had to kill it."

And in the room beyond, stamping on something on the floor, was Malcolm. Zara sat on the bed with her head in her hands. There was no sound apart from the thud of Malcolm's foot hitting the carpet. After a moment, Zara rose to her feet, seemingly unaware of Bea's presence. She grabbed her son by the arm and, quick as a flash, threw him to the floor, where he lay stunned and silent for a moment before he started to scream.

Bea couldn't breathe. She thought she might be sick. She picked Simon up, pushed her way past Paul, who was hovering at the bottom of the stairs, and let herself out of the house.

She helped Simon into the back of the car, let him deal with his own seat belt, and drove hastily around the corner, out of sight, before parking and fumbling in the glove box for the packet of wet wipes she always kept in there. She pulled a couple out, cleaned his fingers, then opened the window and dropped the wipes in the gutter.

She put the music on loud so that she couldn't hear Simon talk and drove home, her stomach still churning. Alfie was asleep on the sofa, snoring like an express train. She and Simon ate cereal for dinner, which Simon thought was a brilliant treat, then she put him to bed. She didn't sleep that night. Simon didn't, either, and she could still hear him banging around in his room at one in the morning. She made no effort to settle him or tell him to stop.

Antonia had said that the test was important because it meant that you could keep your son away from dangerous boys. Bea didn't want her to be right. But she didn't want to let Simon spend any more time with Malcolm, either. He needed a friend who was a good boy. A good example. A boy who wouldn't teach him to do terrible things.

An M— boy.

The first thing she did the following morning was call Antonia.

CHAPTER TEN

ANTONIA

Now

Antonia had debated whether she should go to work that morning or if it would be better to stay at home and spend some time with her sister. Jack had been feeling a bit unwell, too, which had worried her, but in the end, she'd gone to the clinic. They had built their reputation with dedication and hard work, and she wasn't prepared to let anything mess that up, not even Bea. Especially not Bea. And Jack would be all right after a day in bed. She could trust him to take care of himself.

Antonia's role as a counselor and play therapist was one that she took seriously. She was there to support the parents. To give them a sounding board, a space to say the things they couldn't say to anyone else. She also taught them skills that would get them through day-to-day life with an M+ boy in the family. The medications were good, but it wasn't enough to prescribe them and then leave parents to their own devices. They needed help to manage the side ef-

fects, the inevitable judgment from friends and family, the
emotional strain that came from first accepting and then
managing a child with a lifelong condition.

But as she sat down with her second family of the
day, she knew her mind wasn't on the work. How could it
be? She had to force herself to focus, to smile at the nervous-
looking couple, the woman still thick with baby weight,
dark circles under her eyes, her roots starting to show. Her
husband looked better, though there was a tension to the
way he held his body that told Antonia that although he
wasn't doing night feeds, he wasn't doing as well as he was
trying to make out.

"We want to get ahead of the problem," he explained, sitting stiffly in his chair, shoulders straining at the seams of
his expensive polo shirt. He was wearing a big steel watch,
and his wedding ring gleamed brightly against his tanned
skin.

Antonia switched her gaze to the baby, asleep in his car
seat, his head buried inside the hood of a jacket several sizes
too big. All she could see of him was his chin and his tiny
nose.

The woman reached down and fiddled with his blanket,
completely unnecessarily in Antonia's opinion, though she
recognized the move from her own early days as a mother.
It spoke of a fierce urge to release him from the straps and
scoop him up, to hold him against her breasts, to push him
somehow back inside her body and keep him there, perhaps forever. Antonia knew that feeling only too well.

"He's only a baby," the woman said, her voice thin and a

little high-pitched. She glanced across at her husband, who reached out and rested one of his hands firmly on top of hers.

"I know," Antonia said gently. "And I know how over-whelming all of this must seem. But you are in the right place, believe me. The last thing you want to do is wait until there's a problem and then try and find a treatment program that can accept him straightaway. This way, you can visit several clin-ics, see what they have to offer, and make the right decision for you. And with treatment started early, he'll be fine."

"Does it definitely work?" the man asked. "Because I've read some studies online that say otherwise."

Antonia gave him a sympathetic smile. "I can only tell you what I tell everyone who asks me that. Google is not your friend. Please don't look online. You'll only end up not knowing what to do. You've come here because you wanted professional advice. And I'm telling you, as a professional, that the treatment works. When it doesn't, it's because par-ents haven't stuck with it."

He sat up a little straighter. "We're not like that," he said.

"I'm glad to hear it. Now, we offer various programs here. There's medication, of course, but there are also tried-and-tested parenting techniques that we can teach you. We usually recommend a combination of the two for the best result, and of course we can tailor it to suit you and your lifestyle."

The two of them looked at each other. They could go one of two ways at this point: either the father, despite his initial interest, would ask how much it was going to cost, or the mother would get in first and say she wanted the personal-ized program with no mention of money at all. Antonia thought she knew which way they were going to go, though you could never be sure. But she'd gotten pretty good at reading people over the years.

"We just want to do what's best," the woman said. She looked like she was going to burst into tears.

Antonia got up, moved to the other side of the desk, and took the woman's hand. "It's so hard, isn't it? Overwhelming, really. And we understand that, we really do. The thing to remember is that we're on your side and we want the same thing. We want what's best for our boys."

The woman looked down at the baby and didn't look back up. By the time he started crying, the contract had been printed and they had signed it. Antonia told them they could use the room to have some privacy to feed the baby.

She tapped at her phone as she walked out of the office, logging in to the app that controlled the cameras she had positioned around the house. Bea was in the living room watching the television. She couldn't see either Jack or Simon. They were probably both still in bed. Typical teenage boys.

She tapped the icon that took her to the doorbell camera. It was placed at an angle to give her a wide view of the street so she could see the gate and, through it, the front end of Bea's car. As she watched, there was movement on the screen. Another car rolled into view. It was white, with sharp markings down the side, and she recognized who it was immediately.

The police.

And that was the moment when she knew that her sister's visit wasn't merely a social call.

||| ANTONIA

Thirteen years ago

Parenting, November

GIVING HOPE TO BOYS

Meet the men determined to help our boys. Dr. Owen Talbot and Dr. Paul Sloan, cofounders of the Hopeful Futures Clinic, are on a mission to revolutionize care for boys diagnosed as M+.

"We've got the test," says Dr. Talbot. "Now we've got to make sure that M-positive boys are given every opportunity to lead full and productive lives. Otherwise, there's a risk that they'll be left behind." Dr. Talbot, who is thirty-five and married with a son of his own, is determined to make sure that doesn't happen. That's why he and his partner, Dr. Sloan, have set up the clinic, the first of what they hope will be several. It's been a hard slog, both men continuing with their work as pediatricians for the NHS while the clinic was

in development. "We don't want to let anybody down," Dr.
Sloan remarked. "We both believe in the NHS, and we'll
continue to work for it as long as possible. But M-positive
boys can't wait. And with the new guidance from the De-
partment of Health, which allows us to directly supply the
necessary medications, Hopeful Futures will be able to pro-
vide everything parents need while ensuring their child's
privacy."

Setting up the clinic proved to be harder than Antonia
had expected, but she did everything she could to help,
from making phone calls to posting about it on her blog
and starting a website. She wanted Owen to be able to focus on what he needed to do and not have to worry about
any of those things.

She viewed half a dozen offices before she found one that
she liked. It was in a good location, close to the town center
but not so close that traffic would be difficult, and the building also housed a dentist, which she felt gave it the right
feel. It had two offices, one each for Paul and Owen, plus a
space for a reception desk and waiting area. She ordered
carpets and furniture and then took Owen to see it on one
of Jack's days at day care.

"You've done a great job," he said. "We'll have this place
overrun with patients in no time."

"I thought I could run the reception," Antonia said, gesturing to the wide desk with the blue swivel chair behind it,
chosen to match the colors of the clinic name, which she'd
had carefully painted on the wall.

"Lily's going to do that," Owen said. "She's got secretarial experience, so it makes sense."

"Oh, of course!" Antonia said, disappointment sitting heavy in her stomach. She didn't let Owen see it. This was too important to let personal feelings get in the way. And she could contribute in other ways. She kept telling herself that the situation was only temporary, that they were building a better future for themselves, and for Jack, but she was still annoyed by it. She wanted to be a part of this, too, not just sit on the sidelines. After all, it had been her idea. But she wasn't needed. She wasn't useful, not like Lily.

Now Owen was doing his hospital shifts, plus work for the clinic on top. He was barely home at all. She found herself spending more and more time alone with Jack. She didn't mind. She adored her son, and she loved every minute she spent with him. She was lucky and she knew it. How many women had what she had?

But she was tired. Bone-deep tired.

Parenting is tough! she posted on her newly opened Facebook account early one Tuesday morning after Jack spilled orange juice all over the kitchen floor while she was reading an article about an M+ boy who had been kicked out of seven different day cares by the age of four. These were the boys they needed to reach. But how?

Perhaps she could send some brochures to local day cares? Though perhaps toddler groups would be better. Or even . . . prenatal classes. Yes. That was where she should be focusing her efforts. Get parents thinking about it before their boys were born.

"What did he do this time?" Owen asked when he came in. He was in the middle of knotting his tie.

"It was me," Antonia lied as she grabbed a dish cloth and mopped up the spill.

"Don't forget that I've arranged for us all to have lunch together at the clinic today."

"I won't," she promised. "Do you want me to bring anything?"

"Just yourself and Jack," he said, giving her a kiss on the cheek, then turning her head so that he could kiss her properly, firmly, on the mouth. She didn't resist, even though she could feel Jack watching.

"No, Daddy!" he shouted up at Owen.

Owen ruffled his hair and laughed. Antonia laughed, too. Jack had become very possessive of her recently, and although she'd never admit it out loud, she loved it when people said he was a mama's boy. It made her feel like she was doing something right for him. She was more than aware that the clinic was taking some of her attention away from him, and she felt undeniably guilty about it.

"See you at lunch," Owen said, then he picked up his jacket and phone and left. She heard the front door slam shut and looked down at her son, who had his arms wrapped around her legs. He put his little feet on top of her bigger ones.

"Dance with me!" he demanded.

Tired though she was, Antonia did as he wanted, and soon the two of them were laughing loudly. In moments like this, she forgot her exhaustion, the anxiety that hung from her shoulders like a backpack full of rocks. They danced on and on, faster and faster, Jack pulling on her hands until she missed her footing and almost fell over. She caught herself just in time.

"Whoa, little man!" she said to him. "You nearly sent me flying!"

Jack laughed.

"Yes, very funny," she said. She sent him to get dressed. "Shall we go to the toy shop this morning?" she asked him when he came back downstairs.

He liked that idea a lot. He chattered almost without pausing for breath as she drove them there, and they spent a fun hour perusing the shelves, Jack pushing a tiny shopping cart, looking cute in chinos and white tennis shoes. It was a shame Simon wasn't younger, so she could give Bea some of Jack's old clothes. He always looked so scruffy.

She was seeing Bea more regularly now, perhaps every ten days or so rather than once every couple of months. She wasn't sure what had changed exactly, but she'd happily welcomed her sister back into her life. Jack loved Simon so much. His untested status was still a concern, but Antonia made sure to watch him carefully, to make sure he wasn't left alone with Jack. And she hoped that the more Bea saw of the clinic and what she and Owen were building, the more likely she was to stop being foolish about it all.

She and Jack made it to the checkout with a full trolley, and as she paid, the cashier leaned forward to get a better look at Jack. "Aren't you adorable!" she said. "And so well-behaved!"

"Thank you," Antonia replied.

"You can always tell the negative ones," the woman said,

smiling. "They know how to behave themselves. Don't you, sweetie?"

"I'm a good boy," Jack said, smiling up at her before he grabbed his new Nerf gun from the counter.

"I can see that!" the woman said, laughing as Antonia picked up the bag with the rest of the toys and followed him out.

"You'll have to be good when we get to the clinic," she said to Jack as she drove the short distance there. "Be nice to Ginny."

She knew he would, of course, but she still felt that she had to say it. Jack was a normal boy with the typical reaction to girls. He thought they were yucky.

"I am a good boy!" Jack said indignantly, repeating what he'd told the woman in the shop.

It made Antonia laugh.

When they reached the clinic, she parked up close to the entrance, helping Jack down before taking the bag of toys from the trunk and carrying them to the door. She picked out the doll she had bought for Ginny and gave it to Jack. "I don't like dolls," he said, making a face.

"It's for Ginny, silly!"

"Oh," he replied, looking at the box again and picking at the edge of it with his fingernail. "Will it stop her from crying?"

"I hope so," Antonia told him.

She pasted on a smile as Lily rushed to open the door for them. "Antonia!" she said, and gave her a hug. "So lovely to see you!"

She greeted Jack in the same cheery way, dropping to her knees to admire the doll and calling Ginny over to look at it. Antonia put the bag of toys down in one corner. Jack settled himself in front of it. It would keep him busy for a while. Hopefully long enough for her to have lunch without him trying to crawl into her lap.

But it wasn't long before Ginny started to howl. Paul was first to his feet to deal with her. Then the phone rang and Owen excused himself to answer it, leaving Antonia alone with Lily.

"Ginny is doing well," Antonia said. "I love her dress."

"Gorgeous, isn't it?" Lily sighed, a happy, satisfied sound. "She's got a whole closetful. I know it's too many, but I just can't help myself."

"Paul is good with her, too."

"He loves having a stepdaughter. He says it's much easier than having a son. No offense," Lily added.

"None taken," Antonia said, though she felt the sting of it and couldn't help wondering if it was intended. No. Lily wasn't like that, and anyway, she knew that Jack was negative. "How's Malcolm?"

"The same. And growing bigger all the time. It worries me, Antonia. He's so difficult to manage already, and he's only six. What's he going to be like when he's sixteen?"

Antonia just shook her head and bit into a carrot stick.

"He doesn't come to stay with us overnight anymore," Lily continued. "I had to put my foot down there. It's not safe for Ginny."

"Doesn't Paul have him on a program?"

"He does," Lily said. "But, to be honest, I don't think Zara follows it. It's a massive problem. But, what can we do? We can't force her to implement it."

Lily's tales about Malcolm's behavior both repulsed and fascinated Antonia. It was like a car crash that she couldn't look away from. He bit and kicked and broke things. He swore at teachers and shop assistants and lied about everything. He was exactly the sort of boy that the clinic had been set up to help.

"I don't understand that," she replied. "Why wouldn't you do something that could help your child? If Jack were M-positive, I would do whatever it took to make things better for him."

She was interrupted by someone hammering on the door.

"Probably a parcel or something," Lily said, brushing the crumbs off her velvet skirt and getting to her feet. Antonia saw her freeze as she reached for the handle. Whoever was out there banged on the door again, and Lily opened it.

Zara walked in.

She pushed her way past Lily, who moved aside as easily as a leaf blown in the wind and looked around before her gaze landed on Antonia. "Where's Paul?"

"I don't . . ." Antonia began, but before she could finish, a door opened at the rear of the clinic and Paul came out, Ginny on his hip. He was chatting to her in a light and cheery voice filled with love.

The change when he saw Zara was immediate. "Lily," he said, "take Ginny into my office."

Lily rushed forward to take her daughter. She shot one anxious glance backward before doing as he'd asked. Antonia sat perfectly still, and when Jack started to move, she gestured at him to remain where he was. He sank back onto the carpet, a toy car in each hand.

"I need more pills," Zara said.

"You were given a prescription two weeks ago," Paul said calmly. "You should have enough to last for another month at least."

"Yes, well, I don't."

"Why not?"

"Why do you think? Because he won't take them! If I can get him to put them in his mouth himself, he chews them and spits them out. If I try to put them in his mouth, he bites me. I tried hiding them in his food, and he threw it on the floor."

Paul shook his head. "I don't understand why you are so determined to make this difficult."

"If you think it's so easy, take him for a week and medicate him yourself."

He exhaled. "I'll have to get Owen to write a new prescription."

"I'll wait," she said. She folded her arms, the posture of a dangerously furious woman trying to hold in her anger. She was visibly thin, and there was a bruise on her upper arm that looked suspiciously like the handprint of a six-year-old boy.

Antonia might have felt sorry for her if she hadn't ruined Jack's birthday. That, to Antonia's mind, was unforgivable. This was a woman who had everything she needed to manage her son and, for reasons best known to herself, wouldn't do it. No wonder Paul had left.

She scooped Jack up, and she followed Paul into Owen's office. "Anything I can do to help?" she asked the two of them.

Owen didn't take his eyes off his computer. "Get some Riclonfex from the drug cupboard, will you?" He reached into his pocket, took out the keys, and held them out to her.

"How many boxes?"

"Give her three," Paul said. "I don't want her finding an excuse to come back again next week. It upsets Lily."

"Got it," Antonia said, glad to be of help. She went into the office at the back of the clinic and took the boxes from the cupboard, then locked it and went back into reception. She handed them to Zara.

"Thanks," Zara said.

"Is there anything else?" Antonia asked her politely. Just because Zara had barged in here so rudely didn't mean she had to forget her own manners.

Zara stared at her for a long moment. There was fight in her eyes, and Antonia thought she might say more, but she didn't. Her whole body seemed to slump. "No," she said.

After she left, Antonia closed the door and locked it. The relief was tremendous. All the adrenaline that had flooded her body slowly began to dissipate, and she found herself craving a stiff drink. But she was glad she'd been here. She'd kept her calm and dealt with the situation, and both Owen and Paul had had the chance to see her do it.

She slowly lowered Jack to the floor. "That lady is bad," he said.

She rested her hand on top of his head and smiled at him.

Out of the mouths of babes, she thought. "Not *bad*," she told him. "Sad. Her little boy isn't very nice, you see. That's what Daddy does here. He helps little boys to be nice."

"Am I nice?"

"Of course you are."

"Is Simon nice?"

Now, that she couldn't answer.

CHAPTER TWELVE

BEA

Now

Bea was half-asleep on the sofa in the living room, a cup of tea balanced precariously on her lap, when her phone rang, making her jump. Hot liquid splashed onto her thigh, and she moved the cup to the coffee table before she could do any more damage. She'd been miles away, her mind drifting to nowhere, lost in the feeling that right here, right now, there was nothing to be afraid of.

She checked her phone. The screen said it was Antonia.

She sighed, rubbed at the wet patch on her jeans, and debated whether to answer it. She let it ring three times before accepting that she didn't have much choice. Antonia would only keep ringing otherwise. She tapped the icon, and her sister's face popped up on the screen.

"Why are the police looking at your car?" Antonia yelled at her.

"The police? They're here?" Bea leaped to her feet, ran

over to the window, and looked outside. How could Antonia possibly have known that?

"Yes, the police, and, no, they're not there, but they were, and they were looking at your car. I saw them on the doorbell camera."

Her sister's anger was palpable, and for once, Bea couldn't blame her. She rushed upstairs to get her keys, almost forgetting the phone in her hand.

Antonia quickly reminded her of it, her voice barking out, "What are you doing?"

It reminded Bea of when they were children and Antonia had followed her around the house, asking that exact same question. They were latchkey kids. Their father had left and moved in with another woman when Antonia was seven and Bea was three, and their mother worked long hours, which meant that the two of them spent a lot of time alone in the house, with Antonia automatically in charge because she was older. Even when they'd become adults, Antonia hadn't been able to break out of the habit of telling Bea what to do, because when Bea was twenty-one, their mother had died of a stroke, and Antonia had taken on the role full-time.

"Moving the car," she snapped back.

She cut Antonia off, stuck the phone in her back pocket, got the keys from her bag, and went straight outside in her bare feet, waiting impatiently for the gates to open. Her hands were shaking so much that it took her three tries to get the car started. She nosed it along the driveway, toward the garage. She should have just asked Owen for money, bought ferry tickets, taken Simon across the sea to Ireland,

and started again. If she'd done that, they would be long gone by now. But they had no passports and no ID. It was a pipe dream and nothing more.

Opening the garage proved a little trickier, though eventually she found a button on the inside that activated the door. She parked the car inside next to a neat row of trash cans. The door closed behind her, trapping her, but at least she was out of sight, and it was enough for her pulse to start calming down. She held on to the steering wheel and took several deep breaths as her phone rang and rang.

She shouldn't have come back here. She shouldn't have let Simon talk her into it. You could never go back; she knew that better than anyone. But she was so tired of running. Sometimes it felt like she'd started a marathon the day Simon was born, and she was still going with no end in sight.

She finally answered the phone, turning her head so that she wouldn't have to look directly at the screen, where her sister's face loomed large.

"Why are they interested in your car?" Antonia asked.

"I don't know."

"Tell me the truth, Bea. Or I swear I'll phone the police right now and ask them."

"You wouldn't."

"Yes, I would," Antonia said. "You've brought the police to my home. My *home*. So don't tell me that you just wanted to make contact, to see how I am."

"It's . . . complicated."

"That's not good enough."

Story of my life, Bea thought to herself, but she knew this wasn't the time for self-pity. It wouldn't fix any of her problems. Her priority had to be keeping Simon safe. That meant she somehow had to find a way to get Antonia on her side, and, knowing her sister, only the truth would do.

But that didn't mean she couldn't choose how much of the truth that was.

"We've been working at a farm," she said, finally forcing herself to look directly at the screen. That was what everyone called the places that the government had set up to help provide jobs for M+ men. The word might conjure up images of blue skies and acres of golden wheat, but that wasn't the reality. These farms were industrial, not agricultural. They were rough and dirty, offering the sort of hard manual work that no one else wanted to do, and they paid poorly. Very poorly.

Antonia blinked. "A farm?" Her mouth opened and stayed that way, a wet pink cave yawning open on the small surface of the phone.

"Yes," Bea said. The truth was out now, and she couldn't take it back, although she had a sudden and desperate urge to claim it was a joke and they hadn't been on the farms at all. But it would be too little, too late. "There was some trouble, and we had to leave," she continued. "I assume that's why the police were looking at the car. Someone at the farm must have reported us."

She didn't try to hide her fear. She wasn't sure she could.

The image of her sister blurred for a moment, then came back into focus. Antonia had moved. Bea could see a Monet print in the background. "What sort of trouble?"

"Nothing, really. Just . . . an argument about our wages."

"But what were you doing there in the first place? Is he positive? Is that why you were on a farm?"

"No, he still hasn't been tested."

Antonia pinched the bridge of her nose. "Why should I believe you?"

"Because you know me. And if you don't believe me, you can use that fancy computer system you have at the clinic to check."

"That would be illegal, and you know it. Simon isn't our patient. Unless you want to make him our patient?"

Bea got out of the car, slamming the door closed. "And give you permission to test him? No thanks."

"I can't believe that I thought you had come here to see me. That you'd missed me."

"I did miss you."

"No, you didn't. You're a fool, Bea," Antonia continued. "A stupid, stubborn fool. You could have avoided all of this by having him tested years ago, but you stuck to your ideal-istic nonsense. You insisted that it didn't matter whether a boy has the gene or not, that it just matters how he's treated. Well, that hasn't worked out for you, has it?"

"This isn't my fault!" Bea shouted back, her temper fi-nally getting the better of her. "And anyway, the treatment doesn't work! If it did, the farms wouldn't exist, because all M-positive boys would be properly integrated into society, and they'd behave themselves, and they don't!"

"The treatment does work," Antonia said. Her voice was suddenly very quiet and calm, making Bea feel like a raging toddler in comparison. "We help M-positive boys and their families every day. But it isn't a cure. Parents have to follow the program. Boys have to accept the limitations of their condition. It's not our fault if they won't."

She genuinely believed it. Bea could tell. She wasn't going to change her sister's mind. Not that she wanted to. She didn't care what Antonia thought, not anymore. She had far bigger problems than that now. Leaving the car in the street had been stupid. In hindsight she couldn't believe that she'd done it. She'd have to get rid of it.

"Promise me you won't tell Owen that we've been on a farm," she said.

Antonia frowned. "You want me to lie to my husband?"

"Not lie, just . . . I don't think there's anything to be gained by telling him, do you? Please, Antonia. It's embarrassing enough without everyone knowing. He always thought I was a terrible mother, and now I've gone and proved it, haven't I?"

"You should have had Simon tested," Antonia said again. "Years ago. I don't know why you didn't."

"Yes, you do," Bea said, and ended the call.

She had to talk to Simon. As she went into the hallway, she heard footsteps on the stairs. She leaned in, looked up, saw the back of someone running hastily upstairs.

Not Simon.

Jack.

How much had he heard?

CHAPTER THIRTEEN

BEA

Thirteen years ago

As more and more private clinics open up across the country offering help to parents of M+ boys, tonight's episode of Dispatches *asks if we are creating a two-tier society, and what will happen to those boys from families who can't afford access to treatment, as waiting times for NHS appointments have now hit two years, on average. Should private clinics be forced to open their doors to parents who can't pay?*

Bea was unhappy. She didn't want to be. Most of the time, she could ignore it, but sometimes she would lie awake in the middle of the night, listening to Simon and Alfie breathing, and she would think about the fact that the only day care that would take Simon was also the only one that had taken Malcolm before he left to go to primary school, and she would silently cry.

Simon was four now, getting bigger all the time, and was harder to tire out. It was like having a puppy that had to be fed and exercised on a regular schedule; otherwise, it would get bored and destroy the furniture. Day care wasn't enough anymore. She was hoping the move to school would help. But then, she'd hoped regular visits to see Jack would have a calming effect, and so far that didn't seem to be working.

"He needs something to wear him out," she said to Alfie. "He's so full of energy all the time. I think that's why he acts out." She didn't mention the fact that she was also desperate for some time to herself, to quietly sit and read.

"What about swimming?"

"Good idea," Bea said, thinking about it.

She signed Simon up for swimming lessons later that week. It worked for the first few sessions, until Antonia had gotten wind of it and decided to sign Jack up, too. Now, instead of an hour to herself, Bea got to sit on an uncomfortable plastic chair up in the stands at the side of the pool, trying to ignore the combination of chlorine with a mild overlay of vertigo, and listen to her sister yammer on about her favorite topic.

"We've got enough patients now to move from two days to three," Antonia said. "And we're looking for bigger premises. The office we've got isn't working for us anymore."

"How many boys is Owen seeing now?" Bea asked, telling herself she didn't care.

"Eighty-seven," Antonia said proudly. "Can you believe it?"

Bea had looked at the clinic prices online, though she hadn't told her sister that, and she did a quick calculation in her head, her gaze falling on her sister's new handbag as she did so.

"He says at the current rate we'll be close to five hundred patients in another six months," Antonia said. She combed her fingers through her hair, the sharp light bouncing off the diamond tennis bracelet on her left wrist. "He's planning to give up his NHS work completely by the end of the year."

"So who will be helping the parents who can't afford the clinic?"

Antonia pouted. "It hasn't been an easy decision," she said. "In fact, it's been a very difficult one. But Owen can't help everyone." She picked up her bag, rested it on her knee. "Look," she said, "I know the clinic is expensive, and I know you can't afford it. But if that's the reason why you don't want to have Simon tested . . ."

"It isn't the reason," Bea protested, though it was a big part of it now, of course. But she would never admit that to Antonia. The more Antonia flashed her money about, the more determined Bea was to prove that it didn't bother her, that she could bring Simon up just as well without it, if not better.

Antonia carried on as if she hadn't heard. "I brought you something." She opened her bag and angled it so that Bea could see inside. There was a small white box with a printed label. "It's a testing kit. If you do the swabs, I'll order the test through the clinic. We can do it under a false name. No one would have to know."

"Are you high?" Bea said loudly, utterly shocked.

One of the lifeguards shifted position and glared at them.

Bea hunched down in her seat. "You've gone crazy," she said to Antonia. "Seriously. I can't believe you're even suggesting it."

"I'm scared for you," Antonia said, and when she looked at Bea, there were tears in her eyes. "If you only knew what we're seeing at the clinic . . ."

Bea gathered her water bottle and book. She went downstairs and waited for Simon to get out of the pool and then took him back into the changing room and got him dressed. She rubbed him vigorously with the towel. He giggled. *At least one of us is having a good time,* she thought to herself. She certainly wasn't.

Antonia had always been a bit obsessive, Bea knew that. It was one of the many ways in which they were different. Bea had always been content with what she had. As long as she had enough, she was happy. But Antonia needed more. Bea found it strange when she thought about it, how two closely related people could react so differently to the same childhood. But then, perhaps it hadn't been the same. She was several years younger than Antonia, had seen far less of their father before he had left. Most of her memories of him were made up of bits and pieces that other people had told her. They'd had different experiences of their mother, too. Bea had known only the aftermath, only the poverty. But she'd seen the photos of Antonia, her pretty dresses, her dolls. That had all gone, and Antonia had been fighting to get it back ever since. Or so it seemed to Bea.

She pulled Simon's T-shirt over his head, helped him with his socks, waited as he put his pants on himself, and thought about that little white box in Antonia's bag. The sight of it had horrified her. She'd known that Antonia was obsessed with the test, but she hadn't expected her to go quite that far. Perhaps she should be glad that her sister hadn't already attempted to test Simon on the sly. She folded Simon's damp towel, shoved it into his swim bag, and decided that it was time to find some new friends.

CHAPTER FOURTEEN

JACK

Now

They hadn't thought about the car. That had been a mistake. As Jack followed Simon up the stairs, his mind raced, trying to put everything together. He caught up with his cousin, pushed him into the spare room that Simon had slept in, and closed the door behind them, leaning his weight against it to make sure that Bea couldn't come in.

"Did you hear that? The police have been here. Shit, Simon. This is bad. This is really bad."

"Calm down," Simon replied. "It's fine."

"It is *not* fine!"

When he'd told Simon to come here, that they could fix this, he'd never for a moment thought that Simon would bring this sort of trouble with him.

"Yes, it is," Simon told him. "Because I've been tested, remember? All we have to do is keep it together until I get the result." He lifted his arm, sniffed his armpit. "Ugh." He got off the bed and pulled his T-shirt off, turning as he did so, and Jack saw his back. His cousin was skinny, but the muscles that moved under his skin looked well used and hard.

And he was covered in bruises.

Jack stared, his mouth open as he tried to take in the pattern of purple and yellow. He'd never seen anything like it. "Fucking hell, Simon."

"What?"

"Your back. Why didn't you tell me you were so badly injured?"

"Oh." Simon twisted, trying to look at himself. His face went red. He immediately tried to put his T-shirt back on, but it was too late. "It's nothing."

As Jack looked, as he saw all the different colors of the bruising, a thought entered his head that he didn't quite want to believe. "I thought you only got in one fight," he said. He was suddenly aware of every muscle in his own body, of the blood pulsing at his temples. "The one on Saturday. You said . . ."

Simon turned slowly as he pulled the T-shirt back over his head and down his body. "I know what I said."

Jack gestured at him with a shaking hand. "What really happened? Just how many fights were you in?" He saw his cousin flush, saw the muscle tic in his jaw, and knew just how badly Simon didn't want to answer that question. And that he didn't need him to. It was obvious. "What's going on?"

Simon shook his head. He didn't look at Jack. "You won't get it."

"What won't I get?" Jack shouted at him. "Don't treat me

like I'm stupid, Simon, because I'm not. You don't end up
with the police outside the house, or looking like that, because you got into one fight with one bloke. That's not how
life works."

"The fights don't happen by accident. They're organized."

"I don't understand," Jack said.

"People bet on them. Not just the men who work there
but other people. Rich people, like you all. They would all
turn up in the evening and they would watch. I wanted a
piece of that for myself. You can make money from it if
you're clever."

Jack sank to the floor, his legs suddenly wobbly. "But you
get paid to work at a farm."

Simon snorted. "It's not even minimum wage, man. The
whole thing is a scam. M-positive boys are a cheap work-
force, and there are a lot of people getting rich off the back
of it."

Jack had learned a bit about the waste farms at school.
Huge concrete-and-steel structures built alongside motor-
ways. They ran twenty-four hours a day, recycling everything from license plates to old umbrellas. Yes, most of the
people that worked there were M+ men, but they were
suited to hard, physical work; it made their condition easier
to manage, and there were on-site accommodation and
shops and canteens and a doctor. He hadn't been too concerned when Simon had first messaged to say he was working at one. If anything, it had seemed like a good thing.

What Simon was telling him now . . . it didn't fit in with

any of that. "I thought you got looked after there. There are all these facilities on-site . . ."

"You mean the toilets that were always blocked and the showers that didn't work and the food that cost an arm and a leg?"

"You should have told me," Jack said. The back of his throat prickled. He felt simultaneously hurt and angry— hurt because of what his cousin had been living with, angry because Simon had kept it from him. He thought about the message Simon had sent him a week ago, his phone waking him in the middle of the night with the sound of the Joker laughing.

You'll never guess who just showed up here.

For the next three days, Jack had barely slept, living for updates. He could sense the danger approaching his cousin, had imagined the form it might take. He had felt like an important part of Simon's life again. The blood had fizzed in his veins; the world had seemed brighter, charged with energy. His life here with his parents, with school and music and his M– friends—the life already mapped out for him— nice as it all was, it sometimes made him feel like he was going to die of boredom.

To find out now that Simon had kept things from him . . . Jack was all of a sudden aware that although he was a little taller than his cousin, he was no match for him in any other way. Simon was wiry with muscle where Jack was soft. His

hands were rough, his fingers scarred, and there was something in the way he carried himself that made the hairs on
the back of Jack's neck stand up. He wasn't the person Jack
had known at all.

"You let me think that you were in trouble! You let me
think that he wanted to kill you and you had to do it!" Jack
said furiously.

"I did."

Before Jack could reply, Bea opened the door and stuck
her head in. Her gaze landed on Jack. He braced himself,
waiting for her to say something, to ask him what he was
shouting about, but she didn't. She turned her attention to
Simon instead.

"Get in the car," she told him. "We've got things to do."

CHAPTER FIFTEEN

ANTONIA

Twelve years ago

BBC News, Sophie Robinson Reporting

A group of doctors have today raised concerns about drug treatments commonly used for behavior management in boys identified as being carriers of the M gene after hospitals reported seeing an increase in the number of siblings of boys thought to be on treatment programs being taken to the emergency room with minor injuries. It appears that although the treatments are effective, families who have stopped their use due to side effects have seen a rapid escalation of violent behavior. Parents are being urged not to stop treatment without seeking medical advice and to take steps to ensure that their sons comply with treatment.

It came as no surprise to Antonia when, shortly after Jack's fifth birthday, Lily announced that she was pregnant again. "Another girl!" she said excitedly. "I can't wait for Ginny to be a sister. It's going to be amazing."

"Congratulations," Antonia said, hoping that no hint of bitterness showed in her voice. It wasn't that she was unhappy or jealous—far from it. She was perfectly content with Jack and had no desire to have another child. Nor had Owen shown any interest in expanding their family. He often talked about how well things worked with the three of them and of the things they'd be able to do as Jack got older. But it still hurt her to see someone get pregnant so easily, to see them look forward to the birth with so little fear. By all accounts it had been easy for Lily the first time, and she had no reason to think this time would be any different.

"We'll need to get someone in to cover for me, obviously," Lily said. "To be honest, I would stop now if I could."

"Why don't I step in?" Antonia offered.

"Really?" Lily asked. She sounded doubtful. "Are you sure? You don't have any relevant experience, and managing an office is quite challenging."

Antonia told herself that Lily didn't mean to be rude. "I'm sure I can figure it out."

"Of course!" Lily said. "And you can always ring me if you need any help."

Antonia let her change the subject, listened to her prattle on for an hour about strollers, but privately she was already planning the changes she would make. When Owen got home that evening, she told him her idea. Fortunately, he was more willing to listen than Lily had been. But he, too, had doubts.

"What about Jack?"

"He's at school now," Antonia said, trying to hold back

her impatience. Honestly, it was like all of them thought she was useless. "He doesn't need me as much."

"I thought you liked being a stay-at-home mother."

"I do! But the clinic is important to me, too. It's a family business: you, Paul, Lily. I'm the only one who isn't involved, and I think it's time that I was."

"It would make things a lot easier," he said. "Let me discuss it with Paul."

"Did he discuss hiring Lily with you?"

"Not really," Owen admitted. "But she'd been his secretary, so he already knew she had the right skill set."

What skill set was that? Shagging your boss? "Owen," Antonia said, starting to lose patience. "It's answering the phone and sending emails. It's hardly rocket science. I've got a degree in psychology. I'm not stupid!"

"Of course you're not," Owen said, taking hold of both of her hands and pinning them against his chest. "I had no idea you felt left out. You should have said something sooner. If you're happy to take it on, I'll let Paul know. Consider it a done deal."

"Thank you."

The next morning, she took Jack to school as usual, then made her way to the clinic. Lily was surprised when she walked in, but Antonia didn't let that put her off. "Might as well make a start!" she said cheerfully. "After all, you did say that you'd hand it all over now if you could."

Lily worked with her for the rest of that week, saying that she wanted to make sure that Antonia knew what she was doing. Antonia knew by lunchtime on the first day but

didn't point that out. It was nice to get up and put on adult
clothes instead of the leggings and sweatshirt she normally
opted for, to wear a full face of makeup, to chat with the patients when they came in. She found the M+ boys fascinat-
ing. She wanted to be part of this, of what they were doing
here, and now she was. She decided very quickly that she
had no intention of giving it up once Lily came back from
maternity leave.

She redesigned the phone and appointments system. She
hired someone to upgrade their website. She took over the
ordering of the medications they kept on-site and went out
for lunch with the drug rep. And then, in a move she was
particularly proud of, she found a plot of land for sale close
to the town center that would be perfect for a purpose-built
clinic.

Six weeks after she started, Owen told her that Paul had
commented on what a great job she was doing. "I'm so
proud of you," he said. "You've made such a difference to
the clinic, to the way it works. I don't know how we managed without you."

"Thank you, darling," she said, turning into the offered
embrace. "That means so much to me. And I'm so glad that
I've been able to help out."

But that didn't stop Lily from popping into the clinic on
what felt like an almost daily basis. It drove Antonia up the
wall. "She's on maternity leave," she said to Paul one afternoon after coming back from the bathroom to find Lily at
her desk, clicking through emails. "She's not supposed to
be working."

"I know," he said, laughing. "Can't keep her away!"

Antonia suspected that Lily's frequent trips to the clinic might have something to do with the fact that Paul had cheated on Zara with Lily and that he had met Lily at work and that, with the benefit of hindsight, Lily had realized that his wandering eye was a personality feature rather than anything to do with her particular charm.

But it didn't matter.

Whether Lily came back or not, Antonia wasn't going anywhere. She had finally found something, other than being Jack's mother, that she was good at. She was making a difference to the families who came here, and she was making a difference to Jack, too, showing him that his father wasn't the only one willing to step up and help boys less fortunate than him.

If only Bea would accept her help, too.

||| SIMON

Now

Simon followed his mother down the stairs. She was walking quickly, her movements economical. He'd seen her like this before, and it meant only one thing. Trouble. "What's going on?" he asked as she marched into the garage. The car, the one that had caused all the trouble, was parked in the middle of it.

"We need to get rid of this," she said. "Get in."

He did as he was told. Bea pressed a button at the side of the garage, causing the door to rise up, revealing the world outside a centimeter at a time. It seemed to take forever. Bea was behind the wheel with her seat belt on and the engine running before it had made it all the way up.

Should he tell her what Jack had said? He didn't know. It didn't seem the right time to say anything. If he did, it might lead to questions he didn't want to answer, like where he and Jack had been that morning. He'd thought it would be easy to tell his mother that he'd been tested. After all, he was eighteen now, and it was his choice, not hers. But he had spent his entire life being told that the test was wrong, that it would ruin his life, that he shouldn't have it, and he was afraid of her reaction.

So he said nothing.

He slowly slid his seat belt on as Bea reversed the car out onto the gravel. His mouth was dry and his guts cramping as he thought about what Jack had told him, that the police had come to the house. He had thought he was safe here. It had seemed so far away from the farm, like another world, almost. He'd stayed calm in front of Jack, but he didn't feel it now.

Bea spun the wheel, turning the car, and right in the pause when she stopped to change gear, a shout came from behind them and someone banged on the back of the car. Simon twisted round in his seat to see Jack through the rear windshield. His face was red. "Where are you going?" he shouted. He ran to the front of the car and stood there, arms folded, glaring at them.

Bea dropped her window. "Move out of the way."

"Not unless you tell me where you're going!"

"That's none of your damn business! Get out of the way!" She gripped the wheel and began to inch the car forward.

Simon saw the shock on his cousin's face. He lowered his own window and stuck his head out. "Jack, move," he said. "Seriously."

"But . . ."

He undid his seat belt, reached for the door handle. He didn't want to move Jack out of the way, but he would if he had to. His mother was in a scary mood. There was no reasoning with her when she got like this.

Fortunately, Jack got the message. He scampered to the side of the car and stood there, staring down at Simon, his face still flushed, and Simon felt suddenly and unexpectedly bad for him. But there wasn't time to do anything about it.

Bea already had the car in motion, and they were through the gate and out onto the road with a screech of their tires. He swallowed down the saliva flooding his mouth. "Please tell me what's going on, Mom?" he said. "Are we leaving?"

She took a sharp left at the top of the road. Her body was stiff and angular with tension. "The police were looking at the car this morning," she said.

"I know. Jack told me."

"He always was a nosy little shit," she muttered.

"Mom!"

She thumped the steering wheel with the heel of her hand. "Sorry," she said. "It's just . . . this is the last thing we need, Simon. We're supposed to be keeping our heads down. That was one of the reasons we came here, so we could lie low for a few days and try to figure stuff out."

"I know," he said again. He stared straight ahead, unable to look at her, knowing that all of this was his fault. But he couldn't change it. And he knew that he'd had no other choice, not really, and so he wouldn't apologize for it, either.

They sat in silence as Bea drove them into the town center and kept going out the other side toward the industrial estate that ran alongside the railway lines. A couple of roundabouts later, she pulled the car to a stop at the side of the road.

Simon knew this spot. They'd lived not far from here when he'd been a kid, he and his mother and his dad, Alfie, just up the road from the water treatment plant. The smell had crept into the house whenever the wind blew in their direction, which was often. He scratched his head, wondering why those memories had chosen to pop up now.

He hardly ever thought about his dad anymore. Wasn't worth the energy. Alfie had made his choice the day he'd walked out. Simon hadn't let himself feel anger over it. He hadn't let himself feel anything. What was the point? It was just another situation that he couldn't change.

Bea looked behind them, crept the car forward, and took a left turn down the narrow track that led down under the railway bridge. She turned off the engine and got out, leaving the door open.

He'd already had half an idea what she was planning when she'd driven along this road, but now he was certain. "Do we have to?" he asked, swallowing down the sudden lump in his throat.

"Got any better ideas?" she asked him.

"Can't we sell it?"

"Got no paperwork, it isn't insured, and it links us to the farm," she said. "What do you think?"

Simon hung his head. The grass beneath his feet was patchy, littered with butts from hand-rolled cigarettes and little silver canisters. When he'd been a kid, this place had had a reputation for being a hangout for a certain type of person, and it looked like that hadn't changed. He felt tears pricking at the backs of his eyes, the swell of emotion both shocking and embarrassing him. He had to get a grip.

But she was throwing the only thing they had away.

He could stop her. He could tell her what he'd done that morning. But before he could, she turned and started to walk back up the slope toward the road. She was fast, but he kept pace with her easily, even as her breathing started to get loud and he wished that she'd slow down.

"Mom," he said, "I need to tell you something."

"Is it something I want to hear?"

He could just say it. He could just tell her the whole truth of it, all of it, all the things he'd kept to himself, and deal with the fallout. He hated the fact that he'd lied. But he also knew that sometimes lies were better than the truth. That despite the emphasis adults put on honesty when you were a kid, they lied all the time. They pretended they didn't, but they also told five-year-olds that a fat man in a red suit sneaked into their house and left them presents at Christmas.

"Probably not," he admitted.

"Then keep it to yourself, thanks."

"Mom, I got tested this morning."

Bea came to an abrupt halt. She planted her hands on her hips, staring straight ahead, not looking at him. Simon steeled himself. He was ready for her anger. But he didn't get it, which took him by surprise.

"I saw the two of you sneak out," she admitted in a quiet voice. "I wondered what you were doing."

"Are you mad at me?"

She turned slowly and looked at him. "What would be the point?"

"I know you never wanted me to do it. It's just . . . you said it yourself, Mom. We can't go on like this."

"And you really think getting tested will fix it?"

Yes.

The word was on the tip of his tongue. But he didn't say it. "I don't know. But it can't make things any worse."

CHAPTER SEVENTEEN

BEA

Twelve years ago

@TrashTheTest @SaveOurSons. Schools should not be allowed to ask for M test status. This is confidential medical info. #ProtectOurBoys #SayNo

Stephanie says they're asking for test details in schools now," Bea said to Alfie that night as he lay stretched out on the sofa. There was a hole in his sock right over his big toe, and he kept tugging at it. She held up her phone. "Look at what she just posted online."

"You can't believe what people post on the internet," Alfie replied without taking his eyes off the TV. "I read something the other day that said that the prime minister is really a lizard."

"She's not making this up," Bea said crossly. She'd met Stephanie a few weeks ago through a notice on the message board at the local café. Now there was always someone at the other end of the phone if she wanted to go for coffee or just wanted to chat. Stephanie was a normal person with a normal life and normal kids, who had the same sort of money she did, who worried about the same sorts of things. And she was on the same page as Bea with regard to the test, too. When Bea was with her, she felt like she could breathe.

She couldn't say the same for Antonia. Bea had been to visit her new house that afternoon. It had six bedrooms. Bea couldn't get her head around why you'd need six bedrooms for three people, but the bespoke kitchen and the bathroom that looked like it belonged in a Park Lane hotel were undeniably beautiful. It had a gym and a home theater with a sofa big enough to seat a giant. She'd walked through it, trying and failing not to guess the price of everything she saw. There was no denying that the M test had given Antonia the lifestyle she'd always wanted.

And it wasn't just her sister. With every day that passed, the test was becoming more and more popular. It was as normal as ultrasounds and vaccinations. It was just what you did.

No one seemed willing to talk about what they were doing to M+ boys, or the willingness to segregate them and deny them access to parts of life that were open to their siblings and classmates. If anything was going to drive those boys down a dark path, it was their exclusion from society, not their genetics.

But Alfie didn't want to hear it. He always got like this whenever she tried to talk about the test, about what was happening. It felt like the only place she could discuss it was with Stephanie, and most of the time she kept it there. But sometimes it spilled over. She couldn't help it. "This is real, Alfie."

"Don't stress." He reached out and groped for her hand, squeezed it, eyes still on the TV. "It'll be fine."

"Did you not hear what I said? Schools are asking if boys are tested! How is that going to be fine?"

"Have him tested if you're worried."

"Are you insane?"

Simon was in his room, as he had been for the past forty minutes, after kicking one of the cupboard doors in the kitchen so hard that he'd almost broken it. He'd lost his temper because Bea had refused to let him stay up past his usual bedtime to watch a film she considered too violent for him. He had reacted as if it were the end of the world. Bea wouldn't cave. The battle lines had been clearly drawn, and he was going to learn where they were even if it killed her.

She was determined to give him the life that M+ boys couldn't have, and that meant he had to learn how to live it. He had to know the rules, and he had to know how to follow them. Because what was the alternative? Schools today meant workplaces tomorrow. What if they decided that you couldn't get married if you were positive? You couldn't have hospital treatment when you needed it? You couldn't have children of your own?

She didn't blame him for blowing his top tonight, though—not completely. He was always like this after he'd spent a day with Jack. And Jack had been in peak form today, running around the new house, his excitement bubbling over as he'd told Simon they were getting a dog, maybe *two* dogs, and then Simon had had to come home to this house and reality.

"It's still not a big deal," Alfie said gently. "Honestly, Bea, you're overthinking it. Schools aren't allowed to turn kids away on the basis of the test. That would be discrimination. They've got to provide for them. If some idiotic parents want to have a label to attach to their son, let them. It doesn't mean anything. No one cares."

He made it sound so simple. At first, that had been what had attracted her to him: the complete lack of drama. He had seemed to share some of her ideals, too. Now she wasn't sure about any of it. His lack of drama was starting to look a lot like laziness, and all his talk about saving the planet seemed to be an excuse not to shower enough.

She stared at the television, seeing only blurred shapes on the screen, not really paying attention to it. Alfie was right about one thing, though. The test was stupid. And Simon was fine. He was just a normal little boy. He was *probably* just a normal little boy. It was true that he was more aggressive than Jack, but then, she didn't think that Jack had ever heard the word *no* in his life, so he had nothing to complain about. Antonia treated him like he was made out of glass and seemed to think that any attempt to impose rules was akin to child abuse.

"I'm serious, Bea," Alfie continued. "Either have him tested or let it go. You're getting obsessed. It's all you ever talk about these days."

Bea swung her feet to the floor and padded the short distance to the kitchen, where she opened the fridge and took out a can of Diet Coke. The broken cupboard door hung askew. She'd have to go to the shop tomorrow and spend money she didn't have on buying things to fix it before the landlord found out. "I am not obsessed!"

"Yes, you are," he said. "And it's getting boring." He picked up the remote, changed the channel, and turned the volume up, effectively putting an end to the conversation.

The noise disturbed Simon, who stumbled out of his room, pajamas wrinkled up around his knees. "You woke me up!"

Alfie was on his feet immediately. "Sorry, pal." He scooped him up, cuddled him. "Let's get you back to bed."

That was Alfie all over: there for the hugs, never the discipline.

But maybe he had a point. The test was the first thing she thought about when she got up in the morning, and whenever she had a spare moment (and sometimes when she didn't) she was looking for stuff about it online, browsing forums and blogs and news websites. She didn't know what she was hoping to find, really. She just . . . she wanted to know that she was doing the right thing.

Later, Bea looked up the test online. There were no appointments available for an NHS test anywhere local. A private one was £350. She had the money hidden in a tampon box in the bathroom cabinet so that Alfie couldn't lend it to one of his friends and leave them short. She could feel the weight of it, the pressure to do this thing that everyone was doing, to put her son into the appropriate box, even though she'd been here before and had booked a test and canceled it.

She didn't want to be a bad mother. But she wasn't sure

she could afford to be a good one. Suppose she did have him tested, and it was positive. She'd never be able to afford the treatment.

Perhaps she could ask Antonia. After all, her sister had offered her a free test through the clinic . . .

No. If she did have Simon tested, Antonia was the last person she would want to know.

She called Stephanie instead. "Alfie said I should have him tested."

"Don't do it," Stephanie said. "You don't want to. You know that."

"I know," Bea said. "It's just . . ."

They talked into the early hours of the morning, and eventually Bea fell asleep on the sofa, still in her clothes, curled up under the blanket she usually kept draped over the back to hide the threadbare cushions.

"You didn't come to bed," Alfie said quietly the next morning as Simon settled down with toast and jam.

"I was talking to Stephanie." Bea felt terrible, sore, and sour, her skin and eyes aching from the lack of sleep.

Alfie looked at her. There was pity in his gaze, and it made her feel even worse. "This is what I mean," he said. "You could have come to bed, but instead . . . I'm worried about you, Bea. You spend so much time online looking at stuff to do with the test, and then you ring Stephanie, and the two of you wind yourselves up over it. But in the real world, it's not that big a deal. Really, it's not."

"Maybe you're right," she said, as much to make peace as anything. Part of her knew he was talking sense. She did spend a lot of time doing exactly what he'd said. It wouldn't do her any harm to cut back a bit. There was a possibility, if she was honest with herself, that she was losing her sense of perspective.

But her decision to do better lasted for exactly three hours, at which point Antonia rang her. She made the mistake of answering the phone without checking the screen first. Antonia, clearly thrilled that Bea had picked up, jumped straight in and told her that they'd just got planning permission for a purpose-built clinic.

"It's so exciting," she gushed excitedly. The phone was on the floor next to Bea, her sister's voice coming through the speaker as Bea hand-polished the floor tiles of a large conservatory. "We'll have more space, proper parking. It's going to make such a difference for these boys, Bea."

Sure it is, Bea thought to herself. *Your bank balance will be happy, anyway. You'll be able to hire that landscape gardener you were blathering on about.* "Sounds amazing," she said.

"We should all get together to celebrate!"

Bea couldn't imagine anything she wanted to do less than having Antonia's new house rubbed in her face again. But she'd promised herself that she wouldn't try to actively destroy what little relationship they had left. So she let herself be talked into it and agreed to dinner that evening. At least she was getting a free meal, she told herself.

"Antonia told me how well things are going at the clinic," she said to Owen as they sat down at the table. "She said you're having to move to a bigger place. Congratulations."

"Thanks," he said. "To be honest, it was her idea. I would

probably have waited a few more years until we'd expanded our client list, but as she pointed out, if we're going to do that, we need better premises to do it from. And it's not like the test is going anywhere."

Was it her imagination, or was there a hint of a challenge in that? Well, two could play at that game. "I don't know," she said. "People used to think that smoking was a good idea, and look how that turned out."

"Indeed," he said. "But I don't think that's a fair comparison." He looked her right in the eye as he said it, and she was transported back to the hospital the day Simon was born. "This is bigger than just the boys themselves, Bea. This is going to change everything. Think about it. If we get M-positive boys on a treatment program early, before they become dangerous, then we prevent countless hospital admissions. Domestic violence rates go down. That takes pressure off the police. The number of men in prison goes down. Again, less pressure on the system. More men leading useful, productive lives. Surely everyone wants that."

Bea thought that he sounded like he'd been watching too much TV, but she kept that to herself. Alfie had once said that doctors thought they were gods. Listening to Owen talk, she had to agree. "Would you have the test?" she asked him.

"What?"

"You said it would help men lead useful lives, but we're only testing boys. If this is about helping men, then surely it makes sense to test men. So I was wondering if you'd have it?"

He gave her a smooth smile. "The test isn't currently

recommended for adults, except in a few very specific circumstances."

"But surely you're curious."

"Not really," he said. "There's no possible benefit to my
having it. I work, I pay taxes, I contribute to society. I've already proved both to myself and to everyone around me
that I'm not a dangerous man."

You are a coward, though, she thought to herself. *And a liar.*
She was suddenly all too aware of his size, his muscular
forearms, his status as an untested male. It made her skin
feel like it was too tight for her body. She'd thought of Simon as somehow alone in the world, the odd one out, but
he wasn't, was he? Alfie wasn't tested, Owen wasn't tested.
If anything, Jack was the unusual one.

Owen had done something to his son that he wouldn't
do to himself.

Antonia was right. The test did mean something. That
was why adult men were pushing the responsibility onto little boys who couldn't say no, to focus attention away from
themselves. That was why Owen wouldn't have it. That was
why Alfie wanted her to stop reading about it, to stop talking about it.

And that was why she wouldn't.

CHAPTER EIGHTEEN

ANTONIA

Now

They managed to get all patients seen and out the door on time that afternoon, much to Antonia's surprise. It didn't happen often. When it did, it was a gift. She decided to leave her car at the clinic and go home with Owen in his. She enjoyed sitting next to him, seeing the admiring glances that came their way. They were, she knew, an elegant and beautiful couple in a classy and expensive car. Why wouldn't people want to look at them?

"I hope Jack is feeling better," she said.

"I'm sure he will be," Owen reassured her. "In fact, I'm predicting a miraculous recovery."

"What's that supposed to mean?"

"Come on, Antonia. You can't really have thought he was ill this morning. He was faking it so that he could spend some time with Simon."

Antonia pursed her lips. "He knows better than that."

"No, he doesn't," Owen said.

She wanted to be cross, to argue, but she needed to keep him in a good mood. She hadn't told him what she'd seen on the doorbell cam that morning. He didn't know that the police had been to the house.

She wasn't sure how to tell him.

The traffic slowed to a halt ahead of them, and a fire engine went rushing past, lights flashing. A police car followed it, and Antonia involuntarily clenched. But it kept going. It didn't stop.

They crawled slowly forward, Antonia craning her neck so she could see what was going on. "Looks like there's a car on fire under the bridge," she said.

"Again? Goddamn vandals," Owen replied. "Let's just hope no one was hurt."

She checked the local news on her phone for updates. "Doesn't look like it," she said, although the photo of the car someone had posted online made her skin prickle. The make and color were all too familiar. Antonia didn't believe in co-incidences. "Oh my god," she said. "I think it's Bea's car."

"What?!" Owen said, his shock obvious. He twisted in his seat to get a better look. "Stolen and dumped, probably. Or Bea did it herself in order to try and get you to give her a new one. At least it's not parked outside our house any-more. I suppose that's something to be grateful for."

Antonia couldn't tell if he meant that as a joke or not. She didn't laugh. By the time they got back to the house, she was more than ready for a drink, and she headed straight into the kitchen, not even bothering to take off her shoes first. Flash was in his basket next to the French doors, and he came to her side immediately, sitting there in silence, watching her with those dark liquid eyes, waiting for instructions. She ordered him back to his basket, and he went without complaint.

She knew exactly what had happened to the car. Bea had left it under the bridge. It didn't take a genius to work that out. And if Bea had been that keen to get rid of it, then she was more than a little afraid of the police.

It made Antonia's spine tingle just thinking about it.

Jack came rushing into the kitchen just as she was taking a glass down from the cupboard, and she quickly put it back. She didn't want him to see her drinking this early.

"Hello, my lovely boy," she said, and embraced him. "Feeling better, I take it?"

"Yes, fine," he said, shrugging her off. For someone who was supposed to be ill, he did look remarkably cheery. Perhaps Owen was right, and he had skipped school. "I've got something to tell you, though."

Was this the part where he confessed? She steeled herself for it, determined not to be angry. "What is it?"

His face split into a wide grin. "Simon got tested today."

Antonia felt her heart skip a beat. "He did *what*?"

"He got tested. Isn't that great news?"

"Unbelievable," Antonia said. She turned, reached for the glass again, and filled it almost to the brim. Her hands were shaking. "How did you find out?"

"I went to the hospital with him."

Antonia set down the glass and turned to look at her son. "You did *what*? I thought you were ill!"

"Don't be mad, Mom. I thought you'd be pleased he got tested. I know it's what you wanted."

"Yes," Antonia said. "It is. I'm just a little shocked, that's all." She reached for the glass and took a long drink. It helped. Then she rushed out of the kitchen in search of her sister and nephew. This was big news indeed. She found Bea in the garden, playing with the neighbor's cat. She took a moment to watch her sister from a distance.

Oh, Bea, she thought. *What happened to you? How did you end up like this?*

Bea got to her feet as she approached, brushing the grass from her scruffy jeans. Her eyes were wide and wary. The cat bolted. Bea looked like she wanted to follow suit.

"Is it true?" Antonia asked her. "Simon's been tested?"

Bea picked the stray strands of fur from her palms. "Apparently so."

A million thoughts flooded Antonia's mind, many of them cruel. She didn't voice them out loud. She could see how painful this was for her sister. All those years of refusing to have Simon tested, and he'd gone and done it anyway.

"Are you all right?" Antonia asked her.

Bea shrugged. "Why wouldn't I be?"

"Because you didn't want him to have it."

"He's eighteen. There's nothing I could do to stop him. It was always going to be his choice in the end."

Antonia walked over to the roses and gently touched the petals of her favorite pink one. "That doesn't mean that this is easy for you. After all, you must know how it's going to turn out."

"No one knows until they get the result."

"Come on, Bea," Antonia said. She crushed a petal between her fingers. "You're smarter than that. You must know what he is. You wouldn't have refused to have him tested for so long otherwise." Whatever mistakes Bea had made—and there were plenty—she was still someone Antonia cared about. "I know you just wanted to protect him."

"Didn't do a very good job there, did I?"

Bea's voice cracked on the words, and Antonia hurt for her. But there was nothing she could do to make it better. Hadn't it always been inevitable that things would turn out this way?

She took a step toward Bea, wobbling a little in her heels, and then wrapped her sister in a hug. Bea smelled of the Lily of the Valley shampoo that Antonia kept in the guest bathroom. It was an improvement, to say the least. Bea stood stiffly and then slowly put her arms around Antonia and returned the hug.

"You must stay with us until he gets his result," Antonia said. "It's important, Bea. Don't face this alone when you don't have to."

There would be no running away from the truth this time. Simon was going to have to face it—and the consequences for what he'd done to that girl in Cornwall.

Antonia intended to make sure of it.

CHAPTER NINETEEN

‖‖ BEA

Twelve years ago

Statement from the Association of UK Private Schools and Colleges to All Member Groups

Dear head teachers,

After taking legal advice, we have been informed that it is currently legal to exclude boys from your schools on the basis of their M test status. The basis for this conclusion is that M test status is not currently recognized as a protected characteristic in law, nor is it considered to be a disability. We must advise you that this may change in the future and that you may face challenges from parents who do not agree. However, at this moment in time, you may lawfully choose to exclude boys from your institutions on this basis if you feel it is appropriate.

Yours sincerely,
Brian Crofthouse, Chair

When Simon had started school, life had seemed to shift into another gear for Bea. It had been a relief to be out of the world of preschools and the battering that she'd taken when she tried to get Simon a place. Despite what Stephanie had said, the state primary school nearest to the house hadn't asked about Simon's test result. However, private schools had already been pushing M+ boys out for some time, and it was coming for state schools, too. Anyone who thought otherwise had their head in the clouds.

"It's really awful," Stephanie said as they sat together over coffee early one Sunday morning. They'd taken over a corner of Starbucks and were fiercely defending their space. "But I just feel so powerless. I've almost stopped posting on my blog. No one is reading it anymore. And whenever I post stuff on Facebook, I get the most awful comments, accusing me of wanting girls to be in danger. The worst thing is that we're going to have a whole generation of young men who have been pushed out of everything. And that's not going to be good for anyone. But no one wants to talk about that."

Bea took a sip of her coffee. At first, her friendship with Stephanie had been a relief. She could say whatever she wanted about the test without fear. But recently, she had started to feel a bit, well, bored with all of it. They rehashed the same things over and over. Stephanie kept herself entertained with posts on forums and Facebook that provoked online spats (often deliberately, Bea had realized), but none of it was real. None of it, at the end of the day, actually mattered.

It didn't help anyone.

And that made her think of Zara.

It had been a while since she'd last seen her. There had been a couple of coffee dates since the trouble with the goldfish, and a few text messages, but that was it. The friendship hadn't broken; it was more that it had never really got going in the first place, partly because Bea had made no effort to let it. She wasn't proud of herself for that. Maybe she should make the effort, she thought; otherwise, wasn't she just punishing Zara for something she hadn't done, the same as the test punished boys?

She stayed with Stephanie for another half an hour, until her coffee was gone, and then she made her excuses and left. Alfie had taken Simon for a bike ride, and they wouldn't be back until later, so she had some time to herself. She used it to phone Zara. It took her three tries to pluck up the nerve.

"Zara?" she said when the call was answered. "It's Bea Mitchell."

She held her breath, hoping that Zara would want to speak to her.

"Bea?" Zara said. "Wow. I wasn't expecting to hear from you."

"How are you?"

"Same as ever. You?"

Bea bit into her bottom lip to hold back the unexpected tide of feeling that was welling up inside her. "I'm okay," she said. "I thought . . . maybe you might like to meet up?"

"I guess so," Zara said slowly. "When?"

"I'm free now, if you're not busy."

"I've got Malcolm with me. Will that be a problem?"

"No, of course not," Bea lied.

An hour later, she found herself waiting outside the shopping center. Zara was late. Bea was close to certain that she wasn't coming when someone waved at her from a distance, and she saw Zara walking over. Bea waved back, but her attention was on Malcolm, trailing several feet behind.

He was bigger but otherwise the same. What had she expected? The number 666 scorched onto his forehead? A sign on his jacket that said M+, KEEP BACK? No. Both of those things were ridiculous. But the feeling he gave her was unchanged. It was what she and Antonia used to call "the ick": a sensation like ants crawling over her skin, an urge to step away, an undeniable sense of disgust. An involuntary shudder worked its way over her body, but she fixed on a smile as Zara drew close.

"Hello," she said. "It's good to see you."

"You too," Zara said, and she smiled as well, just as quickly, just as false.

It was awkward; there was no denying it.

"How are things?" Bea asked.

Zara shrugged. She was wearing jeans and a black puffer jacket, her hair pulled back into a ponytail that couldn't disguise several inches of dark roots and looked even thinner than Bea remembered. The clothes had expensive logos on them but had lost their freshness, the jeans worn at the seams, the jacket badly mended on the right sleeve. "Pretty shit, to be honest," she said.

"I'm sorry."

"It is what it is," Zara replied.

Bea glanced at Malcolm. She didn't know if she should greet him or not. "Can I buy you a coffee?"

"Sure," Zara said. "Can it be to go? He isn't good in confined spaces."

"Of course," Bea said. She bought drinks for the three of them, and they did laps of the shopping center with the cups in their hands. Zara told her that her ex had remarried and that his new wife had tried to make him cut contact with Malcolm. "He's not allowed to go to their house," she said. "Paul sees him on his own, once every couple of weeks, and half the time he claims he's busy and cancels."

"That's unacceptable," Bea said. Much as Malcolm scared her, no kid deserved that. She wondered what Alfie would do if Simon was tested and found to be M+. Would he walk away and leave her to it? Probably, she thought with a sensation like being drenched in cold water. She couldn't imagine many men who wouldn't.

"Yes, it is," Zara said. "But I can't make him see his son. Believe me. I've tried."

"Are you getting any help at all?"

"He's on a treatment program," Zara said. "I suppose you could call that help. Paul set it up for him. It's all being done through your sister's clinic."

"Does it work?"

"When I can get him to take the meds, yes, it does, but he hates them. Side effects, you see."

Malcolm hadn't said a single word, had just trailed along like a mute animal. Although Bea hadn't liked the earlier versions of him that she'd met, she didn't much like this version, either. "He's very quiet," she said.

"That's because you've caught us on a good day," Zara replied. She said it almost entirely without feeling and with total acceptance. "He took his pills this morning. You should see him when he doesn't."

Bea felt sick. "This is the treatment? This is what it does? And you're still giving it to him?"

She regretted the words as soon as they left her mouth. It had been cruel. Unnecessary. Intrusive. Rude.

"I'm a single mother," Zara said. "Every time I close my front door, it's just me and him. At least this way he's manageable."

"I'm sorry," Bea replied in a quiet voice. "I shouldn't have said that."

"No, you're right to ask," Zara said. "Because I'm not okay with it. I hate that I have to do this. I hate that I can't find a better way to cope with him. But I just can't."

Bea moved a little closer and slid an arm around Zara's shoulders, uncertain at first that it was the right thing to do. The two of them stood there like that for a long time. Malcolm stopped a couple of feet away and did nothing.

"I'm so tired," Zara said quietly.

"I know," Bea said.

When she finally dropped her arm, she could sense that something had changed. It didn't matter what Malcolm was;

Zara was clearly struggling. It had been selfish of her to walk away and leave her to it. And Bea didn't like to think of herself as a selfish person.

Malcolm sucked hard at his straw, slurping at the remnants of his drink. He turned his head and looked up at Bea. He didn't look like a demon. And yet, his M test result said that he was.

Bea had to wonder what his life would be like if no one were allowed to know his M status. If he could have gone to a better day care, a better school; if he hadn't been treated like a monster from birth. And what would Zara's life be like?

Like hers, she realized. Stuck in between.

And if he'd been negative?

Then Zara would be living in a six-bedroom house and dripping with diamonds, just like Antonia.

CHAPTER TWENTY

JACK

Now

Jack didn't want to go to school the next morning, but he knew it would look suspicious if he skipped another day. And Ginny hadn't replied to the messages he'd sent her the evening before or that morning. He wanted to check that she was okay.

He showered, put on his uniform, and went downstairs. There was no sign of Simon. Or the dog. "He took Flash for a walk again," his dad said. He was in the kitchen reading the news on his phone. He didn't look up when Jack walked in.

Jack dropped some bread in the toaster. "Didn't you tell him we've got someone to do that?"

"I did," Owen said as he finished his coffee and picked up his car keys. "But he seemed determined to go out, and it won't do Flash any harm to have extra exercise."

Jack heard the unspoken message and ignored it. Owen was always hinting at stuff like that, as if Jack didn't have enough to do, with school and homework and music. He slathered his toast with butter and jam, then took it upstairs. His mother was in her room, straightening the bed. The door to the other spare room was firmly closed. Presumably his aunt Bea was still asleep.

He sat at his desk and turned on his laptop, wanting to see if Ginny was online. She wasn't. He checked her social media, but she hadn't posted anything new, so he scrolled for a bit, trolled a couple of losers, downloaded some music, and watched a video on violin fingering techniques on YouTube.

After all that, Simon still wasn't back. Nor did he respond to the message Jack sent him. Jack couldn't wait for him any longer, not if he was going to get to school in time to see Ginny before lessons started. Simon's absence worried him. He was supposed to be here, keeping his head down, not acting like everything was fine and he could do whatever the hell he wanted. The test might be done, but they didn't have the result yet, and that was what mattered. Jack knew he wouldn't feel right until Simon had the M App loaded on his phone, his result there for everyone to see.

He brushed aside his mother's offer of a lift and set off in his own car, hoping he might spot Simon on the way, but he didn't, and he got to school still none the wiser about his cousin's whereabouts.

He checked his phone one more time, then strolled into the building, bumping a few sixth graders out of the way as he passed. He found Ginny in the library, giggling away with a couple of her friends. They looked up as he walked in, then they turned to each other and giggled again, hiding their mouths behind their hands so he couldn't see what they were saying. "What's the joke?" he asked.

"Nothing," one of them said. She got to her feet. "See you later, Ginny."

"Yeah," Ginny said. The other girl sat there a little longer, but Jack was able to see her off, too, by sitting in the just-vacated chair and giving her a death stare until she left.

"You haven't answered any of my messages," he said to Ginny. He tried not to let his irritation show.

"Sorry," she said. She flashed him a quick smile. "I've just been busy. Cross-country tryouts are next week, and I've been trying to get some extra training in. That's why I didn't answer. And you said you had a migraine yesterday. I wanted to let you rest. How's your head now, by the way?"

"Fine," Jack replied, sitting back in his seat, his muscles relaxing. He'd overreacted. He could see that now. She wasn't ignoring him. Not that she would. They were too good of friends for that. "Thanks for asking. How's the training going?"

"Pretty good," she said. She adjusted the hem of her skirt. "I saw someone while I was out yesterday morning, actually. Your cousin Simon."

"You saw Simon?"

"Yes. I thought he was you at first." She laughed. "How dumb is that?"

Jack had to take a second to breathe. He tipped his chair back, putting his weight on the rear legs. The back of his neck felt hot. "Pretty dumb," he said.

"Is he back for good, then?"

"No. Just visiting. He and my aunt showed up on Monday night. Totally out of the blue," he added.

"Really? Wow." Ginny sat back in her seat. "I bet your parents didn't like that."

"No, they didn't," Jack said. "Dad was furious. He pretended he wasn't, but I could tell. As for Mom . . ." He lifted his hand to his mouth and mimed knocking back a drink.

Ginny made a face. "Oh, dear."

Jack laughed and the uneasy feeling started to dissipate. It was pretty funny, if you thought about it. His parents running a clinic for M+ boys and making a killing doing it; his aunt refusing to even have Simon tested. He couldn't help but wonder sometimes if Bea had done it just to wind his mother up.

He was almost sorry that was over now.

The bell rang, and the two of them got to their feet and walked over to the biology lab for their first lesson. "Did Alex tell you that we're going to rehearse at his house on Thursday evening?" he asked as they waited outside. "His parents are away, so we can make as much noise as we like."

"Yes, he messaged me."

"I'll give you a lift," he said. She hadn't passed her driving test yet, so she had to rely on other people if she wanted to go anywhere. She'd already let him take her home a few times.

"No need. I've sorted it out."

Before he could persuade her to ditch whoever it was and go with him instead, their biology teacher opened the door and they went in. There was no further opportunity to talk, and they didn't have any other lessons together that morning. He didn't see her again until lunchtime. He was in one of the practice rooms tuning his violin when she came running in.

"Can you take me into town? I've just been told I've got to do a time trial after school and all my gear is in the wash at home."

"Sure," Jack said, quickly slipping his violin back in its case and closing it. It didn't take them long to reach town, and when they got there, Ginny didn't mess around. She went straight past the discount sports store located just inside the entrance of the mall and up to the Nike store on the top floor. They paused only for Jack to scan his M App at the door, verifying his M− status, and then went inside. He sat quietly as she tried on tennis shoes and picked out running gear. There weren't any messages from Simon on his phone, so he sent him one.

Heard you bumped into Ginny Sloan yesterday

That got a response.

Yep

We've been going out for the last six months, Jack typed, then deleted it.

We're kind of a thing. He deleted that, too.

She's

He exited the app as Ginny came over with a bag in her hand. "I'm done," she said. "Thanks, Jack."

"No problem."

A group of boys had gathered outside the shop, and they jeered at Ginny as she and Jack left. None of them were in school uniforms. Jack knew who they were immediately, or rather, he knew what they were. "Piss off," Jack shouted at them. He squeezed Ginny's hand. *You're all right*, he wanted to tell her. *You're safe with me.*

They shouted back and flipped him off. He took out his phone and snapped a picture of the boys before uploading it to the app everyone used to report antisocial behavior. They'd get moved on soon enough.

The test had fixed a lot, but it hadn't fixed everything. At least everyone knew who the dangerous boys were now, and you could mostly avoid them. His school didn't admit boys with a positive test. Other places were allowed to refuse them entry, too, like shops and gyms and bars. Jack knew for a fact that all his friends were negative. But M+ boys clung on anyway, like scum at the edge of a lake.

It made him think of Simon. Was he scum? He certainly looked like an M+ boy, with his scruffy clothes and that bruise on his face. And there had been times when he'd acted like one, too. But Jack had never quite been able to bring himself to believe it. And even if it was true, he'd always thought that Simon was different than the boys his parents treated at the clinic, the ones who needed pills to make them act like normal human beings.

But maybe he'd been stupid to think that. Maybe he'd seen what he wanted rather than the truth, because Simon was his friend. He felt suddenly cold. His cousin had a darkness in him. Only a fool would deny that.

Ginny smiled at him as they got in the lift that would take them up to the parking garage. He smiled back, and it settled something inside him. A girl like Ginny would never be interested in someone like Simon. But that didn't mean Simon wouldn't be interested in her. Of course he would. She was gorgeous and completely out of his league, and if there was one thing Jack knew about his cousin, it was that he coveted things he couldn't have.

Ginny offered to pay when they got to the ticket machine, but Jack didn't let her. He checked his phone again before he got in the car. He had more messages from Simon, though none of them were about Ginny.

Mom is having an argument w yr cleaner

Whats yr xbox password

I'll be glad when this is over and I've got my result

A strange burning sensation started in Jack's chest, and he pressed a hand against his ribs. He didn't know why Simon was so worried. He was going to get the result he wanted, if not the one he deserved.

Jack had made sure of that.

CHAPTER TWENTY-ONE

ANTONIA

Nine years ago

Daily Telegraph

Is the M Gene the New Frontier for Divorce?

A couple known only as R and W is heading to the high court today. R, an investment banker and an heir to one of Britain's biggest fortunes, has been accused of years of domestic and sexual abuse by his estranged wife, W. But with no incidents reported to the police and no medical evidence to back this up, it has become just another case of he said, she said. However, all that could be about to change. W is expected to ask the judge to order R to be tested for the M gene. A positive result would mean that it is likely that W will be awarded a significant figure in damages as well as a divorce, on the grounds of unreasonable behavior, and sole custody of their three children. Legal experts have also said that it could potentially lead to R facing a police investigation and prison sentence.

One chilly autumn morning, Antonia and Owen got to the clinic to find two smashed windows and graffiti all over the front. The police took statements and told them to get CCTV installed. The insurance company paid for the cleanup work.

"We'll just have to accept that this is part and parcel of running a place like this," Owen said when Antonia complained about the bill for the CCTV. The system had cost them thousands. It wouldn't be necessary if people would behave themselves. But clearly that was too much to ask.

Much to her surprise, she found it comforting, knowing that it was there, and the visible cameras and stickers placed on all the windows warning potential troublemakers that they were being filmed seemed to have the desired effect. She began to look forward to going to work once again, no longer worried about what they would find when they got there.

She was on the phone with a client when Paul came striding out of his office, his face like thunder. "I need to see Owen," he said.

Antonia checked her watch. "He should be done in another ten minutes. Your next patient is here, by the way." She kept her voice low, not wanting to draw the attention of the family sitting on the couch in the waiting area.

"They'll have to wait," he said.

That wasn't like him. "What's the problem? Maybe I can help?"

"In my office," he said shortly.

She locked her computer and followed him. He closed the door behind her. "I need to have the test," he said.

Antonia stared at him in disbelief. "Whatever for?"

"Zara," he said. He clenched his teeth. "She wants more money. Claims that what I'm paying isn't enough, as if she isn't already bleeding me dry. I'm already paying for his housing, his maintenance, his medical treatment. Greedy, grasping bitch."

Antonia, who had seen the ring that Paul had recently given Lily for her birthday—a three-carat pink sapphire surrounded by diamonds—searched for some pithy comment, for something to show that she was on Paul's side, but she couldn't find anything. She didn't like Zara and made no secret of that, but she also didn't have much time for men who refused to look after their children properly or who disrespected their mothers by leaving them to struggle. It was too close to her own childhood.

"My lawyer suggested that it would be helpful if I was tested," Paul continued grimly. "Best I do it now before Zara gets hold of the idea. Did you see that divorce case in the news? If you want something from a man, request the M test. If he refuses, you win. If he tests positive, you win. He just has to cross his fingers and hope like hell he's negative, even if he's never done anything wrong."

Antonia unpeeled her tongue from the roof of her mouth. "I'll get a testing kit from the cupboard," she said. They kept a stash at the clinic because many parents asked to have their sons retested in the usually vain hope that the first test had been wrong, though they hardly ever were. The test gave the odd false negative, which was why each involved two separate swabs tested independently. But it didn't give false positives.

She washed her hands, put on a pair of latex gloves, then laid all the pieces out. Paul opened his mouth and she gently swiped the cotton buds against his cheek, collecting cells to be sent for genetic testing.

She wrote down all the necessary details, packaged it up. Then she gave Paul a smile she didn't feel and left the room, taking the box with her. She rang the courier company and arranged for it to be picked up, then had to scramble to soothe the parents who had been left to wait.

The day only got worse from there.

By the time she left to collect Jack, she was in a foul mood. But seeing Jack made things a little better. He came running out of the school, happy to see her as always, and she swept him up into a hug. Lily was at the gate, too, waiting with her youngest daughter.

Antonia made small talk, waving at Ginny when she came shuffling out, skirt swinging around her chubby knees. She decided not to tell Lily that Paul had taken the test. It wasn't any of her business, really. If Paul wanted to tell her, that was up to him. But she did tell Owen.

"What if he's positive?" she asked. "He can't keep working here if he is."

Paul got his test result two days later. It was negative.

Zara didn't get her money.

CHAPTER TWENTY-TWO

||| BEA

Now

The police came back that morning. Owen and Antonia had gone to the clinic, and Jack was at school, so Bea and Simon were alone in the house. Simon was in the home theater playing video games when the knock came at the door, and Bea answered it alone. It was just as well.

But it did mean that all Bea had for support was the dog, and he was no use.

She stared in horror at the two uniformed officers on the doorstep, both male, both much taller than she was. They would be M—, all uniformed officers now were, but that didn't stop her from feeling afraid. But she straightened her spine and told herself that she had dealt with scarier men than these two.

"Can I help you?" she asked when she finally found her voice.

"Bea Mitchell?"

"Yes?" she replied. She wished that she'd lied and said she was the cleaner.

"Can we come in?"

"Not really. This isn't my house."

They looked at each other, and some silent message passed between them, but they seemed to accept it. "We need to talk to you about an incident that happened at a recycling farm in Hilsford four days ago."

Her heart sank. She rubbed a hand over her face, aware of her terrible clothes, her terrible hair, that to tell the truth could only incriminate Simon but to deny it wouldn't help, either. "Okay," she said.

Acknowledge, deny. Acknowledge, deny.

"You were at Hilsford?" the taller of the two asked.

"Yes, I was there."

"And your son?"

"He was there, too."

"Why were you there?"

"I needed to earn a living," she said. She folded her arms. "That's not illegal, is it?"

"Of course not."

Again the two of them looked at each other. Again the silent communication.

"The problem is this, Bea," the shorter one said to her. "May I call you Bea?"

"No, you may not."

A crease formed between his brows. He didn't like that. "There was a fight on the night of the eleventh," he said. "An illegal fight. I understand your son was part of it."

She shrugged. "What's that got to do with me?"

"Where is he?" the other officer asked her.

"I've got no idea," Bea lied. "He's eighteen. Do you honestly think I've got any control over where he goes or what he does?"

She said the words flippantly, trying to hide how angry she was, how frightened, how desperate to close the door before Simon came to see what was going on.

"The boy that Simon fought is in the hospital with brain damage," the taller of the two continued. "It doesn't look good. If he dies . . ."

Bea felt all the blood drain from her face. She clutched at the edge of the door. "Simon didn't do anything," she said faintly, because denial was all she had left now.

"If you see your son again," he said, "we need you to contact us immediately."

Then the two of them turned and walked away. Bea closed the door with a shaking hand and, once inside, could only make it as far as the bottom of the stairs before she had to sit down. She buried her face in her hands and pressed hard against the corners of her eyes, refusing to let any tears leak out.

All of Simon's life, she had tried to protect him. She had tried to keep him close to her as the world grew crueler and smaller for boys, less forgiving, more willing to find them guilty of something, of anything. She knew that she had already given him a less-than-ideal start in life, with his arrival on the floor of a hospital bathroom, and Alfie, and the fact that there had never really been enough money, and the crappy day care and the crappy schools and . . . and . . . and . . .

When he'd been born, she hadn't had him tested partly

because she didn't agree with it and partly because Owen had been the one to suggest it. Later, she'd refused because she couldn't afford the treatment if he got a positive result, and so she'd decided that no test was the better option. And later still, she'd refused because her fear that his result would be positive was so overwhelming. The alternative to that outcome was that her parenting was so awful that she made Simon bad despite his inherent goodness, and she couldn't face that possibility, either.

She had never felt as alone as she did in that moment, sitting at the bottom of the stairs in her sister's big fancy house.

"Mom?"

Bea looked up to see Simon hovering close by.

"What's going on?" he asked.

"That was the police again," she told him. "Looks like our attempt to put them off by dumping the car didn't work. They know we're here. At least, they know I'm here, because I was stupid enough to open the door."

"What did they want?"

"That fight . . . the boy's got brain damage. They don't know if he's going to make it."

"Shit," Simon said, which was Bea's sentiment exactly. "Really?"

"Yes, really."

When he sat down on the step next to her, she put her arm around his shoulders and held on tight. He was hot and bony, and he smelled like soap. "I didn't mean to," he said.

"I know."

But he had done it anyway.

"It's going to be all right, though," he said.

"How, Simon? How is it possibly going to be all right? You got tested. You did the one thing I always told you never to do. If it comes back positive, they will throw the book at you. They'll put you in prison. There won't be a smack on the wrist or community service. You won't be able to claim self-defense. So tell me: How is it going to be all right?"

She waited for him to give her an answer, but he didn't. Instead, he shrugged off her arm and went upstairs. The side of her body he'd been pressed against was suddenly cold. Bea felt like she was going to burst into tears.

There was only one person she could possibly talk to. Only one person who might understand what she was feeling. She got her phone out, found the number, and called it. It rang five times before she got an answer, and she'd almost given up hope that she would.

"Hello," said a familiar voice.

"Zara?"

"Speaking."

"It's Bea Mitchell."

"Oh my god. Bea! How are you?"

"Not good," Bea said. She swallowed tears, took a breath. "Look, I don't mean to be weird, and I know it's been a long time, but can I come and see you?"

"You're here?"

"Yes."

"I'll text you my address. Do you want to come over now?"

The message came through almost immediately, and although Bea noticed that Zara had moved, she thought little of it until she got there. The Zara she'd first met had lived in a detached beast of a house a couple of streets over from Antonia. This current version lived in a third-floor apartment in a concrete tower block. There were grubby net curtains in all the windows and banging music coming from the door opposite Zara's. It didn't frighten Bea, but it did upset her. Whatever had happened to Zara in the past five years hadn't been good.

She rang the doorbell and took a step back, filled with a sudden urge to run away, or at least to be ready to do so if it proved necessary.

Eventually she heard the sound of a lock being turned, and the door opened.

"Zara?" Bea asked, knowing it was her but still needing to check, such was her shock at the change in her old friend's appearance.

Instead of being the picture of perfect health, like Antonia, Zara was a ghost. Her face was drawn, her skin gray, her hair thinning at the temples. The glamorous clothes and beautiful shoes had gone completely, replaced by leggings and a short-sleeved gray T-shirt that only served to highlight how very thin she was. Traveling up her right arm was a long jagged scar, and she was holding her weight on a stick.

"Bea! Please, come in." She moved back awkwardly, making enough room for Bea to squeeze past. She found herself in a tiny living room, a TV and a two-seater sofa with a duvet and pillows on it being the only furniture. To be fair, there wasn't really room for anything else.

Zara didn't apologize for the mess or for herself, and Bea

respected her for that. She knew how utterly horrendous she would have found it to welcome anyone from her old life into the shithole of a trailer that she and Simon had shared on the farm.

"There's a chair in the kitchen if you want to grab it," Zara said.

Bea did as she suggested. She brought the chair in and sat down. Zara awkwardly sat on the sofa—more of a controlled fall than an actual sit—and pulled the duvet over her knees, setting the walking stick down next to her.

"You must be wondering about all this," Zara said.

"It's difficult not to," Bea admitted.

"Malcolm's final gift to me," Zara said. "Four years ago. I was driving him back to the boys' home. He decided he didn't want to go and grabbed the wheel. Drove us straight into a truck coming in the other direction."

Bea tried to speak, but her voice wouldn't work. She had to pause, swallow, and try again. "I'm sorry." It was all she could manage. "Zara, I'm so sorry."

"Why? It's not your fault."

"Did he . . . is he . . ?"

"If you're asking me if he survived it, of course he damn well did."

"Where is he now?" Bea asked softly, hoping he wasn't in the apartment.

Zara's face crumpled. "I don't know." She thumped the duvet, put a smile on her face and a bucketload of cheer into her voice. "Enough about me anyway. I can't believe it's been five years!"

"I know." Bea tried to smile. "Long time. I'm sorry that we just disappeared on you like that."

"Antonia said you wanted a fresh start. I can't blame you for it. I should've done it myself years ago."

It hadn't occurred to Bea that her sister wouldn't have told people the truth about what had happened. "You talked to her about it?"

"Not directly. Paul told me. But to be honest, it was never really discussed. She came back from the vacation without you, it was exciting for about five minutes, and then people moved on. You know how it is."

"Ouch," Bea said, only half joking. But that was what she'd wanted, wasn't it? To be out of sight and out of mind? It still hurt, though, to know how little impact she'd had on these people. But she squashed that down, ashamed to feel it. At least she knew where Simon was. Zara couldn't say the same about her son.

Zara attempted a smile. "Anyway, enough about me. What brings you back to this neck of the woods?"

Bea had come here for help, and she wouldn't get it if she lied. Plus she felt that she owed Zara the truth after the other woman had been so painfully honest about her own situation. It took courage to admit that your son wasn't a good person, to see his flaws. "Simon's in trouble," she said.

It was the first time she'd said that out loud. It felt almost overwhelming. The back of her throat prickled, and she could feel the muscles in her cheeks starting to pinch in preparation for tears. She took a deep breath, willing it to pass.

"What sort of trouble?" Zara asked her gently.

"It's a long story," Bea said. She didn't know how much of it she was truly ready to tell.

"Well, I've got nothing else to do," Zara said.

"We . . . we've been working on a farm," Bea said. It surprised her to find that she didn't feel ashamed about admitting that to Zara. The other woman had never judged her in that way, unlike her sister. "And however bad you think that was, multiply it by ten, and you're about there. Some of the older men set up fights between the younger ones and organized betting on the results. Simon got involved. I ignored it, to be honest, because it meant there was a little extra money. It made things easier, so I didn't ask where he'd got it from. But he was in a fight last Saturday that got out of hand. He beat the other boy half to death." She pressed her fingers against her eyes, trying to push the memories away.

The knock on the door of the trailer. It had been one of the few women who worked there, wanting to let Bea know that there was trouble. Bea had shoved her feet into her boots and run full pelt across the tarmac toward the gathered crowd. The place was floodlit, so it was bright even at midnight, and there had been the roar of male voices, music coming from a car with the windows down, the smell of the nearby factories making the air gritty even in the middle of the night.

The men had formed a solid wall, and she'd had to fight her way through it, elbowing them out of the way, ignoring their complaints. Their excitement had been palpable, bordering on sexual. It was something Bea was aware of, that violence turned some men on, but she'd never experienced it up close before, and it had disgusted her.

And when she had gotten to the middle, she'd found Simon on his hands and knees, spitting blood, the other boy sprawled unconscious on the ground, his face beaten unrecognizable, and her disgust had morphed into flat-out terror.

To know that your son could do that was . . . it was . . .

"Is he still untested?" Zara asked. She was using her attorney voice, Bea realized. She hadn't noticed before.

"Stupid fool went and got it done yesterday." She licked her lips, her mouth dry. She took a deep breath, let it out. "So I guess by the end of the week we'll know if he's a negative boy caught in a bad situation or a positive boy being true to his nature."

Zara's expression spoke volumes. "Are you worried?" The duvet started to slide off her knees. Bea grabbed it before it could hit the floor and carefully tucked it back in place.

"Scared witless," she admitted. "I still can't really believe that he's done it."

Zara reached out and took her hand. "I'm so sorry, Bea. I know it isn't what you wanted."

"I honestly thought I could protect him forever," Bea told her, blinking back tears. "But you can't, can you? Because they grow up and think that they know everything, even though they don't, not even close." She wondered if she should tell Zara that the police had been to the house, that

Simon was in far deeper trouble than she had let on. Some-how she couldn't bring herself to do it. If she said the words out loud, it would be like admitting that Simon was no dif-ferent than Malcolm. "And you still love them. Even though you feel like you shouldn't. Even though sometimes you don't want to."

Zara's phone rang. She answered it, and Bea got to her feet and went into the tiny kitchen, thinking to give Zara some privacy and make herself useful. She filled the kettle and put it on. There was a box of tea bags on the counter-top, and she found a couple of mugs and tossed the bags in.

When she took the tea back into the living room, Zara was staring into space, her hands shaking on her lap. Her face was incredibly pale. Bea knew immediately that some-thing was wrong. "What is it?"

"That was Paul," Zara said, looking up at her with shin-ing eyes. "Something's happened to Malcolm. He's in the hospital."

CHAPTER TWENTY-THREE

‖ BEA

Seven years ago

Instagram post from @RichieHawkinsFootball

It's official, guys. I know rumors have been circulating
for a while now, and I decided it was time to put the
record straight. My son @RobbieHawkinsBaby has
tested positive for the M gene. I decided, in solidarity with
@RobbieHawkinsBaby, that I would have myself tested as
well, and I can confirm that I am also positive for the gene.

We're still coming to terms with this and figuring out
exactly what it means for us going forward as a family,
but I can tell you that we are going to get through this
together. #family #love #Mgene #Mpositiveboy #bekind

Bea shoved her phone back into her bag as the bus turned
onto their road. It hadn't been a good day. It had started
well enough, she supposed: a family breakfast, a successful

trip to the shoe shop, an hour in the library. She and Alfie had even managed to make it through all that without having a fight.

But she could sense one looming now.

She knew what had triggered it. It had been a moment of weakness, the inability to keep her mouth shut when she knew she should have. She'd gone into the big pharmacy on the high street to buy a couple of things for their medicine cabinet at home (not that they had an actual cabinet; it was an old ice cream tub she kept under the sink). Simon was forever covered in bumps and bruises, and she'd needed antiseptic cream and plasters. And there on the next shelf had been a new range of herbal remedies for boys.

M+ boys.

The labels had promised miracles, but Bea hadn't been fooled for a second. *Dose your son with this untested and most likely completely useless stuff, and all your problems will be solved. Only £7.99!*

She had walked straight out of the shop in a cold fury, which Alfie hadn't failed to notice, and he had picked at it until she'd told him exactly what the problem was in words that even he could understand, which had gone down like a lead balloon.

The bus ride home had been filled with tension that hadn't been lost on Simon. He had pushed his way into the seat next to her, turning his back on Alfie, something Bea knew she should discourage but, more and more often, found herself not wanting to.

She felt like the world was closing in around her. The madness was spreading. The M test was cutting a hole through the middle of society, shearing off the boys deemed "other," and she didn't know what to do about it. She was close to accepting that there was nothing that could be done. Not when people could get rich from the test and everything that went with it. People like Owen. And her sister.

She pressed the button for the bell to tell the driver they wanted to get off and ushered Simon to the front, not bothering to wait for Alfie. She just wanted to go home and climb into bed and hide. But when she got there, she was in for a surprise.

Zara was on the doorstep.

The other woman shot to her feet, dusted her backside clean with one hand. Bea could guess what had happened before Zara even opened her mouth. She'd had another fight with Paul. They were becoming more and more frequent. Bea knew why, of course.

"This isn't a good time, Zara," Alfie said shortly, coming up behind Bea.

"I just left Malcolm at Paul's house," Zara said to Bea, as if Alfie hadn't spoken. Her eyes were huge. Mascara streaked her face and her eyes were bloodshot. "He tried to refuse to take him. Can you believe it? I had to literally leave him standing there in the street and drive off. I didn't know what else to do. But I've got to have a break from him, Bea, I've got to. I feel like I'm going mad."

Bea opened the door and ushered Zara inside, Simon following close at her heels. "Upstairs," she ordered him. "Go and read a book or something."

"But, Mom . . ."

"Now!" Bea said.

Simon pouted but did as he'd been told. She left Alfie to make up his own mind about what he was doing and took Zara through to the kitchen, where she put the kettle on. Tea wouldn't make any difference, but at least it gave her something to do.

"I'm sure everything is fine," Bea said, but even to her ears, it sounded flat. "Paul will just have to deal with him. He wouldn't leave him there on the street."

"He's off his medication again," Zara said. "I found it in his room. He's been stashing it. I was so sure that he was taking it. I've been watching him like a hawk. But he's thirteen, Bea. There's not a lot I can do if he doesn't want to take it."

"What did Paul say?" Bea asked

"Paul is refusing to speak to me." With that, Zara dissolved into a flood of tears. "He won't even answer the phone."

Bea glanced across to see Alfie standing in the doorway. The expression on his face said it all. *This is not your problem. Don't make it your problem.* But what choice did she have? Where was Zara supposed to go? Paul's family had cut her off completely, and Bea knew that Zara was an only child born to older parents. Her mother was dead and her father was in a home with dementia. Her friends had all sided with Paul after the divorce. Their social circle had effectively closed Zara out. No one wanted to be associated with the mother of the M+ boy.

"Make some tea, will you?" she said to Alfie. She tried to move past him, but he was blocking the doorway. It was obvious that he wanted to keep her where she was, make her deal with Zara rather than the problem, because as far as he was concerned, Zara being in the house was the problem.

Well, he was wrong.

"Alfie," she said warningly, and he finally relented and moved out of her way. She went outside so that she'd have privacy for the call she didn't want to make. She didn't have Paul's number, but she knew who did.

"It's me," she said as soon as her sister answered. "I need you to get ahold of Paul."

"Nice to hear from you, Bea," Antonia said.

"When you get ahold of him," Bea continued, unable to hide her impatience, "tell him to fucking man up and start dealing with Zara and his son."

She heard muffled voices: Antonia and a man, presumably Owen. That was confirmed when he came on the line.

"What's going on?" he said briskly.

"Zara just turned up at my house. She tried to drop Malcolm off at Paul's house, and he refused to even open the door, so she just left Malcolm outside and drove off."

"For fuck's sake," Owen said, and in that, they were in agreement for once. Bea heard mumbled conversation again, and then Owen came back. "I'll deal with it."

The call ended without so much as a goodbye, but Bea barely noticed the rudeness. Zara had made her way outside and was standing on the doorstep, a cigarette in one trembling hand.

"Owen's going to try to talk to Paul," Bea said. "But I'm sure he would have let Malcolm in the house as soon as you left. He's just a kid. Paul wouldn't leave him on the street."

"I'm not so sure about that. Ever since Paul got a negative test result, he's been acting like Malcolm isn't his problem anymore. I tried to renegotiate the child maintenance payments now that Malcolm is older and his clothes are more expensive and my food bill has gone up, and he didn't want to know. He's decided that it must somehow be my fault that Malcolm is positive, and he's using that to justify paying the bare minimum for him."

Bea's phone rang again. Owen. "Did you get hold of him?" she asked.

"Yes," Owen said grimly. "Malcolm ran off and he doesn't know where he is."

"Is he looking for him?"

"No. He's on his way to the clinic. The security alarm went off."

"And obviously that's his priority, not his son," Bea said furiously, and hung up. How was she supposed to tell Zara that? If she were in Zara's position, she would want to kill Paul for the way he was behaving. She didn't understand how anyone could be so cruel, so selfish.

She took a deep breath, tasting the smoke from Zara's cigarette, feeling it catch at the back of her throat. There was no way around this, no way to spin it. She had to tell Zara the truth. "Malcolm ran off and Paul doesn't know where he is," she said. "Apparently, something's happened at the clinic and he's gone there instead."

"The clinic?" Zara asked. Her eyes went wild. "Oh god. It's Malcolm."

She ran across the road to a dirty BMW with a large

scratch down one side. Bea went with her, getting straight into the passenger seat, tugging at her seat belt as Zara swung the car out into the road with a squeal of tires. It crossed her mind that Zara might not be in a fit state to drive, but they were already moving, so there was little she could do apart from cross her fingers and hope for the best. It wasn't far to the clinic from here. From what she could remember, Paul lived several miles outside town. With a bit of luck, they'd be able to get there first.

"He hates the clinic," Zara said in a high-pitched voice. "He says his dad only works there because he wants to poison all boys like him."

"Poison?"

"That's what he calls the medication. Owen writes Malcolm's prescriptions, but I know Paul is the one deciding what he should be on."

Bea had a sick sense of dread in her gut. It didn't help when Zara took a sharp right, clipping the curb as they went around the corner. She took another right and then a left turn and slammed to a halt in the middle of the clinic parking lot, flinging open the door.

"Malcolm!" Zara screamed as she climbed out, but her voice was drowned out by the alarm. "Malcolm!"

Bea opened her own door and got out slowly. Apart from the alarm, there didn't seem to be anything out of place. But she couldn't shake the creeping sense of unease.

Zara pressed her face against the door of the clinic, trying to see inside, then darted left to the window and looked again. The blinds were closed. Bea doubted that she could see anything. How would Malcolm have gotten into the building, anyway?

"I'm going around the back," Zara shouted at her, and was gone before Bea could suggest that she stop, wait, and think. Anything could have set the alarm off. They didn't know for certain that Malcolm was here. And if he was, Bea wasn't sure that she wanted to find him.

Another car pulled into the parking lot, and she was relieved to see Paul get out of it. A second car drew up alongside Paul's. Bea recognized it immediately as Owen's. She'd never thought she would be in a situation where she would be glad to see him. Then Antonia emerged from the car, too, and she realized that Jack was strapped in the back, and any positive feelings she had evaporated in light of their stupidity. Whatever was going on, it didn't need an audience.

"Is he here?" Paul shouted at her.

"I don't know," Bea told him. "We got here right before you did. Zara went around the back to see if he's there."

Paul swore, the sound carried away by the noise of the alarm, though the shape of the word was unmistakable. He was off and running immediately, taking the path Zara had taken to the rear of the building.

Owen rushed straight to the door, keys in hand. In a matter of seconds, he had it open and was inside. The alarm stopped.

Bea looked at her sister, her face red and shiny, her hair hanging loose from its bun. She'd never seen her look like this before. Antonia was always so well put together. Even her casual appearance was smarter than anything Bea could hope to achieve. "She shouldn't have left him at Paul's house," Antonia said breathlessly. "He called Lily a bitch and said he was going to kick her head in. Scared the life out of her."

No need to ask Antonia whose side she was on. "He's just a kid," Bea told her. "His father has dumped him for a new family. We both know what that's like. I can understand why he's pissed off. Can't you?"

"It's not the same!" Antonia shouted back at her. "You don't know, Bea. You don't understand!"

"Yes, I do."

What Bea didn't understand was the reaction of the adults around him.

But when Paul came back, pushing a struggling Malcolm along the path in front of him, she revised that opinion. Although Malcolm was child-sized, there was something in his face, a raging darkness, that was truly unnerving. She'd only ever seen him when he was in the grip of his medication. She'd never seen him without it before.

Zara was trailing along behind them. She didn't look at Bea. Paul pushed Malcolm toward his car and pinned him against the side of it with one big hand. Zara smacked his hand away, dropped to her knees, and wrapped her arms around Malcolm. He struggled against her grip until she was forced to let go and fell back, sobbing. Paul did nothing.

For a moment, Bea was tempted to march up to Paul and take a swing at him. But something stopped her. It was Owen. He came rushing out of the building, eyes wide with panic. "Call 999," he said. "He's set the place on fire."

CHAPTER TWENTY-FOUR

SIMON

Now

The next morning, Simon got up very early and took Flash to the park before anyone else was out of bed. He managed to avoid Owen this time. He'd lifted a T-shirt and a pair of tennis shoes from Jack's closet the night before, figuring Jack wouldn't miss them. The tennis shoes were a bit big, and he had to wear two pairs of socks, but the T-shirt fit like a glove, snug across the shoulders, and he thought he looked pretty good in it. It helped. His own clothes smelled like the farm, like the cold trailer that he'd lived in. It had always been slightly damp, and the odor had taken up residence in everything he owned.

He didn't want to be the person he'd become there anymore. And in two more days, he wouldn't be. He'd never known time to move so slowly. He needed that confirmation. It didn't matter that he was certain what the outcome would be or that he already had some idea of what would happen afterward. The place he was living in now, the in-between, was unbearable. It made him feel like he was going crazy.

Jack was being weird with him, too. He'd barely said a word the previous evening, hadn't wanted to watch a movie or play a video game, and had spent most of his time glued to his phone.

Simon told himself that he didn't care. He also told himself that he wasn't going out in the hope that he'd see Ginny again and that he wouldn't be disappointed if she didn't show up. He burned off some of his energy and some of the time by taking a longer route to the park, one that took him by the parade of local shops. Only the Tesco Express was open. He had a couple of quid in his pocket, and he lingered by the fizzy drinks, sorely tempted, but in the end bought a pint of milk instead. When he came out, Flash was sitting exactly where he had left him, so Simon decided to let him off the leash. They set off again.

Even though he was grateful to Jack for what he had done, old complaints died hard, and the things about his cousin that had irritated him before still irritated him now.

"He's got no fucking idea," he told Flash through panted breaths as they went through the gates of the park. "Living in that house, never having to worry about anything. He wouldn't last five minutes on a farm. They're horrible. You're cold all the time, and hungry, and you can't sleep properly, ever."

Flash whined.

"He's going to go off and live a wonderful life, and he'll think it's all up to him, but it's not. It's not an achievement if you're M-negative and you've known it since you were born."

They ran farther, Simon speeding up, putting some zip into his strides. His body had started to loosen up, and he could see clearly out of both eyes now. The bruise on his face had gone down a lot. Another week, and it would be barely noticeable.

"It's just not fair," he said to Flash.

"What isn't?"

The voice came from his left, and he turned, slowing his pace a little, to see Ginny alongside him. She was in purple this morning, a long-sleeved top and shorts.

"Life," he said. "Life isn't fucking fair."

"Sounds like you're having a hard day."

"I'm having a hard *life*."

"Probably not as hard as mine is right now," she said, and sprinted off.

Simon shook his head. Then he put on a burst of speed and went after her. He wasn't sure of their destination, but he got ahead of her easily, which made him feel simultaneously pleased and bad about himself, so he slowed down, intending to let her win, but she slowed, too, until they were walking side by side, hands on hips, neither talking until they'd both caught their breath.

"You're in good shape," she said.

Simon blushed, but he was inwardly pleased that she'd noticed. "So are you. Do you run here every day?"

"Pretty much," she said. There was a bench overlooking the lake, and she sat on it, stretching her slim legs out in front of her.

He sat down next to her. It was easier like this, when he

didn't have to look her in the face. But he wasn't sure how close he should sit, how close was allowed, so he positioned himself as near to the edge of the bench as he could without falling off. He looked down at his hands, scarred from the work and the fights, and hoped that she didn't notice. Jack's hands didn't look like that. Neither did his uncle Owen's. "So tell me," he said, "what's making your life hard right now?"

"You wouldn't believe me if I told you."

"Let me be the judge of that."

"Do you remember my stepbrother, Malcolm?"

"Malcolm?" Simon asked carefully. He felt suddenly nauseous. He pretended to think about it, but really he was trying to buy himself time. He linked his fingers together. His palms were moist. "Yeah. I guess so."

"Well, we found out yesterday that he's been working on a farm, and he got himself in some sort of trouble, and now he's in the hospital, and both my parents are acting like the world has ended. I don't understand it. They haven't seen him in years, and I always got the impression that neither of them was bothered by it. They never tried to find him or anything. My mom wouldn't even let him in our house when we were kids."

"Wow," Simon replied. He stared straight ahead, unable to look at her. "That's . . . god. I don't know what it is."

"It's shit," Ginny said. "That's what it is."

He wondered what she would say if he told her what he knew. Nothing good, he was sure of that. "I'm sorry," he told her.

"What for? It's not your fault."

Simon shifted a little in his seat. He felt suddenly too big, too unwieldy, dangerous—all the things his mother had warned him about. Her words rang in his head. *Don't stand too close. Don't touch unless invited. Don't assume. Don't use your size to intimidate. Even a girl the same height as you has thinner bones. Her strength doesn't match yours even if she insists that it does. Control your temper. Control yourself.*

But he hadn't, had he?

"Does Jack come running with you?" he asked, desperately wanting to change the subject.

"Jack? Mr. Sickly?" she laughed. "No. And I wouldn't like it if he did."

"I thought you were friends."

"We are," she replied. "Sort of."

"Oh," Simon said, confused. "You mean you don't know?"

"He's more like . . . an annoying brother, I suppose, rather than a friend. You know. Someone you put up with because you have to rather than someone you'd actually choose to be friends with."

"Harsh."

"He's not all bad. He does help me out with stuff sometimes." She jerked her legs out of the way as Flash came and sat in front of her, tongue lolling.

Simon clicked his fingers, calling the dog to his side. His mouth was a little dry. He unscrewed the lid from the bottle of milk, drank some of it, then wiped the top with his hand and offered it to Ginny.

"No, thanks," she said, so Simon finished it, then squashed the bottle flat and tossed it into the nearby trash can.

"I've never seen anyone drink a pint of milk like that before," she said.

"You haven't?"

"No," she said, and she smiled, and it made him feel all funny inside. Her skin was very smooth, her hair very shiny. He wanted to touch her. He reached for the soft fur on Flash's head instead and sank his fingers into it, feeling the heat and the bone and the life underneath. It helped. But not enough. Loneliness washed over him, strong enough to knock him over if he hadn't already been sitting down.

"I should probably be getting back," he said, even though that wasn't true. He had nothing to get back for. He didn't know why he'd been so keen to see her. Why she'd felt it was important to tell him about Malcolm, about Jack. He started to walk, letting go of Flash's collar, trusting the dog to walk ahead. He didn't run even though his legs still had plenty in them. The reason he didn't run was because Ginny had fallen into step alongside him, and her shoulder kept bumping against his arm. She was a tall girl, almost as tall as he was, and he liked that, he decided. She nudged him with her elbow, and he glanced across at her. He tried not to look at the swell of her breasts under her top. He tried not to notice—honest, he did—but Simon was a boy long deprived of young female company, and he couldn't help himself.

"Do you know how much longer you'll be here for?" she asked him.

"I think Mom wants to stay until the weekend at least."
Though, after that, he had no idea what would happen. He
had hoped they'd be able to stay and start over, but that was
before Jack had started being an ass.

"A few of us are getting together after school for a music
rehearsal. You should come."

"To a rehearsal? I can't play an instrument."

She laughed. "We only play for about half an hour. Mostly,
we just hang out and chat."

"Will Jack be there?" he asked, hating himself for it immediately. He found himself hyperaware of the outline of her
body, the small size of the space between them. He should
just say no, but somehow he couldn't bring himself to do it.

"Probably," she said. "He can give you a lift!"

"All right," he said.

"I guess I'll see you later, then," she said. And then she
broke into a run, and Simon grabbed Flash's collar just in
time to stop the dog from chasing after her. He watched
her until she was around the corner and out of sight, and he
waited a little longer after that before he made his own way
home.

He didn't really understand what had just happened.

But she'd asked him to hang out with her.

So he would.

CHAPTER TWENTY-FIVE

BEA

Six years ago

The Guardian

MIXED-SEX SCHOOLS REPORT DECLINE IN FIGHTS AND SEXUAL ASSAULTS

Schools that have been using the M test as part of their admissions process have reported a drastic decrease in the number of incidences of violent behavior, including fights and peer-on-peer sexual assaults. Women's rights campaigners have welcomed the news, saying that it is a positive step toward the eradication of male violence against women and girls. The minister for education, Jacob Nicolson, refused to comment on whether or not it was acceptable for schools to use the M test in this way but said that he was confident that a full range of educational pathways would remain available to M+ boys.

Despite Malcolm's best efforts, the clinic had suffered only minor smoke damage and was closed for less than a week, but for Bea, the impact was bigger than she could have imagined. There was an investigation, which led to Malcolm being taken to live in a residential home for M+ boys thirty miles away, someplace out in the country where he couldn't do any harm to anyone but himself. Antonia had rung her with daily updates, making sure Bea knew all the details whether she wanted to or not.

What had happened had frightened her sister; Bea could see that. It had frightened her, too. Mood swings were one thing. Arson was something else entirely. And Malcolm was so young. Bea couldn't help but wonder what would happen to him as he got older and bigger.

No one seemed to spare a thought for Zara. In the days afterward, Bea had watched her fade. She became a shell of herself. And then Paul had struck the final hammerblow. He stopped his child support payments. Zara became a frequent visitor at Bea's place, and, after her house was sold because she could no longer afford the mortgage, a permanent resident. It was only meant to be for a few days. Those days stretched out into weeks. Zara tried to get an apartment, but there were problems with her references, and it fell through. As soon as people found out that she was the mother of an M+ boy who had attempted to burn down his father's place of work, they didn't want to know. It was as if they saw Zara as tainted by her son's actions.

"How much longer is she going to be here?" Alfie asked

Bea one evening. At that point, Zara had been living with
them for close to six months. He had taken to hiding in
their bedroom rather than sitting in the living room, where
Zara sat on the sofa with her laptop, tapping away, sending
yet another email to her lawyer, who had stopped respond-
ing to them days ago when he'd realized that she couldn't
pay his fees.

"I don't know," Bea told him honestly.

"She can't stay forever. We don't have room. You've got
to do something about it, Bea."

The place was cramped; Bea couldn't disagree with that.
But she couldn't just kick Zara out. "She doesn't have anywhere to go."

"Which is sad but not our problem."

Bea sat down on the end of the bed, her legs wobbly. "I
can't believe you're saying this. You've always got a fiver for
the homeless guys in town, even when we're living on
grilled cheeses. So how come you've got nothing for a friend
who needs us?"

"What about Simon?" he said.

"This has nothing to do with Simon."

"She's a bad influence," he said. "We don't know what
she was telling that son of hers. What if she starts saying
similar things to Simon, and he ends up doing something
stupid to try and impress her?"

"Malcolm did not start that fire in order to impress his
mother."

"Didn't he?"

"No. He did it because his father is a dickhead."

Bea ended the conversation right there by refusing to par-
ticipate in it any further. She crept into Simon's room, intending to sleep there, but the hard press of her bones
against the floor was too much to deal with, so she got up
and went to sit in the living room with Zara, who was
watching television with the sound off. The flickering light
from the screen danced across her face. She had been an extremely beautiful woman once. Her face had that shape, the
cheekbones you only saw in magazines, the sharp Cupid's
bow. But mothering Malcolm had worn her out.

They didn't talk. Eventually, Zara reached out a hand and
Bea took it, and Zara squeezed and Bea squeezed back. The
next morning, Alfie threw some clothes into a duffel bag
and said that he was going to stay with his brother for a bit.

Bea couldn't find it in herself to care. She didn't beg him
to stay, didn't mope around the house after he'd gone. She
didn't even cry. In hindsight, it was obvious that whatever
she had felt for him had quietly died a long time ago. Simon
had found it more difficult, but he coped in his own way.
Alfie let him down gently, maintained contact with him.
He was good like that. Or perhaps he'd learned something
from the fallout from Paul's behavior toward Malcolm.

So when Alfie rang her a few weeks after they'd broken
up, Bea assumed it was because he wanted to arrange his
next visit with Simon. She was mistaken.

"I've got some news," he said.

"Oh?" Bea replied, expecting it to be a new girlfriend or
a new job.

"I've had the test. It was negative."

It wasn't entirely unexpected, if she was honest, though she didn't know what he wanted her to say. *Well done? Congratulations?* "Okay," she said, stretching the word out, hoping it would suffice, though inside she was furious.

It felt like a betrayal. Not only of her but of Simon. One thing she had always been able to say to her son was that Alfie hadn't been tested, either, that it was normal to not be tested, that he wasn't alone. Now that had gone.

And then it got worse.

"I've got a job up north," Alfie said. "I'm . . . I'm leaving, Bea. Will you tell Simon for me?"

Bea hung up.

She wandered around the house in a daze, looking for something to break, but she couldn't afford to replace anything if she did. She rage-ate ice cream straight out of the tub instead. Simon was going to be heartbroken. And it wasn't just that. The days when Alfie took him out or when he went to Alfie's apartment for dinner were days when she didn't have to feed him. Now she was going to have to find a way to stretch her meager budget even further.

She contemplated asking Zara to contribute a bit more but knew that was a waste of time. Then she considered asking Antonia. Her sister would give her the money, but it would give Antonia a certain power over her that Bea didn't want her to have.

There was only one other person she could turn to.

No. Never in a million years. She'd made herself a promise a long time ago, and she wasn't going to break it. But when she found herself looking at an electricity bill that made her heart pound and her palms sweat, there was no other choice.

After she dropped Simon off at school, she drove to the clinic and parked up in one of the spots reserved for patients. Owen pulled up twenty minutes later, parking in a space that said RESERVED FOR STAFF. He reversed in and out a couple of times until the car was perfectly straight and then got out. Bea got out of her own badly parked car, feeling strangely proud of the fact that two of the wheels were on the line.

"Bea?" he said as she approached. She made herself walk quickly, with long, determined strides. "What are you doing here?"

"We need to talk," she said.

"I'm a little busy."

"Owen," she said. That word was a warning, and she knew that he heard it. He was a smart man.

"It had better not take long," he replied. "I've got things to do."

"It won't," she said, reassuring him. He opened the door and ushered her into the clinic.

The smell of air freshener lingered, so the cleaner must have already come and gone. Owen's office was at the rear, and Bea followed him to it. Once inside, she sat down in the chair in front of the desk. She crossed her legs and tucked her hands between them.

Owen took his time, straightening his tie, assuming what she thought of as his pompous-ass position. "Would you like to tell me what this is about?"

"I need money," Bea said. She'd been determined that she would look at him when she said it. It proved to be more difficult than she had imagined. Her face felt hot, and she knew that she was blushing. She'd promised herself when she found out she was pregnant that she would never ask Owen for help. It was the only way she could think of to make amends for what she'd done. She'd always known that sleeping with her sister's husband was wrong, but for the few weeks that the affair had lasted, she had been pulled in by the excitement of having him pay attention to her.

She had also, she knew now, been young and naive and a distraction from his inability to get his wife pregnant. She'd been convenient.

Owen made a strange noise, somewhere between a laugh and a cough. "I see. And what does that have to do with me?"

For years, Bea had imagined what would happen when they finally had this conversation. She'd known it would be uncomfortable. But she'd also thought that Owen would face it head-on.

"You mean you don't know?" she asked with a fluttering in her stomach. Had she got this wrong somehow? Had Owen really not realized that Simon was his son? Did men really do that? Did they see women they were screwing have babies and not ask themselves, even once, if it could be theirs?

Maybe they do, she thought. Maybe for them it was that easy. She could feel her temper rising. She forced it back. If she blew up, she would immediately be the one in the wrong, no matter what else happened. And that was what Owen wanted, she realized suddenly. He was an intelligent man, and he definitely knew how babies were made. Of course he'd known that Simon could be his.

It was still incredibly difficult to say what she did next.

"I am not playing this game with you. Simon is your son, both of us know it, and it's time you took some responsibility for him."

"I don't know it," Owen replied. He looked her straight in the eye as he said it, but there was an angry flush on his neck, and his Adam's apple moved visibly in his throat.

"I can get proof. You're a doctor. You should know that."

"And I can request the M test is done on any DNA sample taken."

Bea felt her stomach drop. "You can't."

"Yes, I can. And I will if you push me on this. I'll give you what you want this time, Bea, but I won't let you blackmail me."

She pressed her palms against her jeans, gripping her thighs as if she could hold herself in her chair. The room was large and lovely, a big picture window at the back, tasteful prints of clear blue skies and summer trees on the walls, the silver laptop on the desk. It was nicer than her house, far nicer than anything Simon was growing up with or could ever hope to have. Alfie had allowed her to hide from all of this for so long. He had been a shield between her and the reality of her situation, which was that all of it was so desperately unfair that it made her want to cry.

She told Owen how much she wanted and got up and walked out. It was only once she was outside, mentally spending the money as she stared at the personalized license plate on the rear of Owen's BMW, that she began to see how little it was.

But it was too late now.

He'd made it clear that if she wanted to push for more, he would demand proof of paternity, and if she tried to get it, he'd have Simon tested for the M gene. Her fear that Simon would test positive was very present and very real. She thought of Zara and of Malcolm, removed from her care and sent to live with strangers. She had seen Zara's struggle to come to terms with it firsthand. She couldn't face the thought of that happening to her.

She started the car and left the clinic, needing to get to work. The money wouldn't help her if she got fired. Her phone rang as she was driving. She ignored it. It rang again, and this time she pulled into a side street and checked her phone. It was Antonia.

Bea took a breath, pasted on a smile, and answered it. She wanted to prove to herself that she could still act like everything was normal, even after what she'd just said to Owen.

"What's up, Antonia?"

"Owen told me you asked him for money."

"He told you?" Bea asked, sinking into her seat, the smile vanishing. She pressed her fingertips against her forehead. The whole point of going to Owen was so that she wouldn't have to have this conversation with Antonia. It was supposed to be a secret.

"Of course he told me!" Antonia replied. "Honestly, Bea,

I don't understand you sometimes. You know you can come to me if you're in trouble. I'll take care of you. I always have, remember? Who fixed things when you kept getting into trouble with that geography teacher at school? Who sorted out that noisy neighbor last year?"

Bea leaned forward so that her head was resting on the steering wheel, feeling her last ounce of dignity dissolve. If Malcolm hadn't already had a go at burning down the clinic, she'd have been tempted to do it herself.

Only she would make sure that Owen was in it when it went up.

CHAPTER TWENTY-SIX

⦚ ANTONIA

Now

Antonia had found it hard to be upset about the news of Malcolm being in the hospital, although she'd feigned concern as Paul had sat in his office with Lily, his phone pressed against his ear, his whole body tense. She'd taken them coffee and biscuits and quietly closed the door. The clients in the waiting room had known something was going on. She had seen it in the way they'd all suddenly perked up, like meerkats sensing danger on the horizon.

"Do you want me to cancel their appointments?" she'd asked Owen quietly as he hovered just outside Paul's office. Normally, they handled their own scheduling with support from Lily, though that obviously wasn't available right now.

Owen had blown out a steady breath. "How many has he got?"

"Four."

The door had opened behind them, and Paul had come

out. His face was a mask. Lily had followed him. Her eyes had been a little glossy, but other than that, there had been no sign that she'd just received bad news about her stepson.

"I'm so sorry," Owen had said. "If there's anything we can do . . ."

Paul had slowly shaken his head. "I haven't seen him in years," he'd said. "It's just come as something of a shock, that's all, and having to call Zara . . . that never makes for a good day."

"Do you want me to handle your appointments?" Owen had asked him.

"No. I'll take care of it."

And that had basically been the end of it. The two men had gone back into their respective offices, Antonia had gone into hers, and everything had carried on as normal. She'd sailed through her remaining appointments without any trouble.

She'd been somewhat surprised to see Paul turn up for work the next morning, but people handled bad news in their own way. And it was a long time since he'd seen Malcolm, which probably made the news, horrible though it was, easier to handle.

But the truth was that Antonia didn't really care. Since learning that Simon had been tested, she'd felt as if she were drifting on a cloud of silk. All her problems seemed to have melted away. It was only two days until he would get his result, and then things would change for the better for everyone. She was sure of it.

It was still hard to believe that Simon had actually gone through with it, but she'd rung someone she knew who worked at the hospital and got her to confirm it in exchange for a promise of an interview at the clinic. In fact, she really must get around to arranging that. She made a quick note of it on her calendar.

Then, at five, with the last patient seen, she turned everything off and went to find Owen. She wanted him to herself for an hour. "Should we stop for a drink on the way home?" she asked him.

"Actually, I'm going for a quick one with Paul. I think he needs it."

"Oh. Of course!" She did her best to hide her disappointment. "Do you want me to come with you?"

"Probably not," he said. "You should be getting home anyway. We don't really want Jack spending too much time alone with Simon."

"You're right," she said. She smiled, let him kiss her on the cheek—though not on the mouth, because she was wearing a bright berry lipstick today—then went out to her car. Lily had already left, so there was no conversation to be had there, no way to find out any more information or to delay her trip home.

When she got there, she found Bea had gone out, and the two boys were alone in the house. That irritated her immensely, although she did her best to hide it. It wasn't that she was afraid of Simon, necessarily, although she was more than aware of what he was potentially capable of. But she wanted to make sure that he and Bea didn't disappear again before Simon got his result. She'd helped Bea run away from Simon's mistakes before.

She had no intention of doing that again.

She sent Jack upstairs to do his homework, which left her alone downstairs with Simon. It was easy to busy herself in the kitchen and keep Flash close at hand, just in case.

"Where's your mom?" she asked him.

"Dunno," he said. "Do you want any help with anything?"

The offer was unexpected, but Antonia thought it best not to turn it down. She gave him a pile of potatoes to peel, and he set to it without complaint. She supposed that was one thing Bea had gotten right. Jack wouldn't know one end of a peeler from the other. Not that it mattered, really. With the future that lay ahead of him, she had no doubt that her son would have his pick of potential wives, and he was sensible enough to find one who could run the household and leave him free to work.

The same couldn't be said for Simon. Antonia was certain she knew what his future held. She might not have seen her nephew for the past five years, but people didn't change. Simon had been a headstrong, loud, aggressive child. It went without saying that he'd have carried those traits forward to now. And there was plenty of evidence: out of education, working on a farm, a face that looked like he'd gone ten rounds with a heavyweight boxer.

Her phone buzzed, and she wiped her hands and checked it. It was a message from Owen.

Apparently Malcolm was on a farm. That's where he was injured. Can you believe it? Paul spoke to doctors at hospital again just now. Injuries are serious. They're

not sure he's going to survive. Can you rebook Paul's
appointments for tomorrow?

Her pulse sped up a little. Of course, she messaged back.

She risked a glance at Simon. He'd been on a farm, too.
Perhaps they should all be grateful that he wasn't in a worse
state. As much as she wanted to see Simon face up to the
consequences of his actions, she wouldn't wish that on him.

She left him alone in the kitchen and went through into
their home office at the front of the house and started making apologetic phone calls, always her least favorite thing to
do. She was on her third one when she saw Bea walking
along the drive. Her sister's shoulders were hunched, and
her face had the pale, exhausted look of someone carrying a
heavy burden. It couldn't be easy, knowing that your son
was only days away from a most likely positive test result.
She almost felt sorry for her. Almost.

But Bea had done this to herself.

CHAPTER TWENTY-SEVEN

JACK

Now

It didn't escape Jack's notice that Simon had gone out again that morning. He'd heard him go downstairs, had tweaked his curtains to see him heading out with Flash. He'd hastily pulled on shorts and a T-shirt and followed him at a distance. Simon hadn't even noticed.

He'd seen him meet Ginny at the park, seen the two of them sit and chat. The sight of them being so friendly had made him want to throw up. What the hell did Simon think he was doing, getting that close to a girl like Ginny? What gave him the right?

At that point, he'd turned and run home, tears stinging his eyes. His dad had caught him coming in the door.

"Where've you been?"

"Went out for a run," Jack had said, pushing past him. "Need a shower."

He'd kept his head down, hoping his dad wouldn't notice

that he was crying. He could hardly believe it himself. He'd stood in the shower for ages, pain in his chest and his throat as he tried to make sense of it all. Simon and Ginny.

No. He wouldn't let it happen.

He got ready for school but didn't bother with breakfast, his appetite lost to the swell of acid in his stomach, and left half an hour earlier than he usually did. He was the first one in the parking lot. He sat in the car, watched the crows pick at the rugby pitch, and tried to understand what had happened. It wasn't supposed to be this way. It was supposed to be him and Simon back together, friends again, Simon needing help and Jack providing it, just like he always had.

But he hadn't taken this new version of Simon into account. How could he? He hadn't known it existed. In his head, Simon was still twelve, a little older than him, but no match for him in any other way. Jack had better clothes, went to a better school, had better parents. He'd always known that Simon was jealous of him. He'd never expected the boot to be on the other foot, and he didn't like it.

Slowly, the parking lot started to fill up, and he made himself go into the school building, even though he wanted to be anywhere else. Ginny was waiting for him in the common room. And she was smiling. Normally, that would have cheered him up, but not today. He wanted to tell her to wipe that stupid grin off her face.

And then things got worse.

"I saw Simon again this morning," she said cheerily. "He was at the park with your dog. I invited him to rehearsal."

Jack felt like he'd been punched. "What for?"

"Because he's your cousin, and it's polite! I'm surprised you didn't invite him."

"Wasn't sure he'd still be here," Jack said, rummaging in his bag for his swipe card for the vending machine. He felt a little light-headed. Probably the lack of breakfast. He couldn't bring himself to look at her. "Anyway, it'll be weird for him. He won't know anyone."

"He knows us," she said. A group of her friends waved from the corner, and she went to sit with them. Jack opted out. He wasn't in the mood for a group of noisy girls and their stupid conversations about makeup videos and influencers. He wanted to talk to Ginny on her own. No chance of that, though. He sat in a different corner, got his textbook out, and pretended to study, but really he was listening to their conversation, which was all about some shopping trip they had planned for the weekend and who was going and what they were wearing and some other stuff that he didn't care about. When the bell rang, he went off to his class, and Ginny went to hers. He didn't get another opportunity to talk to her.

Why are you avoiding me? he texted her, hiding the phone under the desk so the teacher wouldn't see it.

I'm not, she replied an hour later. See you after school.

She didn't mention Simon again and neither did he. He couldn't imagine that his cousin would really want to go anyway. A group rehearsal wouldn't be much fun for him. What did Ginny think he was going to do, sit and watch

them all and then applaud? She had some dumb ideas sometimes.

When he got home, Bea and Simon were in the home theater watching TV. They both looked up as Jack hovered in
the doorway. Usually he would hang out in here for a bit
before he did his homework, but now he found that he
didn't want to.

"How was school?" Bea asked, not sounding in the slightest bit interested.

"Fine," Jack said. "Usual."

He went upstairs and shut himself in his bedroom. This
was *his* house. So why did he feel like he was the one who
had to hide? He stripped off his uniform, showered, got
dressed in jeans and a T-shirt. It didn't come as much of a
surprise when, a few minutes later, Simon sauntered in. He
didn't even bother to knock. "Hey," he said.

"What's up?" Jack asked him. "I've got homework to do."

"I ran into Ginny Sloan at the park this morning. Can you
believe it? Anyway, she told me about some rehearsal thing
you're doing this evening and said I should come along."

"Do you really want to? It'll be pretty boring."

Simon shrugged. "Might as well," he said casually. "Haven't
got anything better to do. Not until tomorrow, anyway."

When he'd get his result.

Jack didn't want Simon to go. He was sure of that. But he
suddenly found that he was afraid to tell him that he couldn't.
He was afraid of this version of Simon, with his bruises and

his hard hands and the way Ginny had looked at him. He remembered a word he'd read in a book once. What was it again? Yes. That was it. *Cocksure.* Simon was cocksure in every sense of the word, in every way that Jack was not.

It was too late now, but Jack knew he'd never have agreed that Simon could come here if he hadn't been thinking of him as twelve instead of eighteen. He wished that he'd never responded to Simon's messages, any of them.

He wanted, more than anything, to tell someone the truth. But he couldn't.

Because that would mean admitting to his own part in it.

He got to his feet. "Do you want anything from the kitchen?"

"No," Simon said, flopping back on the bed and slinging one arm across his face to cover his eyes. His T-shirt rose up, showing his ropy midsection. There was no fat on him at all.

"Suit yourself," Jack said. He went downstairs, keeping his footsteps light, as if he were a burglar in his own home. He went into the kitchen, got himself a drink, then went into the dining room. It was empty, the air silent and still. He opened the liquor cabinet, lifted out a bottle of vodka from the back, then slipped it into his bag, which he'd left by the front door.

When he got back upstairs, Simon had fallen asleep on his bed, so Jack took his laptop downstairs and spent a couple of hours in the office doing his homework. It was only when it was time to go that he realized that he'd left his violin upstairs in his bedroom.

He crept up there, inwardly cursing himself for his stupidity. His only hope was that he'd be able to sneak in and out without waking Simon, but his cousin opened his eyes as soon as he opened the door.

Simon sat up and stretched. "Is it time to go?"

Jack wanted to say no. How he wanted to say no. But he couldn't bring himself to do it. He couldn't stop looking at Simon's hands and imagining them plowing into someone's face hard enough to put them in the hospital. Someone who could do that wasn't the sort of person you said no to.

They got into Jack's car. Jack started the engine, then couldn't resist reaching for his bag and showing Simon the bottle of vodka. Simon might be tougher, but for a moment it made Jack feel like he still had the edge.

"I thought this was a music thing," Simon said, laughing.

"It is, but we like to have fun, too. You must have done this on the farms," Jack said. The gate opened and he drove out onto the road.

"Not really," Simon replied.

Jack was surprised. "I thought M-positive boys liked to party. There are always stories on the news about the drug and alcohol raids on the farms, that they're more likely to be addicts as well as violent."

He didn't know why he was saying these things. But he couldn't seem to stop himself. Simon's life on the farm—indeed, Simon himself—had always been something he had tiptoed around the edge of. The possibility of Simon's M status being positive had been exciting, a bit like having a distant relative who was a gangster or a bank robber. Close enough to give you some claim to notoriety, far enough away that you weren't tainted by it.

It wasn't exciting now.

"It seems to give you an increased chance of nearly everything," Simon said grimly. "Any bad thing they can say about men at all, it's because of the M gene. But I guess that suits those of you who know you don't have it. You can do whatever you want, and everyone just makes excuses for you."

"I don't do drugs!" Jack said indignantly.

"But you drink, right? Even though you're underage."

"That's different. Everyone does it."

"I don't."

Maybe not, Jack thought to himself. *But you are violent, aren't you?*

Inside the house, a dozen kids were sprawled on sofas and the floor. There were big bowls of chips and pretzels on the coffee table, and glasses and bottles of various soft drinks. The TV was on, and a couple of the boys were playing a video game as the others yelled encouragement or booed.

The two of them walked in, Jack taking the lead. "Everyone, this is my cousin Simon," he said, at the same time looking for Ginny. He spotted her almost immediately, standing by the mantelpiece, munching on a handful of chips. She smiled when she saw him, and that made him feel a little better. Maybe he was being paranoid. She'd probably only invited Simon to be polite. It was the sort of thing she'd do.

"Hello, Simon," everyone chorused at once.

Simon raised a hand and gave them all a wave.

They got out their instruments and practiced for an hour. It was what they had come for, after all. They were starting to sound pretty good. They sounded even better after the stolen bottles of alcohol started to appear.

"I told you, I don't drink," Simon told Jack.

"Don't be such a spoilsport," Jack said. "Anyway, one won't do any harm, will it?"

Jack filled his cup, and he filled Simon's.

And prepared to ruin Simon's evening.

CHAPTER TWENTY-EIGHT

||| BEA

Five years ago

Your car insurance renewal quote for this year is £872.78*

*You may be able to get a cheaper quote if you have a negative M test. Proof will be required.

In the summer after Jack's twelfth birthday, Owen was asked to go to a weeklong conference in France to talk about his work with M+ boys. The first Bea heard of it was when she got a phone call from Antonia announcing that she'd booked a cottage in Cornwall for the week and wanted Bea and Simon to go with her. Ever since Owen had told Antonia that Bea had asked him for money, she had gone out of her way to give Bea stuff, whether she wanted it or not.

Bea didn't want to accept any of it. But she wasn't in a position to say no. Life as a single mother was just too damn hard, and the gifts from her sister were sometimes the only things that made it manageable. But she felt such complete and utter self-loathing about what she'd done. It was like trying to carry a sack full of rocks all the time. She hadn't felt this heavy, this cumbersome, this sick of herself since she'd been pregnant.

"Owen's going away for work," Antonia said happily. "I thought the four of us could do something nice together. It's all booked, so you don't need to worry about anything. My treat."

Before Bea could reply, Simon came bounding down the stairs with his phone in his hand. "Jack says we're going on vacation with them!" he said, giddy with excitement. "Is it true, Mom? Is it true?"

She could hardly say no after that. Simon had never had a proper vacation before. She bought shorts and sun cream and comics for the journey, packed their clothes into a garbage bag, and wedged it into the back of Antonia's car at six in the morning. It was a long way, and Antonia wanted to get an early start.

Jack's school had broken up earlier than Simon's, and Antonia had persuaded Bea to take Simon out of school a couple of days early so that they would miss the worst of the traffic. Bea phoned reception from the car, making an excuse about a stomach bug, her toes curling inside her tennis shoes as she did so, but the receptionist didn't kick up any fuss. Bea still didn't relax until they were on the motorway, far from anyone who might spot Simon and ask why he wasn't at school.

The first hour went quickly, but the rest of the journey seemed to stretch on forever, and by the time they got there, all of them were stiff, hungry, bad-tempered, and desperate for the restroom. Still, the view from their little white cottage with its bright yellow door and shutters went a long way toward fixing that. They ate fish and chips from a place around the corner, then packed the boys off to bed.

The two of them were sharing a room, which meant bunk beds and a heated discussion about who got to go on top. Antonia rushed upstairs as soon as the sound of two angry boys filtered down. Bea reluctantly followed her up. She was of the opinion that Jack and Simon were old enough to sort out their own disputes. What she really wanted to do was to sit outside with a glass of wine and listen to the waves breaking on the beach.

"Let Jack have the top bunk," Antonia said. "He's younger than you. It's only fair."

Younger, smaller, premature, blah blah blah, Bea thought to herself. She gave Simon a look, and he dropped his gaze to the floor, but she could see the anger in his scrawny body. She took him downstairs as Antonia continued to fuss over Jack, and she gave him a glass of milk and one of the big cookies that she'd brought.

"There are some battles you can't win," she told him. "Especially not against your cousin."

"Why not?"

"That's just the way things are," she told him.

"Is it because he's M-negative? Does the test make him better than me?"

"No," she said. "He's not better than you. But Aunt Antonia paid for this vacation, and we're only here because she invited us, so we've got to go along with what she wants even if it seems unfair."

"He always gets his own way."

Bea rubbed his back. She could feel how tense he was, and it worried her. He'd never spent a whole week with his cousin before, just a few hours here and there, and she always made sure to remove him as soon as his temper started getting the better of him. And there was no denying that Simon had a temper. It exploded more often than she cared to admit, and no one pushed his buttons quite like Jack.

"I know he does. Believe me, I know. Unfortunately, there's nothing we can do about it. Just . . . grit your teeth and get on with it, and we'll have a nice time, I promise you."

Simon scowled. She hugged him. "Eat your cookie. Tomorrow we'll get up early and go down to the beach, just you and me. How does that sound?"

He had never seen the sea before, and he'd talked about nothing else for weeks. He seemed to think that he was going to run straight in and start surfing like a professional. She didn't have the heart to disillusion him. He didn't have many pleasures in life, her son. His world was very small because she couldn't afford to show him anything bigger, not like his cousin, for whom the world had seemingly no edges at all. He needed this.

He was almost thirteen now, and although the great growth spurt of puberty hadn't begun, she could see his body starting to change. Manhood was coming, and there was nothing she could do to stop it.

"Let Jack have the top bunk tonight," she said. "He'll soon change his mind when he has to get down to go to the bathroom in the night and he stubs his toe on the ladder. Mark my words, one night in there, and he'll be begging to sleep on the bottom."

"Fine," Simon huffed. He'd recently had braces put on his teeth, silver against white, another sign that he was no longer a little boy.

He was growing up.

Bea had no idea yet how much.

Jack didn't give Simon the top bunk in the end, but there were more interesting things happening by then anyway. It turned out that the cottage next door had been leased to a family with three girls. The eldest, Becca, was a year older than Simon. They were all shy at first, awkward, but by the end of the day, all of them were mixing together because Becca had her own surfboard and was willing to let them try it.

More than that, Simon got his first taste of the sea, quite literally, when a wave swept him off his feet. Bea had a moment of panic before his head appeared, his hair plastered to his face. He fell on the sand at her feet, laughing. "Did you see?" he said. "Mom, did you see?"

"I did," she told him.

"It's brilliant," he said, and ran straight back in.

At one end of the beach were a series of rock pools

stacked up against the harbor wall. When the tide was out, they were covered in children scrambling over them like ants in brightly colored shorts and T-shirts, and soon Jack and Simon and Becca were among them.

Bea and Antonia sat in front of a striped windbreak. Antonia played with her iPad as Bea pretended to read a Jackie Collins novel she'd picked up in a consignment store.

"They seem to be having fun," Antonia said. "It's nice for the two of them to have some time together. I know we haven't always seen eye to eye, Bea, and I know we're very different people, but I want you to know that you're important to me, and Simon is, too. Our boys . . . they need each other."

Bea shaded her face with her hand and searched for them. There they were in the middle of digging a hole that was already waist-deep. At least, Simon was digging. Jack appeared to be doing little more than watching. Becca stood next to him, chattering away.

"Sometimes I worry that we're pushing Jack too much," Antonia continued. "He works so hard."

No, he doesn't, Bea wanted to tell her. *You do everything for him. He only has to ask for something, and you buy it for him. You don't even make him tidy his room.*

But she said nothing. Over the past year, she'd come to understand just how dependent she was on her sister's generosity and how fragile their relationship truly was. Every day had become about keeping her head down, surviving to the next paycheck, and keeping things going just a little longer. Plus she was hardly in a position to comment on anyone else's mothering skills. Just look at her son, with the ratty haircut she'd given him the day before, and his second-hand swim trunks.

Nor could she rate herself as a sister.

It was killing her slowly, breath by breath: not just the things that she was unable to give Simon but the things that she was unable to give herself. She was so tired. And it seemed that every month there was something in the news about the M test, some new way in which the world had been made worse for boys who had tested positive, which made it even more difficult for her to do the one thing that could potentially fix so much. She turned another page of her book and stared at it, though none of the words registered in her brain.

"They seem to be getting along well," Antonia said as the boys came charging across the sand toward them, Becca following a little distance behind.

"They do," Bea agreed. She fumbled in her bag for her purse, predicting that they were coming to ask for money for ice cream. She'd put a little aside to pay for treats. It only seemed fair, given that Antonia had paid for everything else.

The three of them went scampering off to the ice cream truck with the tenner clutched firmly in Simon's hand, and Bea went back to her book. The rest of the day passed without drama. Unfortunately, the same couldn't be said for the evening. Bea cooked, one of the downsides of being in the cottage and with her sister, who was used to a fully equipped kitchen and didn't seem to know what to do with a blunt knife and a couple of crap saucepans, all of which were standard for Bea. The boys, exhausted from their day at the beach, went up to bed without complaint.

Antonia had just settled down on the sofa with her usual glass of wine (she'd even brought her own glasses) when she suddenly jumped up, rummaged in her bag, then rushed upstairs. Bea assumed a tampon emergency, especially after she heard the bathroom door close. She sank back into her seat. She'd put a lot of garlic in the food, at Simon's request, and she could still taste it. Antonia probably had some gum in her bag. The beautiful tan leather tote sat at the side of the sofa.

Bea took a peek inside. There were all the usual things: a fortune's worth of makeup, Chanel sunglasses, perfume, tampons, enough painkillers to knock out a horse, and a couple of boxes of what looked like prescription medications. She completely forgot about the gum as she stared at them. She felt a little light-headed.

She scurried back to the sofa as she heard Antonia hit the top step, tucking her feet up out of the way as if she could distance herself from the contents of that bag, from all of this. One thought solidified in her mind. Those medications. She'd heard of them before. And one thing was clear that hadn't been until now, although perhaps it should have. Her sister wasn't well.

As soon as that settled into place, other things began to shift, too, so that she saw them from a new angle. Pieces of Antonia's life began to make sense. It was a frightening thing to acknowledge, which was perhaps why she had put it off for so long. Once you knew about something awful, once it became certain, you were then left facing a very difficult decision: whether or not you were willing to do something about it.

CHAPTER TWENTY-NINE

ANTONIA

Now

It was the phone call that every mother of a teenager dreads receiving. The one that comes late at night, the panic in the familiar voice unmistakable, the terror it prompts rising inside like sickness. "Mom, something's happened."

"Where are you?" Antonia asked Jack.

"At the hospital," he said.

"Are you all right?" She was already out of her seat, looking for her bag, her keys, her shoes.

"Yes. I'm fine. It's Ginny. Can you come? Please?"

"Is Simon with you?"

"No, he's not here."

Antonia pressed a hand against her chest. The thought of Jack alone in that place was almost overwhelming. She could feel the powerful thump of her heart against her palm. "I'm on my way," she said, gesturing fiercely at Owen, who had also leaped to his feet and was watching her keenly. He moved in closer as she took the phone away from her ear. "That was Jack. Ginny's in the hospital," she said.

"What happened? Has she had an accident?"

"I don't know. Can you call Paul and make sure he knows? I've got to go."

He took her hand. "You've been drinking."

"Not that much." She shook him off. "I'm fine." And nothing, absolutely nothing, was going to stop her from going to Jack when he needed her.

It didn't even occur to her to ask Owen if he wanted to go with her or to wait for him. When Jack wanted her, it was like no one else in the world existed. She ran out of the house, got into her car, and headed to the hospital. She parked in the drop-off space by the door and sprinted inside.

"My son is here—Jack Talbot," she said breathlessly to the woman at reception. "With Ginny Sloan."

The woman tapped at her keyboard, peering at the screen through pink plastic glasses. Her bosom was so big it practically rested on the desk in front of her, and there was a half-full cup of coffee to one side, which she paused to take a sip from.

It was taking too long. Why was it taking so long?

Antonia gave up and went into the waiting room to look for Jack. It took her a moment to spot him because it was busy. There he was. She ran straight up to him. "Jack!" she said, flinging her arms around him and hugging him tightly. "What's going on? Is everything all right?"

"I'm not sure," he said. He gestured to a pair of double doors. "They took her through there. Lily got here about ten minutes ago, but she wouldn't let me see her."

"What was it? An accident?"

He hung his head. "Someone brought a bottle of vodka," he said. "She must have had too much. I don't really know, to be honest. She seemed fine, and then . . ."

Antonia took a deep breath, let it out again slowly. To learn that it was nothing more than typical teenage behavior was a huge relief. "You did the right thing bringing her here. Were you drinking?"

His face went bright red. "I only had one, I swear."

Silly boy. She rubbed his arm. "Well, these things happen," she said. "Ginny isn't the first girl to overdo it, and she won't be the last. Hopefully, this will give her enough of a scare that she won't do it again. And neither will you." She looked him straight in the eye. "Will you, Jack?" she said again, a little louder.

"No," he mumbled.

"Good."

"Can we wait until we know she's okay?" he asked.

"Of course we can," Antonia said, and she led him to a couple of empty seats in between a pasty-looking couple in hoodies and a middle-aged man who was fast asleep with his mouth wide-open and his arms folded over his ample gut.

She inspected the seat before she sat down and tried to put as little of herself as she could in contact with it, crossing her legs and holding her bag tightly. At least she'd gotten changed earlier and wasn't still in her work clothes.

Jack couldn't sit still. He kept shifting positions in his seat, his feet dancing all over the place, and Antonia had to put a hand on his shoulder to calm him. "It's going to be fine," she said quietly. "She's in the best place. They'll take care of her."

"I hope so," Jack replied, tugging at his hair. "Lily was really mad, though."

"But it's no less than Ginny deserves for being so foolish."

Someone came through the double doors, and both of them looked up, Jack already halfway out of his seat, but the woman walked off in a different direction, and he sank back, clearly disappointed. "I wish they'd just let me see her."

"I'll find out what's going on," Antonia said, patting his hand.

"They won't tell you anything unless you're family. I tried."

"Your father is a doctor, Jack. He used to work at this hospital. Trust me, I'll be able to find out."

She got to her feet and walked briskly over to reception, but before she could get there, Lily came out of the double doors. She was wearing leggings and tennis shoes with a sweatshirt that said HOPEFUL FUTURES on the front in big white letters. She looked awful.

"Lily!" Antonia called. Lily's eyes were red, and most of her mascara was on her cheeks. Antonia searched in her bag for tissues and offered them.

"Thanks," Lily said. She dabbed at her face. "God, this is the last thing I needed today."

"How is she?"

"Throwing her guts up," she said grimly. "But she'll be all right. I don't think she'll be drinking again in a hurry, though."

"Who brought the alcohol?" Antonia asked. "This was supposed to be a rehearsal, not a party."

"She won't tell me," Lily replied. Her phone rang then, and she pulled it out of her pocket and checked the screen. "It's Paul. I'll talk to you later."

Knowing that Lily was here and that Ginny was otherwise okay, Antonia saw no reason to stay any longer. She beckoned Jack over. He'd remained in his seat while she talked to Lily. *Probably worried that he might get told off,* Antonia thought. She had no plans to punish him herself. He'd done the responsible thing. He'd brought Ginny here and stayed to make sure she was all right. Where were the rest of her friends, after all? Nowhere in sight.

"Let's go home," she said to him.

He kept close as they walked out together, avoiding a woman in a pink robe who was talking loud and fast into her phone and a tattooed young man with his hand wrapped in a blood-soaked towel.

"Where's your car?" she asked him.

"In the staff parking lot," he said miserably. "I've still got my pass from when I did work experience."

"We'll take mine, then, and collect yours tomorrow."

She wanted to talk to him, and she knew from experience that he often said things in the car when they weren't face-to-face that he wouldn't say otherwise. It was one of the reasons why she still liked to take him to school sometimes.

Now that things were starting to calm down and she knew that he was safe, she had questions and she wanted answers. When they got to her car, a couple of paramedics in dark green uniforms stood next to it, arms folded. "You can't park here," one of them said.

"It was an emergency." Antonia waved them off and got in, driving off while Jack was still struggling with his seat belt. She could sense all of a sudden how tired he was. He needed to be taken home and tucked into bed. He might be almost eighteen, but in many ways her son was still a baby. He turned his head away from her and looked out the window.

"What is it, Jack?"

"Simon," he said.

Antonia felt every muscle in her body tighten. "What about him?"

"I think . . . he took Ginny upstairs when she was really drunk, and by the time I realized, it was too late."

"Too late for what?"

His shoulders started to heave. "What do you think?"

"Oh my god," Antonia muttered. This was far worse than she had thought.

"And the worst thing is," Jack said, "he's going to get away with it."

She reached out and touched his hand. "I promise you,

Jack, if he did something to Ginny, he is not going to get away with it."

"He will," Jack said, "because when he gets his test result tomorrow, it's going to be negative."

"You don't know that."

"I do." He sniffed. "Because I took it for him."

CHAPTER THIRTY

║║ BEA

Now

Simon hadn't come back and he wasn't answering his phone. Bea didn't know where he was. Her son had caused her a lot of sleepless nights over the years, and it looked like those days weren't over yet. She could hardly believe it. He was supposed to be getting his test result tomorrow. He should be here, with her, watching the hours slowly slip by, and instead he was god knew where doing god knew what.

Something was up, that much was obvious. She had heard Antonia rush out of the house, had heard her car start up. She'd been caught by surprise when she'd slipped downstairs and found Owen in the living room, a glass in his hand, staring out the window into the night. She could smell the dark peaty aroma of single malt whiskey. The heavy brocade curtains were still open, the drive floodlit.

"What's going on?" she asked him from the doorway.

He turned quickly, as if he hadn't realized she was there.

"A friend of Jack's had a bit too much to drink and ended up in the ER," he said. "He's with her. Antonia's gone to make sure he's all right."

"Is Simon with them?"

"No, I don't think so," Owen replied. He took a sip from his glass. Bea wished he'd offer her one. "Why?"

"He went out with Jack earlier and he hasn't come home."

"I'm sure everything's fine."

Bea came farther into the room. She stood in the middle of the rug, her toes digging into the thick pile, not too close but not too far away, either. "Are you?" she asked him.

"He's a teenage boy, Bea. This is what they do."

"This is not what *my* son does."

Owen drained his glass and set it down on the mantelpiece with a sharp tap. There was a mirror hung over it, huge, spotlessly clean, and he watched her in it. "No," he said. "Your son gets in fights instead. Look, Bea. I deal with a lot of mothers and a lot of teenage boys. Take it from me. Making their mothers' lives a misery is what all of them do. It's how they prepare you to cut the apron strings and let them leave home."

"Is that what you'd tell Antonia if Jack disappeared?"

"Jack isn't Simon."

There was a white baby grand in the corner with a neat arrangement of photos on the top. Antonia and Owen's wedding. Jack as a baby. Jack as a toddler. Bea picked one up, the silver frame heavy in her hand, and prepared to throw it at him, but he was too fast for her. He had his fingers locked around her wrist and the photo in his hand in a split second. She struggled against his grip.

"Don't," he said quietly, dangerously. "You're a guest in my home, Bea, and there's only so much that I am prepared to put up with."

"My. Son. Is. Missing."

As she said those words, the truth of them hit her, and she could feel panic rising. Bea wasn't prone to that emotion, and she didn't quite know what to do with it. Her legs were suddenly unsteady, and Owen caught her by the elbows and steered her down onto the sofa.

"Breathe," he told her. "Just breathe, Bea. Have you tried his phone?"

"Of course I've tried his phone!"

He took his own from his pocket. "What's the number?"

She reeled it off for him, and he called it. As expected, he got no reply.

"I told you," she said. "He's not answering."

Owen ended the call and stared down at his phone. "He gets his test result tomorrow," he said quietly. "Perhaps he's nervous about it, and he's gone somewhere he can be on his own."

"Now you're just being ridiculous." Bea had heard enough. "You really don't know him at all, do you?" The panic was subsiding, and numbness was taking its place. She got to her feet. "Where are your car keys?"

His brow creased. "I'm not giving you another car, Bea!"

"Give me the damn keys, Owen. I need to go out and find my son."

He didn't move, but he didn't need to. Over the past few days, Bea had been discreetly watching her sister's husband.

Owen was a man of routine. The keys were in a silver bowl
on a glass-topped table just inside the front door, where he
put them every evening when he got back from the clinic.

She made a run for it, and she almost made it, but Owen
was quicker, and he stopped her with an arm around her
waist before she could get there. She fought against him, of
course she did, an elbow to the gut that produced a satisfy-
ing grunt. Simon wasn't the only one who had learned the
importance of sticking up for yourself on the farm. She made
another grab for the keys. She caught the edge of the bowl
with her fingertips, and it went flying, hitting the floor with
a bang, then a clatter. She couldn't see where the keys had
landed.

She felt Owen's arm slip from her waist. Her heart was
still racing. She knew he could stop her if he really wanted
to, despite all her bravado. He had a good eight inches of
height on her. The same as her son.

"Why aren't you worried?" she shouted at him. "Why
doesn't any of this scare you? You're his father, Owen. Why
don't you care?"

Bea couldn't bear to be in this house with him a moment
longer. She stumbled forward, yanking open the door and
running out into the warm night. "Simon!" she yelled, although she knew it was hopeless. He wasn't there. She was
almost at the end of the drive when she heard Owen calling
to her. She turned to face him.

He held up the car keys. "Come on," he said. "I'll drive."

She was tempted to ignore him and search on foot, on
her own. But she was tired of being the only adult in Simon's

life, of having to carry that burden alone. She needed some-one else to share the load for a while.

But as she got into the passenger seat, she couldn't help but wish that she hadn't. All these years, keeping those words to herself, not even allowing herself to think them, knowing that Simon was her responsibility and hers alone, so ashamed of what she'd done. Sleeping with her sister's husband. It was like something out of one of those trashy soap operas that she and Antonia used to watch when they were teenagers. Antonia had been entranced by the splashy clothes and the shoes, but for Bea it had been something else that had pulled her in. She'd wanted to be loved, the way the men in those programs loved the women—passionately, dramatically—no matter what the cost. What an idiot.

And in the end, Antonia had gotten both, and she'd got-ten neither.

All she had was a dangerous son.

||| ANTONIA

Five years ago

> *After months of speculation, the government today announced*
> *that it will not be making changes to the Equality Act to include*
> *M test status as a protected characteristic. Although the test it-*
> *self is not a legal requirement, many schools and workplaces*
> *have been using the test as part of their selection process for sev-*
> *eral years. Men with negative tests can also get cheaper health*
> *and life insurance, and some bars and nightclubs have also*
> *started asking for proof of a negative test as a requirement of*
> *entry. Campaigners say this is the end of men's rights in the*
> *UK, as it will effectively legalize discrimination against men*
> *who have tested positive for the M gene.*

It happened on the last day of the vacation. In hindsight, Antonia would see that it had been inevitable, that trouble had been brewing for days. She would wish that she had ended the trip early. She would wish, when she lay awake in the night, thinking it over, that she had never gone at all.

She and Bea had been in the cottage. Bea had been upstairs in the bath, and Antonia had been sitting on the window seat in the living room, watching the swooping flight
of the seagulls through her binoculars. The tide was coming in, the sand flat and exposed, the birds noisy as the
beach cleared and the temperature began to drop.

They'd had a busy day. Jack and Simon had gone out
straight after breakfast. They'd been back twice for food
and money but hadn't stayed long either time. Their feet
had been caked in sand, and both of them had stripes burned
onto their cheeks and shoulders. Antonia had fussed around
with sunblock and T-shirts, and then they'd gone again.
Part of her had worried that she should have kept Jack inside
to prevent further exposure, but it was the last day, and he'd
been having such a lovely time with his cousin, and it was so
nice, for once, just to be able to sit with only her thoughts
for company.

Bea hadn't said anything about the pills in her bag. Antonia had no doubt that her sister had seen them. Her bag had
been unfastened when she'd come downstairs after checking on Jack. And there had been a marked shift in Bea's behavior. She'd softened her voice and started to play mother,
offering Antonia cups of tea and refusing to let her wash
up. Antonia had let her. It had been quite nice, really, and
after all, she had paid for the vacation. She deserved a little
TLC in return.

The week had given her a lot to think about. It was the
first time she'd really seen her nephew close-up. She'd been
expecting, by this stage, to have a better understanding of

him, but she didn't. He remained a mystery. How could he
be so very different from her son? But then, Bea was different, too. She was so strict with Simon that sometimes it
made Antonia wince. Antonia knew that she personally
could not live that way, nor would she want Jack to.

Time drifted on a little more, and eventually Bea came
downstairs, her hair wet and her face pink. "Where are the
boys?" she asked, yawning.

"Out," Antonia said, setting down the book that she
hadn't been reading. "They're playing with that girl from
next door, I think, down in the rock pools."

"Still?" Bea said. "The tide will be coming in soon. They
should be out of there by now."

"Another ten minutes won't hurt," Antonia said. She
stretched, picked up the binoculars, and zeroed in on the boys.
Yes, there they were, and there was the girl, too. She could see
them taking turns jumping into the largest pool.

"I'll go and get them," Bea said. She had left her shoes by
the door, and she shoved her feet into them, combing her
hair with her fingers as she did so.

"I'll come with you," Antonia said.

"No, you wait here," Bea told her. "I can do it. It won't
take long. Why don't you stick that popcorn I brought in
the microwave, and we'll see if there's a film on the TV?"

"Good idea," Antonia replied, and she gave her sister a
smile, and Bea smiled back. Bea closed the door gently behind her, leaving Antonia alone in the cottage. She looked
around at the amateur paintings of the beach that decorated the walls, at the pieces of driftwood and shells that lay

on the fireplace, at the row of battered crime novels that the owner had left for guests should they want to read one. It was tiny compared to home, and she would be glad to get back to her big bed and to the bathroom she didn't have to share and to Owen, but she was glad that they'd come. She could tell that things would be different for her and Bea going forward.

Outside, the sky was streaked with red and orange, and there was not a cloud to be seen. The sun had felt wonderful on her skin, and she'd gotten more of a tan than she'd expected, which was an added bonus. She picked up the binoculars and searched again for the boys. Jack and the girl were in the water now, with Simon on the rock, waving at them. He looked to be in a temper about something.

She shifted her gaze. There was Bea, just reaching the bottom of the steps, about to step foot onto the sand. Back to the children. The tide was getting closer now. They really ought to be out of the water. Thank god Bea was on her way to get them.

And then she saw . . . no. It couldn't be. She had to be imagining it. "No!" she shouted, shifting position, moving to her knees, pressing the binoculars hard against her face, barely noticing the pressure. She hammered on the glass with her free hand. "No, don't! Stop!"

But she could only watch helplessly as Simon roughly hauled the girl out of the water. Antonia could tell from the angle that her head was going to smack straight into a rock that hung over the edge of the pool even before it did.

"Oh my god," she said. "No."

All this time she'd allowed herself to think that everything was all right, that there was no danger. She could not
have been more wrong.

She dropped the binoculars and scrambled to the door,
flinging it open and running outside. She sprinted down
the steps barefoot. Running across the sand was much,
much harder, and her lungs were screaming before she was
even halfway there. "Bea!" she yelled. "Bea!"

Bea turned in the distance, shielded her eyes with her
hand, and waved at her, but the wave slowed and then she
dropped her arm, and she looked toward the rock pools as
Antonia pointed at them and yelled, and somehow the message must have got through, because Bea started to scramble across the rocks, the wind whipping at her hair.

Antonia was slower to get there, hindered by her bare
feet. The rocks were sharp and slippery in places, and she
had to grab on to stop herself from falling in, and a couple
of times she failed and her foot plunged into cold water,
rubbery seaweed tangling around her ankle.

But she kept going. She could see Bea ahead, her bright
yellow T-shirt making her easy to spot. She saw her sister
drop to her knees and knew what she was going to find
even before she got there. The two boys, side by side, shiv-
ering, hands clutched to their chests as if they didn't know
what to do with them, and her sister bent over the supine
figure of the girl, rubbing her face and talking to her, the
words stumbling over one another as she begged her to be
all right.

"Move aside," Antonia said, kneeling down next to her

sister. "I learned CPR at the clinic." For several long minutes, she fought and fought to bring that little girl back to life, but she was too far and too long gone. Blood leaked from the wound on her head and slowly spilled onto the rock below and her eyes stared lifelessly up at the sky.

When Antonia accepted defeat, Bea shoved her aside and tried to copy what she'd done.

"Bea, you need to stop. It's not working."

"Shut up," Bea said fiercely. "Have you got your phone? Call an ambulance!"

Antonia squeezed her sister's shoulder, aware that the two boys were watching. "She's gone."

"No!" Bea howled. But she took her hands off the girl, sat back on her haunches. Her face was utterly white. She looked like she was going to pass out.

It made Antonia afraid for what she had to do next. But she had to do it. There was no other way out of this. She'd seen what had happened, what Simon had done. "Listen to me," she said. "Go back to the cottage, get your stuff, and leave. Take my car. The keys are on the table."

Bea turned her head and looked at her through wild, terrified eyes. "What are you talking about?"

"Bea, I was watching. I saw . . . I saw what happened. You've got to get Simon out of here before someone calls the police."

She hadn't thought her sister could get paler, but she did. "Go!" Antonia urged her. "Simon, go with her. No arguing. Grab your stuff and leave. Go. Now!"

A look passed between Simon and Bea, and for a moment,

Antonia couldn't breathe. "For fuck's sake, he's not tested!" she shouted. "What do you think they'll do to him, Bea?"

That was all it took.

Bea grabbed Simon's hand. The two of them scrambled away from the rocks, down and out of sight. Antonia turned to Jack, who was still standing there, shaking violently now. She climbed around to him, tried not to look at the body of the girl at their feet, and hugged him. "We've got to take care of things now," she said. "Do you understand? For Simon. We've got to protect Simon. If the police catch him and test him and it's positive, his entire life will be over. We're not going to let that happen."

He nodded. "But it was an accident," he said. He looked up at her, and she saw the fear in his eyes.

"It won't matter, darling," she said. She had to force down the bile in her throat as she lifted the girl and slid the body back into the pool. She waited as long as she dared, then she carefully took her phone from her pocket and called the police. Within a matter of minutes, she heard sirens, and people started coming down onto the beach to see what the fuss was about, and the parents of the little girl were with them, and nothing, nothing could have prepared Antonia for that.

She whisked Jack away from all of it, stumbling back across the sand to the cottage, and by the time the police came to talk to her, she had her story straight. A tragic accident. Jack had been too far away to stop her from jumping in, and she'd hit her head, and there was nothing he could do, he'd tried to get her out, but she was too heavy. She wrote Simon out of the story completely. It seemed the right thing to do at the time.

It wasn't until they were alone and Antonia had locked herself in the bathroom that what had happened finally hit her. Her mouth was suddenly very dry, her tongue sticking in place, and she felt a little dizzy. She ran her wrists under the cold tap and splashed water on her face. It helped. So did an assortment of the pills from her bag. She also gave something to Jack to help him sleep, and then she went into the kitchen and got herself a glass of wine.

From her bedroom window, she could see the beach. Lights and torches were everywhere. The crowd was still gathered. The whole scene had a spooky, dreamlike quality, aided by the lowering sun, which had cast everything in soft shades of pink and orange. In the distance, the sea was perfectly calm, but in here Antonia could feel her guts churning, and she thought for a moment that she might be sick. She forced it back with another glass of wine.

At least Bea had listened to her for once. There was some consolation in that. The bedroom had been cleared out, as had Simon's things, and there was no sign of the car. Bea had left nothing behind at all, not even a note. It was as if she had never been there.

All that was left to do was for Antonia to call Owen and tell him what had happened.

CHAPTER THIRTY-TWO

|||SIMON

Now

Simon didn't make it back to the house until the following morning. He only realized that he'd been out all night when he woke up in the park, damp with dew, stiff from having slept on a bench. His head felt like his brain was trying to climb out of it, and his digestive system burned from his throat to his ass. He sat up, slowly, painfully, for a moment lost and quite confused, before pieces of the previous night came flooding back. Jack. The vodka. The house. Ginny. Had he kissed her? He thought he might have kissed her. And maybe some other stuff, too. That part had been good. Better than good. "Fucking hell," he said, and laughed, although there was no one around to hear him. It took a few deep breaths before he was steady enough to try standing up.

His legs held. It was a start.

He had to go back to Antonia's, and when he got there, he would have to face his mother. Unless . . . unless he got back before she woke up. He could go straight to bed and pretend that he'd been there for hours. He talked himself into believing that was his way out, that it would happen, and it got him all the way back to the front door. He let himself in, trying to be as quiet as possible, wincing at every sound, every move he made like thunder in his head.

At least he was going to get his test result today. It wasn't all going to be shit. But for now, he didn't even make it past the bottom of the stairs. Bea came straight out of the kitchen. He had forgotten how quickly she could move when she wanted to. She grabbed him by the front of his T-shirt. "Where the hell have you been?"

"I . . . I went for a run," he said.

"All damn night? Don't lie to me, Simon."

Simon didn't have a response for that. He was starting to feel a little queasy, now that he was back inside Antonia's perfumed house. "I don't feel well," he said.

"That'll be the alcohol you spent last night guzzling. Get upstairs," Bea said. "In the shower. Cool your head. And then we need to have a serious talk, Simon, about what happened last night. That girl you were with ended up in the hospital with alcohol poisoning. Jack seems to think you had something to do with it."

"I didn't!" he said, but he faltered when he saw the look on her face. "Jack brought the vodka. It wasn't me, Mom. I swear."

"Tell me exactly what happened."

A bed. A warm girl. And some stuff that was none of his mother's business. "Nothing happened," he told her. "There was just . . . everyone was drinking, and I didn't want to be the only one who wasn't. I didn't do anything bad to her, and if he's saying I did, he's lying. It's . . . I'm getting my result today," he reminded her. He hoped it would go some way to making her less angry with him, but her expression suggested that he was wasting his time, and it didn't seem like the right moment to tell her that everything was going to be all right.

He turned and ran upstairs. He spent a long time in the shower, standing with his head resting against the tiles as the water beat down on his shoulders, then he cleaned his teeth twice. His mouth still tasted foul, but it was the best he could do.

He needed to check his phone, see if his result was on the M App yet. He hoped so.

But when he went back downstairs, there were voices in the kitchen, and something in their tone made the hair on the back of his neck stand up. He stopped and listened, but he couldn't make out any of the words. Then someone came out of the kitchen.

It was a man he didn't know, probably about the same age as Owen, with a face like a bulldog chewing a wasp. He didn't belong in this house any more than Simon did, with its classy furniture and pale carpets. But that wasn't what told Simon that something was very, very wrong.

It was the uniform.

Simon started to tremble. He couldn't seem to stop himself. For the past five years, ever since the vacation, he'd always had this reaction whenever he saw a police officer. But on all the other occasions, his fear had been misplaced.

But it wasn't now.

"Simon Mitchell? You're going to have to come with us," the man said.

"What? Why?"

"Because, I'm afraid to say, Malcolm Sloan died last night as a result of the injuries you inflicted on him at Hilsford Farm last Saturday."

Simon felt his legs give way. He sank down onto the step. "He died?"

He'd never meant for that to happen. And the worst of it was that he knew it was his own fault. No one had made him fight Malcolm. He'd chosen to do that all by himself. In fact, some of the other men had warned against it, saying that there was something nasty in the other boy, something they didn't like. But he hadn't listened. Why hadn't he listened?

He was bundled into the back of the police car and driven to the station. No one said a word. The radio crackled on and off, but other than that, nothing. He felt dizzy. All he could think about was the look on his mom's face as they'd led him to the car.

"Don't say anything," she'd yelled at him. "You hear me, Simon? Not a word!"

He'd let them fold him into the back. It was as if he'd lost control of his body. He belonged to these people now, the two men in uniform in the front of the car. The world outside seemed strange and far away. The two of them ignored him, occasionally talking to each other, their radios burbling on and off, but otherwise, it was as if he weren't there.

He leaned over and threw up on the floorboard.

That got a response out of the two of them.

Fortunately, they were almost at the station when it happened. The back door was opened and Simon was helped out. Then he was steered forward with a heavy hand on his shoulder. He realized that he was wearing handcuffs. He wasn't even sure when they'd been put on. "Am I under arrest?" he asked.

"Yes," said the larger of the two. "We told you that earlier when we read you your rights. You told us you understood."

He didn't remember that, but he supposed that he must have done it. He was taken inside and put in a cell. He had to give them his shoes. They asked for his phone, but he'd left it at the house. They gave him water. And then they closed the door, and he found himself alone with nothing but four cream-colored walls, a steel toilet, and a bench that was stuck to the wall. He told himself that he wouldn't be in there long enough to need to sit down, but no one came to let him out. Time seemed to lose all meaning. The electric light was harsh, and his head was very sore, and he felt like he'd been drinking battery acid.

He got to his feet again, hammered on the door until his hands hurt. Eventually, someone came and opened the little flap in the middle of the door and glared at him. It was a woman with a heavy fringe and round cheeks like a hamster.

"Stop making that racket!" she said.

"I want my mom."

"Someone will be along to talk to you shortly," she said. "Sit down and be quiet."

She slammed the flap shut.

Simon was left alone.

Eventually—it might have been an hour; it might have been two—the door was opened, and he was taken to another room elsewhere in the building. This, too, was windowless. There was a table in the middle of it, and chairs, and sitting in one of the chairs was Owen, and in the other a woman he didn't recognize who wore a dark suit and had short gray hair that looked like a helmet.

"Sit down," said the policeman standing behind Simon, giving him a little push.

He stumbled forward. Owen pulled out the chair next to him, and Simon collapsed into it.

"Are you all right?" Owen asked him quietly.

"What do you think?" Simon was gripped by an overwhelming urge to cry. He dug his nails into the palms of his hands and concentrated on the sting.

"Did you say anything to them?"

"Mom told me not to."

"Good," Owen said.

Simon didn't understand what his uncle was doing here, but he was grateful for it. Somehow Owen's suit and tie were reassuring. It made him feel like he had an adult on his side, someone the police would have to take seriously in a way they would never take his mother seriously.

The two officers sat down. One of them set an iPad on the table. The other fiddled with a bundle of paper. The first reached across and pressed a button and said something about a formal interview and then made everyone say their name and their reason for being present.

"Michelle Long," said the woman in the jacket. "Attorney for Simon Mitchell."

"Doctor Owen Phillip Talbot," Owen said, unbuttoning his jacket as he spoke.

"And your relationship to Simon?"

"Father," he said.

Simon almost fell out of his chair. He turned and looked at Owen, who studiously ignored him. "No, you're not," he said, forgetting that he wasn't supposed to be saying anything. "My dad's name is Alfie Collins!" He turned back to the officer. "Alfie Collins," he said again, determined to make them listen.

"I'm sorry, Simon," Owen said. "But that's not the case."

His throat felt like it was closing up, and he reached for the plastic cup of water that had been placed on the table in front of him and tried to drink some. It went down the wrong way. It took him several minutes to recover, and everyone just sat there and waited and stared at him as he coughed, his eyes stinging.

"But you're married," he said, as if that made it impossible, though of course it didn't.

"Yes," Owen said. He didn't try to explain it, to justify it. He simply sat, rigid in his seat.

How could he be related to this man? To this stuck-up, arrogant dickhead? Simon put his head in his hands, terrified that he might cry, or worse, that he might punch Owen in the face. He wanted to talk to his mother, though he didn't know what he would say to her. All his life, Bea had been the one person he could rely on. Now even that had gone. He didn't feel angry. He just felt utterly let down, and ashamed that he'd ever trusted any of them.

"Right," the officer said after several minutes of silence. "Ready to continue? I assume you know why you're here, Simon."

Don't tell them anything. "Not really."

"On the night of April twelfth, an organized fight took place at a warehouse in Hilsford. Do you know anything about that?"

"Tell them 'No comment,'" the woman in the suit said before Simon could answer.

"No comment," he said.

"There were four fights that night," the officer said, continuing as if he hadn't heard. "It's our understanding that these were a regular occurrence. Was that your experience?"

"No comment."

"Was it your first fight?"

"No comment."

"We'd like to have a doctor take a look at you, just to check you over. Will that be all right?"

"I've already checked him over myself," Owen said. "He has no serious injuries."

The officer paused. "As I'm sure you appreciate, we'll want to do our own assessment."

No, Simon thought. *No, I don't want you to. You're not touching me.*

"Of course," Owen said.

The woman scribbled something on her notepad.

Simon sank miserably into his chair.

"At the end of one of the fights, a man called Malcolm Sloan was left with serious injuries. Life-threatening injuries that would have been obvious to all present. By the time the police arrived on the scene, the other man involved in the fight had already left."

"We know you were there, Simon," said the other officer. "We know that you were the other man. And this will all go a lot easier for you if you just tell us what happened. We're not trying to catch you out here. We're trying to help you."

That was a big fat lie if ever he'd heard one. Still, he sat tight-lipped and didn't say anything. The conversation went on for another hour. He knew because he was watching the clock on the wall. They kept coming back to the same statements. *We know you were there. Just tell us what happened. We just want to help.*

But if he didn't say anything, didn't tell them anything, they couldn't prove anything.

And then, all of a sudden, the conversation shifted.

"You got tested for the M gene earlier this week, didn't you?"

At last. Now everything would get sorted. "Yes," he said, figuring it couldn't do any harm to answer that one question.

"Why did you do that?"

He shrugged. "I decided it was time."

"We have the result of your test here." The officer with the bundle of paper placed a page down in front of him. Simon stared at it. He scanned the information, picking out his name and his date of birth. That all looked correct.

He read to the bottom.

And there it was in black and white, the result.

Positive.

He blinked.

"No," he said, shaking his head. "That can't be right."

"What can't be right, Simon?"

"The result," he said before he could stop himself.

The woman leaned over and whispered something to Owen.

"I'd like to have a word with my son in private, if you don't mind," Owen said.

He looked at the woman in the suit, and she looked at the officers, and the two of them got up and left. "Five minutes," one of them said as he went through the door.

Simon slumped forward, his elbows on the table, still staring at the test result. "It doesn't make any sense," he muttered.

The woman got up and left, too, and then it was just him and Owen in the room with the bright light and the gray walls—Owen, who was apparently his father—which was so obvious when Simon thought about it that he couldn't think about it at all.

"Why doesn't it make sense?" Owen said to him.

"Because . . ." Simon stopped. "It just doesn't."

"Because Jack took the test for you," Owen said quietly.

Simon had promised he would never tell. That was the deal he'd made with Jack. And he always kept his promises. But Jack hadn't kept his, had he? He'd promised Simon a negative result and given him a positive one.

"Yes," he said. "Jack took the test."

CHAPTER THIRTY-THREE

ANTONIA

Now

Jack came shuffling into the room, hair a mess, still in his pajamas. "What's going on?"

Antonia rushed over and wrapped her arms around him, pulling him close. "The police just took Simon."

"They did? Why?"

She didn't want to tell him, not when he was obviously tired and hadn't had anything to eat. But she didn't have much choice. "Do you remember Paul's son, Malcolm?"

She felt him stiffen. "Yes."

"Well, he died yesterday, and the police think Simon had something to do with it. The two of them were working on the same farm and they got into a fight somehow. Simon did a terrible thing, Jack. I know he's your cousin and I know you've always wanted to help him. But he isn't a good person. I've . . . it's something that I've known for a long time. And I think you've known it, too, haven't you?"

"Yes," Jack said, his voice breaking on the word. "I mean, not always. Sometimes. But last night . . ."

Antonia took his hand and held it tightly. "Promise me something. No matter what happens, do not tell anyone that you took the test for Simon. No one can know. I know you only wanted to help him, but you have to understand how much trouble you could be in if anyone finds out. It could hurt the clinic, too."

"I won't," he said. "But he's going to get a negative result, isn't he? Which means he's going to get away with all of it."

"Try not to worry too much about that," Antonia said. "Even boys with negative tests have to face the consequences of their actions if they do something terrible. It's not a get-out-of-jail-free card, after all."

"But it won't be the same!"

"No, it won't," she agreed, and when she tried to hug him, he let her. She made him pancakes, and then the two of them sat and watched TV. It didn't seem right to make him go to school, not with everything that had happened. She hadn't gone to the clinic for the same reason. After a while, Jack's phone buzzed. It was Ginny. Antonia saw her name pop up on the screen, although Jack didn't let her see the message.

It didn't surprise her when he got to his feet. "She wants me to go over there," he said. "Wants to talk to me about last night."

"You're such a good boy," she told him as he headed for the door. "Drive carefully!"

Jack was her baby, her only, her darling boy. Hard-earned

and long waited for. She had never allowed herself to see his flaws. She had refused to acknowledge their existence.

But they were there anyway.

She tucked the last of the dirty cups into the dishwasher, turned it on, and then slowly made her way upstairs and into her son's bedroom. It was a place she'd walked in and out of freely until he'd hit puberty, and Owen had told her she couldn't do that anymore. After that, Jack was given a warning to remove anything he didn't want other people to see before the maid came in. Not that there was much to worry about. He was surprisingly neat and tidy for a teenager, his clothes always hung neatly in the closet, shoes packed away in their boxes, his devices positioned neatly on his desk. He was, as she had told him, a good boy.

She didn't know what she was looking for when she started quietly opening his drawers, shifting their contents from left to right, her fingers seeking corners where things might be hidden. She looked under the bed, in his bathroom, and in the bathroom cabinet. The bottle that held his vitamins sat on the shelf. He had no idea that Antonia had filled it, just as she did every month, discarding the beige ovals for something far more helpful.

She moved on, back into his bedroom. The only place left to look was his bedside table, and she hesitated before going in there. It seemed almost too far. There hadn't been anything unexpected anywhere else; why would there be something here?

She slowly pulled open the drawer. Unlike the rest of the room, it was messy and filled with detritus: playing cards, old pens, Warhammer figures, Nintendo cartridges, a half-eaten packet of cough drops that had started to dissolve. There was nothing unexpected or out of the ordinary.

Everything was as it should be. And yet she knew that wasn't true. Nothing about this day was as it should be. The police had come to the house and taken her nephew away, which she had expected, but her husband had chosen to go with him, which she had not. Her son was at the house of a girl who had spent the previous night in the hospital with alcohol poisoning. Unpleasant though not unusual, as anyone who had ever been seventeen would know.

But Jack's involvement in it . . . that was a cause for concern.

Because Antonia knew something about her son that no one else did. Not even Jack himself.

She took one final look around the room. There was nowhere else left to check, except . . . her eyes fell on Jack's bag hanging on the back of the door. She unzipped it and rummaged through the contents.

Her fingers closed around something at the bottom of the bag. A glass bottle. She withdrew it, already knowing what it was, and she cursed her son for a fool when she looked at it. It was an empty vodka bottle of the exact same brand that she always bought.

She didn't need to check the liquor cabinet to know where it had come from.

What she did next seemed to happen in a blur, her body moving of its own accord, as if she were watching herself from a distance, like she was sitting in the dark at a movie theater, the action unfolding on a screen in front of her. She could almost smell the sweet, sweaty aroma of popcorn.

She left Jack's room and went into Simon's. It was tidy, too, but probably only because he had so little to make a mess with. There were a few clothes piled on the chair in the corner. The duvet was folded up on the bed. A duffel bag sat in the corner.

She picked it up, loosened the strings, and pushed the empty bottle inside. She hadn't heard the front door open. She hadn't heard Owen come into the house or his quick footsteps as he came upstairs. She was too distracted by the noise in her head.

"Antonia?" he asked.

She didn't know how much he had seen. She could only hope that it hadn't been so much that she couldn't talk her way out of it. But those hopes were quickly dashed. Owen strode into the room and picked up the bag, his hand diving inside it before she could say anything to stop him. He fished out the bottle. He looked at it for a long time before he turned to her. "Why were you putting this in Simon's bag?" he asked. His voice was dangerously soft. Antonia had never heard him speak like that before, certainly not to her. She hadn't even been aware that he had it in him.

"I wasn't!" she said. The words fell out of her mouth before she could stop them, and she almost found herself believing them.

"I saw you do it."

"No, you're mistaken. I just found it there. I was trying to decide what to do! I'm so worried about what happened to

Ginny." She grabbed his hand, squeezed it. "Jack said that Simon kept trying to get her to drink, and . . ."

Owen let out a strange noise. He dug his fingers into his hair and then dragged his hands down over his face. "Where would Simon have gotten alcohol?"

"I don't know! He's been working at a farm! He probably got it there. Everyone knows that alcohol abuse is rife in those places. And he's eighteen! There's nothing to stop him from buying it." Her chest was heaving, and she clutched at the diamond pendant she wore around her neck. "I don't understand why you're asking me these questions. We should be taking this straight to the police."

She snatched at the bottle, but Owen held it out of her way. Then he pushed past her, knocking her shoulder with his upper arm, a hard contact that seemed terrifyingly deliberate. He went straight into their bedroom. The first place he searched was her chest of drawers, and he didn't do it neatly or carefully. Clothes dropped to the floor around his feet, beautiful silk scarves and soft cashmere cardigans tossed aside like garbage.

"Stop that!" she ordered him, but he didn't listen. She rushed over to him, grabbed his arm, but it didn't work. He got hold of her, pushed her over to the bed, and sat her firmly down on it as if she were five years old.

He thrust a finger in her face. "Sit there and shut up!" He went back to the chest of drawers. Antonia sat silently, praying that his temper would burn itself out quickly, that he'd realize how vile he was being before he searched any further. She could see the lean muscles of his back straining against the fabric of his shirt, and a faint line of sweat seeping through between his shoulder blades.

He abandoned the chest of drawers and turned to her bedside table. She saw what was coming as if she were in a car, watching a crash about to happen. He pulled open the top drawer, where she kept her underwear, her secret stash of receipts, the vibrator he didn't know she had. He found all of those, and perhaps that might have been bad enough if he hadn't pushed his hand right to the back of the drawer and found where she kept the pills. It wasn't all of them; there were more in her handbag and more still tucked into the toes of a pair of winter boots at the back of the closet. She was always afraid that she would run out, and so she kept a plentiful supply at hand, perhaps too many if she was forced to think about it, which she was now.

Owen picked up the packets. All the fight went out of him, and he sank down on the bed next to her, the mattress dipping slightly under his weight. "I knew you were going to be a lot of work when I married you," he said. "But I thought I wanted to do that work. I wanted you. You had everything you needed to be an excellent doctor's wife."

Antonia felt, in the pit of her stomach, that he'd just dished out a terrible insult, but she couldn't quite figure out what it was.

He didn't look at her, seemingly transfixed by the box in his hand. "How long have you been stealing from the clinic?"

"I haven't! I would never do that!"

"So if I go over there right now and stock check, compare what we've got with the prescriptions and orders, I won't find any discrepancies?"

Antonia crumpled then. Tears had always worked in the past, and she thought they would work now, but they didn't. Owen got up from the bed, went over to his closet, and pulled out the backpack he normally took to the gym. He packed an assortment of clothes into it.

"What are you doing?" Antonia asked him, watching in horror as he carefully folded one of the white shirts he wore to the clinic. The question was redundant; what he was doing was obvious, although she found it difficult to watch and even harder to believe.

"What I should have done a long time ago," he said. He didn't sound angry or sad; the exact opposite, in fact. There was a relaxed calm about his posture and his tone of voice. He zipped the bag closed. He didn't look at Antonia, not once. "I'm leaving you."

"What? Owen, no. You can't."

He turned then and looked at her, and she saw for the first time the touches of gray at his temples and the creasing at the corners of his eyes, and she realized that he'd aged, and she hadn't even noticed. "You altered Jack's test result," he said. "I haven't figured out how yet. But I will. He's positive. And you've been treating him for it."

She could lie. But somehow she knew that it would be pointless. "Please don't tell him," she said.

Owen just picked up his bag and walked out.

CHAPTER THIRTY-FOUR

||| JACK

Now

Jack parked outside Ginny's house and strolled along the path to the front door. He'd stopped to buy a bunch of flowers on the way, some pink and purple ones that he'd liked the smell of in the shop. He knocked on the door, glad not to have his hands empty. He'd been so angry when he'd found Ginny with Simon the night before, and he wanted to make sure that she forgave him for it.

When Ginny opened the door, he saw immediately how pale she was. Her eyes were rimmed with red, and he could tell that she'd been crying. He put a hand to the door and pushed it farther open. "Are you okay?"

She nodded, but she didn't meet his gaze. "I guess you heard what happened."

"To Simon?"

"No," she said, confused. "To Malcolm."

"Right. Yes, of course. Sorry." It hadn't occurred to him that she'd be too bothered about that. After all, she hadn't seen him in years. It wasn't like they were close or anything. They weren't even proper siblings. But he kept those thoughts to himself. He held the flowers out and she took them.

"Thanks," she said, though she didn't look at them or smell them, which he found a bit irritating.

"My parents are out," she said. "They took my sister to stay at my grandparents, for a few days while they get things sorted. I told them I didn't want to go. They're mad at me for getting drunk last night. How was I supposed to know he was going to die? They just said he was in the hospital, and I didn't think it was that big a deal. M-positive boys are always having fights and accidents and ending up there. You see it in the news all the time, but they don't *die.*"

Her voice broke a little on the last word, and she shook her head and turned, rushing off toward the kitchen. Jack toed off his shoes before he followed her, checking his reflection in the hallway mirror on the way and taking a moment to smooth back his hair. He definitely looked better than Simon, with his smashed face and thug haircut, which made the fact that she'd let Simon take her upstairs all the more baffling.

He wondered what Ginny would say if he told her that the police had come for Simon that morning. That her brother had been the one to put the bruises on Simon's face and that Simon had been the one to put him in the hospital. That Simon and Malcolm were basically the same. How he wanted to tell her.

When he got to the kitchen, he found her cramming the flowers into a vase. It gave him a chance to get a proper look at her. Her body was hidden inside jeans and a massive hoodie. She wasn't wearing any makeup, and her hair didn't look like it had been brushed that morning. He was disappointed that she hadn't made a bit more effort. "I was worried about you last night," he said, watching as she chucked tea bags into mugs and made drinks for both of them.

"I told you, I'm fine. I just had too much to drink, that's all."

She pushed past him and went into the living room, where she flopped down on the sofa. The TV was on. She'd been watching *Friends*. It was the episode where Ross bought himself a pair of leather pants. Normally, it had her in stitches, but she wasn't even smiling now. And there was a plate of untouched beans on toast on the floor close to where she sat. It had obviously been there for a while, because the beans had gone dull and gritty-looking. Jack's stomach turned over at the sight of it. She didn't seem fine. Not even close.

"Did Simon get home all right?" she asked.

Why was she asking about him? "Simon?"

"Yes. I . . . I didn't get a chance to talk to him before he left. I wanted to make sure he's all right, but he's not answering his messages."

"Don't you remember what happened?"

She paled and bit down on her lower lip, tugging her cuffs down over her hands and hiding them. "Well, I, mostly . . . I was *really* drunk, Jack."

"You went upstairs with him, and you were . . . well, it's a good thing I came looking for you."

Her eyes were suddenly huge in her face.

"I got rid of him for you," Jack continued. "You don't need to worry that anything happened with him, because I made sure it didn't. Honestly, Ginny, you really should be more careful about who you mess around with."

"I like Simon," she said faintly.

"You don't know Simon. A girl like you should never be with a boy like him. It doesn't matter, anyway. I'm the one who took care of you."

"But I thought . . . I thought . . . So you're saying I didn't have sex with Simon? But I definitely . . . Then . . . who?"

Jack just stared at her. "You can't tell me you weren't up for it," he said quietly. "Did you honestly think I was going to say no?"

Ginny slopped tea on the front of her hoodie. "Shit," she muttered, and quickly put the cup down, rubbing at the front of her clothes with her fingers. It didn't have much impact on the wet patch. Her eyes were wild and she licked her lips, as if they were suddenly dry. "But I would *never* have sex with you!"

"Well, you did."

She bent her knees, wrapping her arms around her legs and hugging them tightly as if she were trying to make herself smaller. "No," she said. "I don't like you that way." She sniffed, and Jack realized that she was crying.

He put down his own drink and moved closer to her, and he reached for her hand, and she snatched it back, and he didn't like that. He didn't like it at all. He grabbed for it again, this time finding her wrist and locking his hand around it. He could feel the slender bones inside the cool, dry skin, and he could smell the sour taint of old alcohol as it leaked out of her pores.

She tugged at his grip, trying to break free. "Stop that!" he told her sharply. She went immediately limp, and he was able to slide both arms around her and hug her. "It doesn't matter," he said. "Okay? I'm here. I'll take care of you. Don't I always?"

He smoothed the hair back from her face, saw her recoil. It made him want to punch her. He let go, shocked at himself, at the force of his reaction. When he got to his feet, he saw her staring up at him. Her fear was obvious.

"What are you looking at me like that for?"

"I'm not looking at you like anything!" she said quickly, but it was a lie, and they both knew it. She fidgeted with the ends of her hair, her cheeks red.

Jack stared at her for a moment longer. "Yes, you are," he told her. "You're looking at me like I did something to you." But he hadn't. Not anything she hadn't wanted, anyway. Yes, she'd been drunk. He wasn't denying that. But she'd been flirting with him for months, he knew she had, and she'd only gone up there with Simon so that he would get jealous and go up there and find them. That's just how some girls operated. Manipulative bitches.

"What are you trying to say, Ginny? That I did something to you?"

She didn't reply, merely shrank back in her seat, hair falling across her face, hands twisted together in her lap.

"Fuck you," he said bitterly, all of a sudden sick of her. "All I did was try to help you, and this is the thanks I get. And by the way, the police came and arrested Simon this morning. He was at the same farm as Malcolm. He's the one who put him in the hospital in the first place. Simon killed him. That's the sort of boy you like. What the fuck does that say about you?"

He turned and walked out. He got into his car, started the engine, then turned it off, took out his phone, and called Simon. The test result should have come back by now, which meant that the police would have let Simon go. The anger that rose up inside him at the thought of it was almost overwhelming. Simon was going to get away with all of it, and Jack was the reason.

It rang four times before anyone answered, but when they did, it wasn't his cousin. It was Bea.

"Bea?" he said when he heard her voice. Why did she have Simon's phone? He took a deep breath. He'd get nowhere if he showed Bea his rage. "I was just ringing to see how Simon is."

"Simon?" she said, and she started to laugh. "You're asking about Simon?"

"Is he all right? I'm worried about him."

"That might work on your mother, but it doesn't work on me. I know the truth, Jack."

"What do you mean?"

She laughed again, and it was a cruel, unpleasant sound that made his blood run cold. "I know you took the test for him."

"You should be grateful," he told her. "I did him a favor. Not that he deserves it."

"It came back positive," Bea said, and hung up.

CHAPTER THIRTY-FIVE

SIMON

Now

Simon had been taken back to the cells and left there. He lay down on the bench with his arms wrapped tightly around himself and tried not to cry. He didn't manage for long. But at some point it ended, subsiding to dry shudders that wracked his body every few seconds. He felt both hot and cold. Empty and sick. He had been in some difficult places before—some rough, horrible places—but none of them had been like this. He had never been more alone or more frightened.

He wanted his mom.

Why hadn't she told him that Owen was his father? Why had she let him think that it was Alfie? He didn't understand any of that. And if Owen had known, which he obviously had, why had he let Simon live the life he had? Why did he get to be poor when Jack got to be rich and have everything he wanted?

And then there was the test result.

It had all seemed so simple a few days ago. The perfect plan, as long as they could get away with it, and they had. The woman at the hospital hadn't even batted an eye when Jack said he was Simon, when he answered the questions about name and date of birth and let her swab the inside of his mouth.

Slowly, Simon sat up. The floor was cold under his feet. They'd taken the laces from his tennis shoes, leaving them loose and uncomfortable, so he'd kicked them off and they lay over by the wall, two pristine white shapes. They weren't really his, though. They were Jack's.

Just like that goddamn positive test result.

He sat with that thought for several minutes, letting it settle in, then he began to rewind back through his life with his cousin with that knowledge guiding him. It was like taking a step to the left and looking at everything again. All of it had been a trick. All of it. Jack had been the magician with a card up his sleeve and a trapdoor beneath his feet. Smoke and mirrors, Simon thought to himself. The fucking emperor is naked.

But how? Jack couldn't have done it himself. His official test said he was negative, always had. Simon had seen the app on his phone, the one that let Jack into all the places that Simon was not allowed to enter. And other people must have seen it, too, and believed it, because otherwise Jack wouldn't be at that fancy school with girls like Ginny.

Start at the beginning. Could Jack's test have been wrong? No. He didn't believe that. The tests were incredibly accurate, two swabs taken each time and both tested separately to avoid false negatives, and Owen was a doctor. He would have made sure that it was done properly.

But somehow it had been screwed with.

Owen was a doctor.

Who owned a clinic for M+ boys.

Who was his dad, not just Jack's.

Simon put his head in his hands and silently howled.

Now he knew why he and Jack looked so much alike. They were basically brothers. It was like that stupid story, *The Prince and the Pauper.* Or *The Man in the Iron Mask.* One gets an amazing life; one gets an awful life. It was funny how in those stories the rich, spoiled boy always turned out to be rotten on the inside.

But surely if Jack was M+, there would have been signs.

Had there been signs?

Maybe.

Though if he thought about the boys he'd known from the farms, he would have to say no. Everyone knew that M+ boys couldn't control their aggression unless they were on a bucketload of medications. But Uncle Owen had a clinic that had a cupboard full of them. And then there was Aunt Antonia with her enthusiasm for supplements and vitamins.

Had Owen known? He'd have to say no to that, too. Owen had been just as shocked as he was when the test result came out positive, maybe even more so.

Which left only Antonia.

And then something else occurred to him.

Jack doesn't know, Simon realized. *He's M-positive and he doesn't even know. He's been lied to his whole life.* And more than that, Simon realized that meant that he himself was still an untested boy.

After all this, he still didn't know what the hell he was.

And that meant that there might be a way out of this.

His skin broke out in goose bumps. He shot to his feet, went to the door, and banged on it until the flap was opened and someone looked in. It was a different woman than the one who'd been there earlier, this one bony with a face that had the texture of a leather sofa. "What?"

"I want to see my mom."

She raised a sharply drawn eyebrow.

"Please," Simon said. "I need to talk to her." He ran a hand over his head. "Or anyone. The man who interviewed me earlier. There's something he needs to know. Please?"

He held his breath, desperately hoping she'd listened. The flap was slammed shut, and he heard her walk away. He leaned forward, put his head against the cold metal, and wanted to punch something so bad. So he did. He curled his hand into a fist and hit the door as hard as he could.

Pain sang through every single bone in his fingers and up into his arm. He staggered back to the bed and sat down, cradling his wrist in his other hand. And then he started to cry again. What else was there to do?

When the door opened a long while later and the policeman who'd interviewed him earlier looked in, Simon got slowly to his feet.

"What did you want to tell me?" the man asked.

"I need to see my mom first."

"All in good time."

The policeman stepped back, and Simon could tell he was about to close the door again. No. He couldn't stand it. He had to get out of here. "My cousin took the test for me," he blurted out. "Jack Talbot. We went to the hospital together, and he's the one they tested. Not me."

There. He'd said it. His chest was heaving as if he'd run a marathon, and he could see spots in front of his eyes. He fought for air.

"Is he, now?"

"Yes. The positive test is his, not mine. Please. You've got to believe me."

He could hear himself begging, could see the look of disbelief on the officer's face and realized that the man had heard this story before, probably more than once, and was no more likely to believe it than he was to believe in the existence of the tooth fairy.

The door was slammed shut. Simon was left alone again. The room swam. He sat. He paced. He sat on the floor and put his feet up against the wall. He drummed his fingers against his thigh, finding a good rhythm. He thought about everything and nothing.

The door opened again and a female officer looked in. Simon shot to his feet. "I want my lawyer," he said. It was the only thing he'd been able to think of other than asking for Bea, who obviously wasn't coming, or Owen, who he wasn't sure he ever wanted to see again. The officer closed the door without saying anything.

His mom had always told him not to get tested.

He wished that he'd listened.

And then, when all sense of time had finally left him, when it could have been an hour later or just as easily the middle of the night, the door was opened again, and the policeman stuck his head in. "Come on," he said.

Simon was taken back to the interview room, the same one as before, with the gray walls and the table that was bolted to the floor and the camera in the top corner. There was no sign of Owen. Instead, his mother was sitting at the table. He couldn't decide if that was better or worse. She didn't look up when he walked in. He was directed to the empty chair next to her, and he sat in it.

He bit his lip and tried to hold himself together. It got easier when Bea reached out under the table and took his hand. The woman attorney was there, too. She'd changed her jacket from red to black as if they were at a funeral.

"Where's Owen?" he asked quietly.

"Gone home," Bea told him.

"Is it true?"

She didn't ask him what he meant. "Yes," she said. She still didn't look at him. He wanted to know more. But somehow he realized it was pointless. He couldn't even convince himself that it mattered. It was just one more thing to add to the mess. He thought about Alfie and felt like a fool for missing him. Was that why Alfie had abandoned him? Because he'd known that Simon wasn't his?

Simon decided that he hated adults. They couldn't be trusted, any of them. He sank lower in his seat, his spine curving, and folded his arms. There were coffee stains on the tabletop. He wondered who had left them and where they were now, if they were from another boy faced with a test result that meant that it didn't matter what he said, everyone was going to think the worst.

"Present, D.C. Swann."

The woman attorney spoke up next. "Michelle Long, attorney for Simon Mitchell."

"Beatrice Victoria Mitchell, mother of Simon Mitchell."

There was a pause, a silence. Simon sighed. "Simon Mitchell," he said, reaching out to scratch at the coffee stain with his fingernail. Or should he have said Talbot?

The policeman said some other stuff, the date and time, which gave Simon a jolt. He'd been here for almost twenty-four hours. How could it have been that long?

"Right, Simon. We've already talked about the incident on the farm and Malcolm Sloan. Have you got anything else you'd like to tell me about that?"

Why hadn't he said anything about the test? Simon glanced across at Bea, desperate for her to give him some clue, some direction. But she didn't. And that was when he began to understand that he was on his own. If he was going to get out of this, he would have to do it himself.

"I told you my cousin took the test for me," Simon said. "Have you checked on that yet?" He sat back in his seat and held the officer's gaze, waiting for him to respond.

"I've asked one of my colleagues to look into it."

"And?"

The officer sighed. "You need to stop messing with me now, Simon," he said, his tone suddenly sharp. "Your cousin's test is negative. We checked the register. And quite frankly, I've had enough of your attitude. We know you're positive. We know you were at the farm where Malcolm Sloan was injured, and we've got plenty of witnesses who will confirm that you were the one he was fighting. So tell me the truth."

Simon flicked a glance at the door. He wanted nothing more than to flee. He'd done it before, and it had always gotten him out of trouble, hadn't it? He'd run from the farm and from the vacation in Cornwall and, if he was honest, from the house last night after Jack had caught him with Ginny.

But there was no running away from this.

All that was left was to tell the truth.

"Yes, it was me," he said. He sensed Bea stiffen in the seat next to him. But what could he do? He saw the attorney shake her head, although she didn't look at him. She took her glasses off and put them down on the desk, as if she didn't need them anymore, as if there were no point. "I'm the one who fought him."

And he'd do it again if he had to.

"Would you care to explain why?" the officer asked him.

Simon lifted his head and looked at him. "Why did I fight? Because I didn't have any money and I wanted to make a bit more. Because the trailer we were living in leaked, and it stank, and I wanted to move us to somewhere better. And because I was hungry all the time. Because my dad walked out on us when I was twelve, and there's been no one but me to look after my mom since then, except that he wasn't my dad, because my dad was there all along, sitting in his fancy house and ignoring both of us. Or are you asking why I fought Malcolm in particular?"

He could tell that he'd shocked the officer, and that prompted him to carry on.

"He threatened to kill my mother," Simon said. "I made sure he couldn't."

CHAPTER THIRTY-SIX

ANTONIA

Now

Antonia was in her bedroom. She hadn't moved since Owen had walked out. The scattered clothes and pills still lay where he'd thrown them.

He knew that she'd changed Jack's test. He *knew*.

Everything she'd worked for over the past seventeen years was falling apart. What if he told someone? What she'd done was illegal; she was more than aware of that. She got up and went to the window, half expecting to see police cars rushing down the street, sirens blaring, but it was just as empty and quiet and normal as always. She jerked the curtains closed and paced the room in the darkness.

Her phone rang.

When she saw that it was Jack, she answered it immediately.

"Hello, darling," she said, swallowing her fear, keeping her voice calm. "Where are you?"

"Is it true?" he asked.

"Is what true?"

"That I'm positive."

Antonia sank to the floor, her legs unable to hold her up. "What makes you think that?"

"Bea told me."

Of course she had. "Don't listen to her. She doesn't know what she's talking about."

"You're a liar," he said. "You're a fucking liar."

The phone beeped as he cut her off.

She remained where she was, motionless, trying to process what had just happened. Her skin felt too tight for her body. Her hands started to shake. Her baby boy knew that she had lied to him. She had to find him. Had to help him. He was her angel, her only son, and he was hurting. He needed her. She scrambled to her feet, tapping at her phone as she did so, dialing his number.

She listened to it ring as she ran downstairs, grabbing her bag and keys and shoving her feet into her tennis shoes. She didn't bother to fasten them. It went to voicemail.

She tapped into the app that would let her track Jack's phone, then got into her car and started to drive. Her heart was racing. If he was where his phone said he was . . .

It took almost thirty minutes to get there, the longest thirty minutes of Antonia's life. She drove into the parking lot and dumped the car in the middle, not caring who she blocked in, then ran through the trees and up the grass to the bridge. She thought she saw a flash of blue before she got there, the exact same color of the jacket that her son had been wearing when he'd left the house earlier. When he'd just been a teenage boy going to see the girl he liked after she'd given him a scare the night before, because she'd been stupid and he'd had to take care of her. A boy who'd just had his first proper taste of what it meant to be a man who understood how to take care of women.

When she saw him sitting on the wall, she burst into tears. She slowed to a walk. She was terrified that she would startle him. "Jack?" she called gently. "Come down, darling. It's all right. I'm here."

A train thundered along the track below them, and she had to wait for it to pass before she could say anything else. The air moved around her, and she could feel it sucking at her skin, and she knew that Jack would be able to feel it, too.

"How is it all right?" he shouted back.

She moved a little closer. She sensed that she would have to be careful. She knew M+ boys almost better than anyone. They had to be handled carefully. They were prone to explosive fits of temper, had trouble controlling their emotions. They often acted rashly for reasons they couldn't explain afterward. But Antonia knew how to manage them. Hadn't she spent the past decade figuring out exactly how to do that?

"It might seem terrible at the moment, but it isn't. The important thing is not to do anything you might regret."

He let out a sound a bit like a sob. "You told me I was negative. My whole life, I thought I was okay. That I was one of the good ones. Not like the other boys, the ones at the clinic. I didn't have to worry. But that's not true, is it?"

"Come down, Jackie," she said. "We can't sort this out with you up there and me down here."

"Sort it out? How the fuck are you going to sort it out, Mother? I'm positive! Aren't I? Go on. Admit it. Tell the truth for once."

"I need you to come down first."

"Tell me the truth!" he screamed at her.

Antonia winced. She could hear the faint rumble of another train in the distance and knew, suddenly, how important it was to get him down before this one arrived. Before someone noticed that he was up there and rang the police. Before Jack was put in a situation where he might say or do something that he couldn't take back.

"Yes," she said. "You're positive."

There was no point in lying. Not now that his father and Bea both knew the truth. And Simon would know it, too, wouldn't he? It wasn't something that Antonia could contain, no matter how much she might want to. This had been inevitable since the moment that Jack took the test for his cousin.

But she would still do whatever she could to fix this for Jack.

His shoulders slumped, and all the air seemed to leave him at once. Shudders wracked his body. Antonia reached up, grabbed the back of his jacket, and pulled. She expected him to resist, but in the end, he didn't. He let her pull him down, let her put her arms around him. She managed to get one of his arms across her shoulders, and she walked him back to her car, where she found herself facing an irate man who she had blocked in. Fortunately, he took one look at Jack and backed off.

Antonia folded Jack into the passenger seat. At least now that Jack was with her, he was safe. No harm could come to him while he was in her care. She wouldn't let it.

"Why did you do it?" he asked her. His voice was hoarse. His face, when she glanced across at him, was red and sore. She could smell the cologne he'd put on earlier when he'd gone to see Ginny, intermingled with the sour smell of fear. "Why did you let me think I was negative?"

"I did it for you," she told him. "Because I am your mother, and I love you, and I wanted you to have a good life."

"But you let me think I was negative!"

"I took care of you. I helped you manage it. You're just as good as a negative boy, Jack."

She didn't think this was the time to mention that she'd had him on a treatment program since the age of three. She'd explain that to him later when he was calm. It was important to make sure that he continued with it. He'd need it for the rest of his life, after all.

"I've never worried about anything I did," he continued. "I knew I was negative, so I knew I wasn't capable of doing anything bad. Even when I did bad stuff, I told myself it was fine."

"But you've never done anything bad," Antonia said, though even as she said the words, she knew it was a lie.

"Haven't I? What about the girl in Cornwall?"

And there it was. "That was Simon," she told him desperately.

Jack just shook his head. "No," he said. "Simon tried to help her."

Antonia gripped the wheel tightly. "You're wrong," she told him. "I was watching you through the binoculars, you see. And you're wrong." It was then that something occurred to her, something that could fix this whole mess. In fact, it was already fixed. And the more she thought about it, the more obvious it was. She reached out and patted Jack on the knee. "Simon did it," she told him again. "Just like he killed Malcolm. There's no getting away from that. So if you think about it, when you took the test for him, you actually did something amazing. You made sure that he'll be punished for it. You made sure that the world will see him for what he really is."

Unbelievable as it seemed, her son had finally given her what she'd always wanted.

A positive test result for her nephew.

CHAPTER THIRTY-SEVEN

BEA

Now

Malcolm's funeral was held two weeks after Simon was arrested. It was the longest two weeks of Bea's life. Simon had been taken to a prison twenty miles away. Bea had thought she wouldn't be able to see him, but Owen had come to her rescue and given her a car. When he'd turned up at the house with it, she had almost cried with gratitude, even though it was so little in the grand scheme of things. She'd let him get away with giving Simon nothing for far too long. That had been her mistake, and she would have to live with it.

Nevertheless, she was sorry for the part she had played in this whole sorry mess, and she told him so. She'd never intended for any of this to happen. When she'd come back here, she'd been looking for a way out. For help. Antonia had always been able to fix things for her in the past. Whenever it had gone wrong, anything from a skinned knee to a tin of peaches she couldn't open to math homework that seemed impossible, her sister had stepped up to take care of it.

But no one could fix this—not for her, anyway.

She visited Simon every day for the first week, then every other day for the second. On her most recent visit, they'd hardly spoken. They had just sat opposite each other until their allotted time was up, and then she'd left. She'd managed to make it all the way outside before she'd started to cry. God, what a horrible mess it all was.

But she couldn't change it.

She got dressed in a black suit that she'd found in Antonia's closet, holding the pants together with a safety pin and leaving the blouse untucked to cover the fact that they were too small and wouldn't fasten. She stuffed her feet into a pair of her sister's heels, wobbled around the house for approximately five minutes, then took them off and put her tennis shoes on. If people didn't like it, that was their problem. If they didn't think she should be at Malcolm's funeral, that was their problem, too.

Owen had come to collect Jack and Antonia earlier that morning. Although Owen was still staying in a hotel in town, Bea was predicting a reunion in the not too distant future. After all, no one else knew that Jack wasn't really negative. As far as the rest of the world was concerned, Simon was the evil child, and Jack was still perfect.

But Bea could hardly stand to be in the same room as her nephew. She was still at Antonia's only because she was afraid to leave her sister alone with him. She told herself she was being stupid. He was the same boy she'd always known.

But he wasn't, was he?

Maybe the test did mean something after all.

Maybe that was too much for her to think about right now.

She asked herself why she was so afraid of him now, what had changed, and couldn't find an answer.

It wasn't like he'd actually done anything wrong.

Simon was the one who'd done that.

She got into her car and drove to the funeral home where Malcolm's service was being held, turning the radio up loud so that she wouldn't have to listen to her thoughts. It was with great reluctance that she got out of the car once she arrived.

She could see Paul and Lily at the top of the steps in front of the building, but it wasn't them she wanted to talk to. She'd never had much time for Paul, and although she was desperately sorry for what Simon had done, she couldn't help but think that perhaps some of this could have been avoided if Paul hadn't ditched his son at the earliest possible opportunity. It was a bit late for him to play the caring parent now.

She waited by the gates with her head down until they'd gone inside.

In the corner of the garden of remembrance next door, almost hidden by the high stone wall, she could just make out Zara. Bea approached her slowly. She didn't even know if Zara would want to see her. But there were things that she wanted to say.

Zara was wearing a black blazer, her hair pinned up messily on the back of her head, the streaks of gray even more obvious. Her face was makeup-free, and she held a cigarette that was leaking a steady stream of smoke, apparently forgotten about. She looked up as Bea walked over.

"Hello, Bea," she said. "I imagine you're having a shit day, too."

"That would be an understatement," Bea said. "How are you?"

"Honestly? I have no fucking idea. When I've figured it out, I'll let you know. How's Simon?"

"Eighteen and in prison," Bea said. "What happened to us, Zara?"

"M-positive boys happened to us."

Although Simon's test result was actually Jack's, Bea hadn't told anyone. She found herself increasingly unable to believe that it wasn't the right one. Hope had gone. She'd clung on to it for far too long anyway.

"Do you mind if we walk a little?" Zara asked. She pointed to the path that led to the rear of the funeral home, away from the entrance.

"Of course not," Bea said. "But I think it's about to start in a minute."

They walked slowly along the path, Zara leaning heavily on her cane. "Let them all sit in there and pretend they gave a damn about him while he was alive," she said. "I'll say my goodbyes later, in my own way. You know, it's a funny thing. Even after everything he did, everything he was, I still loved him. Isn't that strange?"

"I don't think so," Bea said. There was an old wooden bench nearby with a plaque on the rear and several bunches of flowers leaning against it. Zara hobbled over to it and sat down. Bea remained standing. "I think that's the burden we carry as mothers. We grow them inside us, and we know them in a way no one else does because of it. You know that old story about Eve, how she was punished with pain in childbirth because she made Adam eat the apple and destroyed his innocence?"

"I've heard it," Zara said.

"I don't think it's a punishment," Bea said. "I think it's a warning. It's nature's way of showing us just how much our children can hurt us, right from the beginning. I remember that Simon . . ."

She stopped.

"Bea, it's all right," Zara said gently. "You've lost your son, too. I know that. And I know that you're not responsible for what he did. I know what Malcolm was like. It could just as easily have been the other way around. You could be saying goodbye to Simon today, and I could be sitting here trying to make you feel better."

Bea's legs felt suddenly wobbly. She sat down beside Zara. For the past two weeks, visiting Simon as often as she had, she'd been able to push her feelings aside. It was easier to feel numb. "No one else even seems to have noticed he's gone. Not even Jack, and he adored Simon." She wanted to tell Zara more. She wanted to tell her all of it, about the test that Jack had taken, about everything. But she didn't know if she was ready for that. So far, it had been kept in the family. None of them seemed to know what to do with it.

"Ginny asked about him," Zara said.

"Ginny?"

"Paul's stepdaughter. She's called me a few times recently. Wanted to talk about Malcolm, I think, and was too afraid to ask Paul. She told me that Simon didn't seem the sort of boy who would do something awful."

Bea didn't know what to say to that. Because Simon was that sort of boy. And he had done awful things. "Is she here?" she asked.

"No," Zara said. "She told me she couldn't face it. She said she was sorry, and she knew she should be here, but she didn't want to be around other people right now. There was some sort of incident the night Malcolm died, apparently. She got drunk at a party and ended up in the ER. Jack took her. I think Paul and Lily are still giving her a hard time about it."

"I remember," Bea said.

That was the night Simon had gone missing, when she'd thought that his failure to come home was the worst thing that could happen, right up to the point when the police had knocked on the door and then arrested him.

Bea had to wonder what sort of relationship Ginny had with her own parents that she had felt the need to phone her father's ex-wife and apologize for her behavior, but then she remembered how Paul had treated Zara and suspected that she knew the answer.

"I think Jack has been pestering her, to be honest," Zara said.

"He has?"

"Yes. She said something about M-negative boys being able to do whatever they want, and there's no point complaining because no one will believe you."

An alarm bell began to ring quietly somewhere in the back of Bea's mind, but she barely heard it, because from inside the funeral home, the sound of music and voices could be heard. She recognized the song. It was one that she used to hum to Simon when he was tiny. Zara reached out and took her hand, and the two of them sat there in silence. Bea was surprised to find that she was crying.

Eventually, the music stopped. "I guess it's time to go," Zara said. She got hold of her cane and pushed herself into a standing position.

"I guess so," Bea said.

She didn't know if she would see Zara again. But she was glad that they'd been able to spend this time together. At the front of the building, they found the others waiting, a crowd in expensive black all pretending to mourn a boy who none of them had really cared about. It struck Bea then how much of this was for show. It wasn't real.

Not in the way that Zara's grief was.

Jack stood with Owen, talking to Paul and Lily and several other people who Bea didn't know but who she assumed to be more relatives. There was a preteen girl who reminded Bea of Malcolm somehow. He was there in the shape of her mouth, the color of her hair. She had to be Paul and Lily's younger daughter. There was no sign of Antonia. And as Zara had said, no sign of Ginny, either. Bea remembered a young girl with distinctive red hair, but there was no one here who matched that description.

Owen caught her eye, acknowledging her with a slight dip of his chin, but other than that, there was no sign that they knew each other or just how intimately. He had an arm around Jack's shoulders.

It was hard for Bea to witness.

But she forced herself to look, even as the unfairness of it cut her to the bone.

She could no longer deny the truth. Antonia had been right.

She should have had Simon tested years ago.

Jack had been, and Antonia was able to manage his behavior as a result. She'd been able to give him every possible opportunity, even the benefit of a negative test. Antonia wasn't the one who had failed as a mother.

Bea was.

CHAPTER THIRTY-EIGHT

ANTONIA

Now

Antonia drove away from the funeral home, one hand on the steering wheel, one hand fiddling with the pin that held her hat in place. She finally managed to work it free and tossed it and the hat onto the passenger seat.

She'd told Owen that she didn't feel well and wanted to go home. He'd offered to drive her, but she'd said no, that it was important for him to stay and support Paul and Lily. They needed to put on a united front. Life would go on after this day, as would the clinic, and they had to do what was necessary to protect that. He hadn't argued.

She wasn't sure yet if their marriage would survive, but so far, the signs looked good. He was at least talking to her, and although he hadn't moved back into the house, she suspected that it wouldn't be long before he did. She missed him terribly. And she refused to believe that he would throw away their marriage over Jack's test. In time, he'd come to see that she'd done the right thing. After all, look at what had happened to Paul and Zara—Malcolm's positive test had ruined them.

And it had been the right thing for Jack, too. Although it had been hard for him to accept at first, he was beginning to come to terms with it. He was vigilant about taking his medication and made sure that she witnessed him swallowing the pills each morning. Antonia took that as a good sign. He was learning to manage his condition. He wanted to manage it.

There was just one problem that still remained.

Ginny.

Antonia had been hoping that she'd come to the funeral. She'd been disappointed and surprised when there was no sign of her and had said so to Lily.

"She's being awful at the moment," Lily had replied. "Honestly, Antonia, we just don't know what to do with her. But ever since that night when she ended up in the hospital, it's like she's become a different person. She's rude, selfish, unhelpful. Jack came to see her the other day, and she refused to come out of her bedroom. Can you believe that? After everything he did for her. Paul had a few things to say to her after that, I can tell you."

Antonia could well imagine. Paul wasn't one to mince words.

"I just don't understand it," Lily had continued. "I thought she liked Jack. But I found packaging for the morning-after pill buried in her bathroom bin. She was so drunk, maybe something happened between them and she couldn't remember."

Some other members of Lily's family had arrived then, and Lily had gone to talk to them, leaving Antonia alone with her thoughts. She had spent several minutes looking at the flowers, making sure that the wreath she had ordered had been delivered. Yes, there it was. Ivy and white roses. Quite lovely, really, far too good for a boy like Malcolm. In fact, all of this was too good for Malcolm. As far as Antonia was concerned, he was a thug and an arsonist, and his was not a life to be celebrated.

Some boys could not be saved.

And others . . .

Her gaze had fallen on Jack, who was sitting with his father, their dark heads close together. At some point, she and Owen would have to talk about the fact that Jack and his cousin were so very similar and that Owen had gone rushing to Simon's side when he'd been arrested. But not yet. Not today.

Today, she had other concerns.

And now here she was outside Paul and Lily's house. It was a frilly Victorian estate, complete with a turret far too dark and dusty for her taste, though a perfect match for Lily, who seemed to imagine herself as some sort of romantic heroine from a gothic novel half the time, solely responsible for rescuing Paul from the mad wife.

She parked in the shade of a tall privet hedge, marched up to the front door, and rang the bell. She had to ring it twice more before she finally got an answer, pinning a cautious smile in place when she heard the lock turn.

"Hello," Ginny said, holding the door open a few inches.

Her hair hung lank and unwashed around her face. "My parents aren't here. They've gone to the funeral."

"I know," Antonia said. "Actually, it's you I wanted to see. Your mom said you aren't feeling well, and I wanted to make sure that you're all right. Is it okay if I come in?"

She saw Ginny hesitate, and she put a hand against the door, taking a step closer to make sure that she didn't close it.

"I suppose so," Ginny said, though her reluctance was obvious. She stepped back out of the way, opening the door wider, and Antonia moved quickly.

The entrance was decorated with dried teasels and old black-and-white photographs in ornate frames. A tall grandfather clock stood to one side. Antonia saw none of that.

"I'll put the kettle on," Ginny said, shuffling off toward the rear of the house. Her jeans were too long and dragged on the floor. She was wearing an enormous cardigan even though it wasn't particularly cold. Antonia couldn't help but wonder where she'd gotten it from.

The kitchen, in keeping with the rest of the house, had brass taps and a huge sink and stove. Ginny moved around it easily. Antonia stood and watched her. Now that she was here, she wasn't sure how to start the conversation.

How did you ask a girl if she thought your son had raped her?

Because that was what it came down to, really. The truth was what people believed it to be. The world believed Jack to be a good boy, an M— boy, and so that was what they saw. All his behavior was filtered through that lens. No one ever questioned it.

Just like Bea hadn't questioned it that awful night in Cornwall when Antonia had told her that she'd seen Simon pull the girl from the water, hitting her head against the rock in the process. What she'd neglected to mention was what she'd witnessed in the minutes leading up to it. Bea had never asked about that. There had been no reason to.

But this girl who stood in front of her—twitching around this ridiculous kitchen with her unwashed hair and trembling hands—made Antonia feel afraid. "Ginny," she said, "I know this is probably not the right time to ask this, but there's something that's been bothering me. It's about the night you ended up in the hospital."

Ginny went as still as a statue. The water overflowed from the kettle, and she just stood there, doing nothing to stop it. Antonia stepped forward, took it out of her hand, and turned the water off. She took hold of Ginny's chin and turned her head, forcing the girl to look at her, nails digging deep into the flesh. "What happened?" she asked again, sharply this time.

Ginny didn't answer. She didn't have to. It was obvious.

What Antonia didn't know yet was what she was going to do about it.

But she would do anything to protect her son.

CHAPTER THIRTY-NINE

||| BEA

Now

It was difficult for Bea to break the news of Ginny's death to Simon. She wasn't even sure she should do it. Perhaps it would be better if he didn't know. But she'd had enough of secrets. It was impossible to keep them. And they only did harm in the end.

She drove to the prison that morning with a heavy heart. Owen had moved back in after the funeral, and not long after that, Bea had found herself on Zara's doorstep. It was impossible for her to be in the house with Owen, to see him with Jack.

Zara had opened the door, looked her up and down, and let her in.

They hadn't known about Ginny until the next day.

"Suicide," Zara had said. "Killed herself while everyone was at the funeral. Dear god. That poor girl."

Bea hadn't known what to say. She hadn't known how to

process it. It seemed that no one had seen it coming. No one had known just how much pain Ginny was in or why.

"I don't understand," Simon said when she told him. She'd said it quickly, plainly, not knowing any other way. "Why would she do that?"

"I don't know," Bea said. "She was having a difficult time. Maybe it all got to be too much for her."

"No," he said fiercely, shaking his head. "She wasn't like that."

"Simon, you have no idea what she was like. You didn't know her."

"Yes, I did," he said. All of a sudden, he was more alive than she'd seen him in weeks—since he'd been brought here, in fact. "She was there when I went out with the dog in the mornings, and we talked. She was nice. And I know for a fact that she would never do anything like that. She had all this stuff she wanted to do, athletics and stuff. And she was happy. She was fun. When I went to that music thing . . ."

He stopped then, as if he realized that he'd said too much, and his face went red. He seemed to shrink back in his seat.

"What about the music thing?"

He picked at his nails.

"Simon," she said. "Spit it out."

"She was happy," he said again. "She told me she was glad I was there, that she'd been hoping to see me, and I know I was drunk, Mom, and she was, too, but we didn't do anything she didn't want to do. I swear we didn't. Then

Jack came in and caught us, and he was so pissed off, and he was screaming at her."

"Then what happened?"

"I don't really know," Simon answered, angling his head and looking at her nervously. He swallowed. "I kind of . . . I left her alone with him."

"Oh, Simon," Bea said gently. She wanted to reach out and hug him. A man in a man's prison but still a child in every way. How had it come to this?

"The thing is," he continued, "I keep thinking about stuff. Old stuff. From when we were kids. Things he did that I always shrugged off because I thought he was negative."

Bea could hear a sudden low buzzing in her ears. She felt pinned in her chair, unable to move. Her hands were cold and her palms were clammy. Because she'd been having similar thoughts. Flashes of memory in the shower as she lay on Zara's sofa in the middle of the night, as she combed her hair. All the times that she'd given Jack the benefit of the doubt or let Simon take the blame when it was obvious now that she shouldn't have.

All the times she had let her son down.

"Do you remember when we went on vacation?" he asked. He leaned forward, his voice lowered to a whisper. "The . . . the girl in the rock pool?"

She forced herself to answer. "Yes."

"I thought I did it," he said. "I pulled her out of the water, and I did it wrong, I must have, because she hit her head on the rock, and I always thought . . . I thought . . ." He paused, then seemed to gather himself. "Jack was in the water with her, Mom. He kept pushing her under, and she kept telling him not to, but he said he was only playing, and then he pushed her under and held her down there for ages, and when she came up, she wasn't talking or anything, and that's when I pulled her out."

"But Antonia saw what happened," Bea heard herself say. "She saw the whole thing."

It was like one of those coloring books she'd had as a child, where each page was covered in interlocking shapes, and you filled in the ones with a dot in them with a felt-tip pen, and you'd see the image that had been hiding there all along. She saw it now inked in bright shades of red, like blood on a rock, like Ginny Sloan's hair, like the agony of childbirth and the joy that followed it.

Antonia changing Jack's test result. Watching him drown a girl in a rock pool.

Missing from the funeral.

She saw what her sister had done, and she knew why.

But she had no way to prove any of it.

Bea had once thought that the day Simon had been born had been the most difficult day of her life. Now she knew she was wrong. None of that came even close to what lay ahead. Simon's case had finally come to court. What happened to him next was going to be decided by the people inside the building on the other side of the road.

She stood watching the traffic rather than the door, let-

ting the movement of the cars lull her mind into silence. She
had barely slept the night before. She straightened up as Simon's lawyer approached, her gait stiff due to her high-
heeled shoes. The woman's jacket was bright blue today
with gold buttons down the front (which struck Bea as unnecessarily gaudy in the circumstances). She didn't smile but
acknowledged Bea with a brisk nod of her head. She pulled
her papers along behind her in a wheeled black briefcase.

"Good morning," she said. "Are you all set for today?"

"I guess so," Bea said.

"It's important that he sees you there. He needs to know
he has your support. The next few days are going to be very
difficult. But we'll discuss all that before we go in. I've re-
quested a private room where we can talk."

"I've been visiting him regularly," Bea said. "He knows
that I'm on his side."

"And his father?"

"Things are a little bit complicated there, I'm afraid."

Owen was paying the bill for all of this, acting like Simon's
father for the first time in his life, but refused to do more
than that. Bea couldn't help but wonder what could have
been achieved had Owen decided to help Simon sooner, but
she knew that there was no point in going down that road.
The past couldn't be changed. Owen's decision to ignore Simon and her decision to let him were mistakes they both had
to live with.

And hard as it was for her to believe, he'd gone back to
her sister and Jack, and the three of them were playing
happy family, carrying on like nothing had changed.

But it had.

She followed the lawyer inside, waited as she talked to the woman at the desk, then walked with her along a narrow corridor with a linoleum floor and windows that looked like they hadn't been opened in years. The lawyer took her to a cramped little room with a table and four chairs and closed the door behind them.

Bea waited patiently as the lawyer opened her bag of papers and withdrew a fat folder with a blue cover. *Simon Mitchell* was written on the outside in bold black letters.

"Can I have a look at this?" Bea asked, reaching for it. She opened it before the woman had chance to answer. There, on those printed pages, were all the details of her son's life from birth until now. She slowly looked through them all. She touched his photo, his dear, familiar face. The pain of missing him was like a physical wound. She wondered if Zara felt the same way about Malcolm.

In the end, she told the attorney everything she knew, everything she suspected. She wanted her son back. That took priority over everything else, even Antonia. She told the woman that her nephew was M+ and that her sister had somehow covered it up. That Antonia had been medicating him since he was tiny, possibly stealing drugs from the clinic to do so. That Jack had taken the test for Simon. She told her about the girl in Cornwall and about Ginny.

And she told her about Malcolm.

The attorney listened, the expression on her face unchanging. Bea was unable to read her. At the end, she took off her glasses, set them down on the desk in front of her, and rubbed her eyes. "As I see it," she said, "our only option is to ask for Simon to be tested again."

"Will the judge allow it?"

"Perhaps. There's no guarantee. If Owen would vouch for him, we might have a better chance, unfair as it is. Do you think he might be willing to do that?"

"I don't know," Bea said honestly. But there was only one way to find out. She checked her watch. She had a couple of hours before the hearing was due to start. If she was going to do this, she would have to move quickly. Owen would be at the clinic at this time, so if she was going to catch him, that was where she needed to go. "I'll see what I can do."

She didn't quite run out of the building, but she might as well have. Fortunately, her car was parked close by. She didn't bother with her seat belt and put her foot down to get through several lights that were probably red. She didn't care if she got caught. There was nothing they could do to her that was worse than what had already happened.

When she got to the clinic, she parked by the entrance and ran straight inside. She barely noticed the people in the waiting room. "Where's Owen?" she snapped at the woman who was sitting at the reception desk.

"Do you have an appointment?"

Bea didn't have time for that. She plowed straight on to the rear of the clinic, where she could see a door with Owen's name on it. She opened it and went in. Fortunately, he seemed to be between clients, because he was standing by the window, his phone pressed to his ear. "I'll have to call you back," he said.

Bea closed the door and stood in front of it with her arms folded. It was funny, she thought, how things changed and how they stayed the same. A little over eighteen years ago, Owen had come to her door wanting something from her. She had given him comfort, and he had given her Simon.

Circumstances had taken Simon away from her.

Now she wanted to know if this man would give him back.

"What do you want, Bea? I'm busy."

"I want you to help Simon."

He moved around his desk and sat down. "Help him how?"

"The attorney thinks that we may be able to have him tested again," she said. "There's a chance that we might be able to get him out of this mess. But we'll need to get the judge to agree, and she thinks we'll have a better chance if you vouch for him."

She could hear the faint murmur of voices coming from elsewhere in the clinic. She was aware of the movement of the leaves on the tree outside the window and the row of medical textbooks on the shelves by the door and Owen's framed certificates hanging in a neat line on the wall.

There had been a time when it would have intimidated her. When she'd have shrunk down in her seat, wanting to make herself smaller, painfully aware of her inferiority. Not anymore. She understood now what hid beneath the glossy facade of this place. She knew her sister's true motives for building it.

All of it had been for Jack.

"Well?" she asked. "I'm on the clock here, Owen. He's due in court in just over an hour."

He set his elbows on the desk, steepled his fingers together. "The thing is, Bea, that he did what he's been charged with. He beat Malcolm Sloan to death. Whether you feel that was deserved or not, whether you believe it was what Simon intended or not, he did do it."

"I'm aware of that," Bea said through gritted teeth.

"It also appears that he raped Ginny Sloan. And that, for me, is the line in the sand. The point of the test was to protect women. What Simon did to her that night was instrumental in her decision to take her own life. The autopsy showed that she had drugs in her system, a sedative we sometimes prescribe here at the clinic for boys who are having issues with sleep. We're assuming she got it from here. That shows planning. It wasn't some spur-of-the-moment thing. That's how much what Simon did affected her."

Bea could hear the blood swooshing loudly in her ears. The roof of her mouth had gone suddenly dry, and she gripped the armrests of the chair so tightly that her knuckles went white. "What was the name of the drug?"

He told her.

She closed her eyes. She couldn't look at him as she said what she had to say next. "Antonia had a box of that in her handbag, you know. When we went on that fucking awful vacation. I went in her bag to look for gum because Simon made me put garlic in the food, and she had all these boxes in there. I thought they were for her. They weren't, though. They were for Jack. Obviously. We know that now."

When she opened her eyes, she saw that he was watching her. Something had shifted in his gaze. "I don't think

Simon raped Ginny; I think Jack did," she said. "And I think that Antonia was so terrified that she'd tell someone that she went to Ginny's house when everyone was at the funeral and did something she shouldn't have."

"Stop talking, Bea," he said, his voice low and dangerous.

But she didn't. She'd been told to stop talking before, and she remembered what it meant. That you were getting a little too close to the truth. "And I think you know, don't you? How long has she been stealing from the clinic, Owen? How long have you been turning a blind eye? What made you decide to cover for Jack and throw Simon to the wolves?"

She wasn't expecting an answer.

He rubbed a hand over his face. "I thought when Simon said that he'd been tested that everything was going to be okay. That, finally, there was going to be an end to it. You see, I watched you parent him badly for years, and I never said anything. All those chances to have him tested, and you refused at every turn. I even gave Antonia a testing kit and told her we could do it discreetly; did you know that?"

"That was *you*?" None of this made any sense to Bea. She'd always had the impression that Owen wanted her to keep her distance just as much as she'd wanted to. Antonia was the one who had always talked about the test, who had pestered her to do it. Not Owen. He'd shown no interest at all from the moment she'd broken it off with him, which was the day she found out she was pregnant. "But you threatened to have him tested when I asked you for money."

"Because I didn't want my wife to find out that I'd cheated on her, and it was the only way I knew to get you to back off!" he said. He didn't shout, not quite, but it wasn't far off. He exhaled loudly, tipped his head back, and muttered something in the general direction of the ceiling. "You brought Simon up badly, Bea. You made him what he is. You gave him a hard and horrible life when you didn't have to. All you had to do was have him tested, and none of this would have happened."

"I don't understand," she said. "What are you trying to say, Owen?"

The answer, when it came, was too little, too late.

"I tested him," he said. "In the hospital, the day after he was born. I came in while you were asleep and took the swabs. I got someone I knew at the lab to run them without recording the result. He's negative. He could have had a good life, Bea, but you were so afraid that he was one of the boys who turns out to be dangerous that you took that away from him."

"So you'll vouch for him?"

"No," he said. "I won't. He needs to face the consequences of his actions. And so do you."

"What about Antonia? And Jack? What are the consequences for them?"

||| ANTONIA

Now

It had been less than a month since Bea and Simon had turned up on her doorstep, but it seemed much, much longer, and Antonia was exhausted. It was hardly surprising, really, given what she'd had to cope with. Her calm, ordered life had been turned upside down. And what she'd always feared had come to pass: Jack knew the truth about his test. And so did Owen. He knew she'd logged on to his computer that day she'd visited him at the hospital when Jack was a baby and changed his test result. Lying to Owen about the result had been a split-second decision. Figuring out how to fix the problem properly had taken significantly more work. It helped, of course, that Owen had always used the same password for everything, and that he'd left her alone in his office so that she could feed Jack without an audience. But there had still been several very anxious minutes as she logged on, searched for Jack's record, and worked out how to alter it.

But perhaps it was good that Owen finally knew the truth. The treatment was lifelong. It wasn't something that could be abandoned when a boy left home, particularly as it was now known that once medication was started, stopping it would lead to major spikes in violent behavior.

She'd seen that for herself with her son. The first time had been on that vacation in Cornwall. The change in routine and the lack of privacy had meant that he had missed a couple of doses. She'd thought that she'd gotten away with it—until that last night, when she'd watched him drown a teenage girl. But her protective instincts had kicked in, and she'd been able to manage the situation. It had been all too easy to convince her sister that Simon was to blame and get her to leave. After all, Simon knew what had really happened, even if he hadn't understood it at the time, and she wanted him as far away from Jack as possible.

So when Bea and Simon had shown up on her doorstep, the peace of the previous five years had been shattered in an instant. She'd had to think quickly. But it had all worked out in the end. Simon was in prison, where he belonged, where he couldn't harm Jack. And although both Bea and Owen now knew the truth about Jack, there was nothing Bea could do about it, and nothing Owen would do about it.

Ginny had been a problem, but Antonia had managed that situation, too. She was secretly quite proud of herself for it. It had been easier than she'd anticipated to slip Ginny the tablets and, when she'd become drowsy, to walk her upstairs, to help her strip to her underwear, and to slide her into the bath. She'd left the water running while she looked for a razor and removed the blade, and if her stomach had turned a little at what came next, it hadn't been anything she couldn't get past.

It was, she had told herself, something that Ginny was halfway to doing anyway. All Antonia had done was to make it painless and easy for her. If anything, she'd done the poor girl a favor. She obviously wasn't coping, and she couldn't go on as she was, letting herself slide, hiding herself away, unwashed and in ugly clothes.

It had made things difficult at the clinic, as Paul and Lily needed to take time to grieve, but that was only temporary, and Owen had already interviewed half a dozen pediatricians who were interested in making the move to private practice. He'd hired a new office manager, too.

So, all in all, things could have been a lot worse.

Even Jack seemed to be coping. Antonia waved as he came out of school and crossed the parking lot toward her. He gave her a small wave in return.

"How was school?" she asked him as he got into the car.

"It was fine, Mom," he said quietly. "It's just a bit weird, that's all, Ginny not being there."

"I know," she said. "It's strange for all of us. But it will get easier in time."

"I'll be glad when I've finished, though. I've had enough of this place now."

Antonia knew what he wasn't saying, too. Rumors had spread like wildfire at the school about Simon and about Ginny, and her son had been tainted by them. The other boys were wary of him now, and the girls wouldn't talk to him. "You'll be through with your exams soon enough, and then you'll be off to college," she reminded him. "It'll be a fresh start. And no one there will need to know anything about any of this."

They sat in silence the rest of the way. Jack leaned his head against the window. He looked tired. Perhaps he needed some adjustment to his medication. That was easy enough to do. They had a new drug at the clinic that promised fewer side effects and better sleep. She hadn't tried it on him yet. Perhaps it was time.

She was distracted as she drove along their street and narrowly missed the neighbor's silver tabby cat as a result. She turned into their drive and slammed on the brakes, also narrowly missing an unexpected car parked very much in the way.

"What are the police doing here?" Jack asked, suddenly alert.

"I don't know," Antonia said, but her heart was pounding. "Let's go and find out, shall we?"

She unfastened her seat belt and got out. The door opened as she walked up to it. It was Owen.

"What's going on?" she asked him. "Why are you here? You're supposed to be at the clinic until five. Has something happened?"

He stepped down onto the porch. Two men followed him, huge and in uniforms.

"Owen?"

"They're here to talk to you about the drugs that have gone missing from the clinic, Antonia."

His tone was clipped and cold. "The new office manager

has been going through the records for the past fifteen years, and it seems that we've ordered far more medications than we've prescribed or disposed of. He wondered where they could have possibly gone."

She took a step back. "It's not unusual for things to go astray," she said. "Anyway, Lily was the one who did the original records."

"With your assistance, as I recall," Owen replied.

One of the policeman inched forward, and Antonia saw the keen look in his eye. She turned on her heel and ran back to her car. She reversed out onto the road at speed, and then she sat there, one hand gripping the wheel, the other on the gearshift, staring into the distance. The temptation to put her foot down and go was almost overwhelming. She could do it.

It would be so easy to leave it all behind.

Someone moved in front of the car. It was Jack. He stared at her through the windshield. Her son. Her lovely son.

Her dangerous M+ son.

She had spent seventeen years trying to protect him. And she'd succeeded, hadn't she? Even though the cost had been so very, very high. As she looked at him, at his dear, familiar face, she tried to tell herself that it had been worth it.

And found that she was no longer certain of that.

She tried to tell herself she didn't need to be afraid of him, either.

But she was. Not just of the things that he had done but

of the things that she had done for him. She could never outrun them. They would always be with her. It didn't matter that she'd been clever, that no one could prove it, that no one suspected. She would always know that she'd not really carried out CPR on the girl in Cornwall, that she'd led Ginny upstairs. She didn't regret those things. They were choices she'd made to protect Jack, to make sure that neither of the girls could tell anyone what had really happened.

But if she stayed here with him, how long until he figured it out and turned that temper on her? She'd stopped believing that she could control him with love a long time ago. She'd tried to manage him with medication, and that hadn't worked. She'd bought herself a protection dog, trained to obey commands that only she knew, but that no longer seemed like enough, and she wasn't sure she could order Flash to defend her from Jack, if it came to that.

When Owen opened the door, she got quietly out of the car and let them take her away.

All Bea had ever wanted was to protect her son. That was it. To do her job as a mother and do it well. She loved him so much. He had been precious to her from the moment of conception. She had felt it happen, that unexpected flash of biological magic inside her body, had secretly known he was there long before any test had confirmed it. The first time she had held him in her arms, she had promised she would always take care of him. She would never let anyone hurt him. She would keep him safe from the world, a world that hated boys, that tested them at birth and punished them for crimes they might never even commit.

But she had failed.

It seemed inevitable in hindsight. She had always been fighting a battle she was one day destined to lose. Because when she'd refused to have him tested, she'd left herself with doubt. He'd once told her that she always thought the worst of him, and he'd been right. She'd constantly looked for signs that he was M+. And because she'd looked, she'd seen them.

Had been persuaded to see them. Even when they weren't there.

She couldn't help but wonder what her sister had seen when she'd looked at Jack, the M+ boy who thought he was harmless. It was several weeks since she'd last seen Antonia. A lot had happened since them. Things that Bea would never have predicted and still found hard to believe.

Antonia had been arrested for stealing drugs from the clinic. Apparently, the new office manager had noticed some discrepancies. A lot of discrepancies, actually—enough to have him asking some difficult questions. And that had led to other questions about the drugs that Ginny Sloan had taken before she died and how she'd gotten ahold of them.

It would be close to ten years before Antonia left prison.

"Why did you do it?" Bea asked her now. They were separated by the breadth of the table and a sheet of Perspex made cloudy by too much cleaning, and it seemed like she was seeing her through water.

"I didn't have a choice," Antonia said quietly. Her voice, once so sure, took up hardly any room. She'd faded over the past few weeks. Her once-perfect hair showed several inches of dark roots and hung almost to her shoulders. Her nails were unpainted, and she wore baggy sweatpants and a matching sweatshirt. The jewelry was all gone. Even her wedding ring.

"Of course you had a choice!" Bea told her.

"Like the choice you made, you mean?" Antonia asked. "Putting your own son in prison?" She shook her head, and lank strands of hair swung lifelessly around her cheeks. The weight she'd lost made her cheeks sink back into her skull, and when she shifted in her seat, she seemed entirely concave, as if her body were folding in on itself.

"At least I'm honest with myself about what my son is."

For the first time, Antonia looked at her properly. A ghost of a smile played across her mouth. "What you made him into, you mean."

"I'm not the one who tried to hide from the truth, who pretended that it didn't matter."

"Aren't you?"

"No, I'm not. That's why you're in here and I'm not."

"Maybe you should be." Antonia leaned forward, her nose almost pressing against the screen. "You lied to Alfie, let him think he was Simon's father when he wasn't. You ran when you thought Simon killed that girl in Cornwall rather than stay and let him face the consequences. And you ran from the farm after he got into that fight with Malcolm."

"I didn't run," Bea said tightly.

"Yes, you did! You came straight to me, like you always do, expecting me to sort out your mess." She laughed, which turned rapidly into a deep hacking cough. "It's almost funny if you think about it. Simon persuaded Jack to take the test for him, and they did it right under your nose, and you didn't suspect a thing."

It surprised Bea that, even now, Antonia still couldn't see it. She still hadn't worked it out. "Where do you think Simon got the idea from in the first place?" Bea asked her.

"What?"

"I'm the one who suggested that all Simon's problems could be solved if he got someone negative to take the test for him."

Antonia stared back at her in stunned silence. Bea could almost see her mind working as she unraveled the events of the past few weeks, everything that had led them here, to this. All of it starting from that one casual comment, said to her son late at night. She didn't even know if she'd been serious at the time. But the seed had been planted.

And Simon, smart boy that he was, had done the rest.

She intended, when the time was right, to push for him to be retested. Zara had offered to support her with her request, and the attorney felt it would be enough to have the request granted. But not yet. He had killed Malcolm. And if Bea had learned anything over the past few weeks, it was that the worst thing you could do for a boy was to let violence go unpunished. At some point, her son was going to reenter society as a negative boy with all the benefits and privileges that entailed. But she didn't want him to think that he was entitled to them.

She wanted him to understand that being negative didn't mean he was perfect. It didn't mean that he could do whatever he felt like and get away with it. He needed to understand that sometimes the world forced darkness out of people anyway.

"So you're right, Antonia. I lied to protect my son. But so did you. You let everyone think that Jack was perfect when he's far from it, isn't he?"

"It's not his fault. He can't help what he is. You've got no idea what I gave up for him, Bea."

JAYNE COWIE

"You didn't give up anything. You sat there in your big fancy house with your doctor husband and gave your son things he had no right to. I'm the one who sacrificed, Antonia. Who did crappy jobs so I could support my son, who . . ."

She stopped herself just in time. She didn't want to talk about Owen. Not here. Perhaps not ever. There were some things that didn't need to be said out loud.

Antonia sat back, folded her arms, and laughed. "You think you understand sacrifice? You don't." She jabbed herself in the chest. "This is what sacrifice looks like, Bea. This is what it means to love your child, to do anything for them. I'm in here for Jack! To make sure that he gets to live the life he deserves. As far as everyone is concerned, I'm the nutty mother who was self-medicating with drugs stolen from her husband's clinic, who lost it and killed the girl who rejected her precious only son. But you? As soon as it got tough, you walked away. You've left Simon to rot."

Bea got to her feet slowly. "Do you really think this is easy for me, Antonia? Because it's not. And I'll tell you something else. Sometimes sacrifice means letting your children face the consequences of their actions, even when it destroys you to do it." She walked quickly to the door. But just before she got there, she turned.

"You know, I never believed in the test," she said. "I thought we should let boys show us who they are before we judge them. But I judged Simon anyway. I assumed he was bad—I let you convince me of it—and when he found himself in a difficult situation, he behaved exactly how I'd taught him to. That was my mistake. But if I've learned anything over the past few weeks, it's that the test is important. It does matter. Positive boys are more dangerous than negative ones. And there's an M-positive boy out there with a negative test result, and it would be wrong of me not to do something about that, wouldn't it?"

ACKNOWLEDGMENTS

It seems a long time since I started writing this book, but at the same time, it feels like it was only yesterday. I'd like to thank first of all my editors at Berkley and Century, Jen Monroe and Katie Loughnane, for all their help and support. This book was a collaborative effort, right from pitch to finished product, and it wouldn't have been possible without your amazing editing skills and patience.

My agents, Allison Hellegers and Ella Diamond Kahn; Alli, for all the great work you've done for me in the US, and for your support with this book. Ella, for all the unseen work you do, for handling bad news so I don't have to, and for your intelligent and sensible advice.

My family. My husband, who still thinks being a writer is a good career choice despite all evidence to the contrary. My daughter, a young woman on the cusp of adult life, both smart and beautiful, born prematurely, now taller than me. And my son. You made your entrance exactly as planned, in our living room, on your due date, and I am lucky to be your mother.

I'd like to not thank COVID, which I caught in the summer of 2022 while on a deadline. You were not helpful, and I hope we never meet again.

And finally, everyone else who has worked on *One of the Boys*—the copy editors and publicists, the marketing team and cover designer—your input is invaluable and much appreciated.

ONE OF THE BOYS

JAYNE COWIE

Discussion Questions

———————

Behind the Book

———————

On My Bedside Table

———————

READERS GUIDE

DISCUSSION QUESTIONS

1. It's quickly accepted that the way to manage boys who test positive for the M gene is to medicate them. Do you think that this is an acceptable thing to do to a young boy?

2. When Bea first opts not to have Simon tested, she's in a very vulnerable place, having just given birth. Does society place too much pressure on women in this situation to make decisions about their children that may have lifelong repercussions? Is it the right time to test?

3. When Antonia first posts about Jack's test result on her blog, she faces some unexpected backlash and is accused of wanting a designer baby. Is this a fair comment?

4. The three boys in the book are treated very differently by their parents and the world around them. How much difference do you think parenting makes? Are violent men born, or are they made?

5. Antonia and Owen both support the test; however, they also benefit from it financially. To what extent do you think this influences their belief in testing? They claim to want to help boys and their families, but is this really their main motivation?

6. Despite the treatments on offer, boys who test positive are quickly marginalized, pushed out of playdates, preschools, and, later on, public spaces and workplaces. Is this an inevitable consequence of this sort of testing, and is it justified?

7. Should girls be tested, or is it fair to test only boys, given that men commit the overwhelming majority of murders, violent assaults, and sexual assaults, and make up the majority of the prison population?

8. Should Owen have told Bea that he'd tested Simon? What difference would it have made if he had? Or was Bea right when she decided to parent Simon with no preconceptions?

9. Although the origin of the M gene isn't explored within the book, Zara is held accountable for Malcolm's M+ status and for his behavior. Do you think it's likely that mothers would be blamed in this way?

10. Would you have your son tested?

This book was definitely a difficult second album. Where do you go next, after you've written a story about a curfew for men as a possible solution to male violence? The answer, in the end, was to go there again, but instead of writing about romantic relationships, to write about mothers and sons. All violent men start life as newborn baby boys, vulnerable and clueless. They've all got tiny feet and hands and sweet button noses. Just like all babies, they cry when they're hungry, they're comforted by the sound of their mother's voice and the smell of her skin, they can't tell the difference between night and day, and they wet themselves.

But at some stage they become something different. They become men who frighten and inflict injury, often on their wives and daughters—men who manipulate and control. But why? What makes these men different? Is it something in their environment, in the way they're brought up and the way the world has treated them, or is it something actually inside them? Are they, for want of a better expression, born this way?

Since Rosalind Franklin took the first X-ray of human DNA in the early 1950s, we've been fascinated by the idea that not just what but who we are is embedded in the nuclei of our cells. The idea that behavior also has a genetic component has been widely accepted by the public and used to explain everything from intelligence to artistic creativity to personality. We've got some evidence from twin studies (identical twins separated at birth are often found to be very similar despite their different upbringings), but we've barely even scratched the surface when it comes to identifying specific genes that control any of these things, and it's likely to be very complicated, involving not just one gene but several, working together in many different ways. (That's not to say that we won't have the answers at some point in the future. But it is worth bearing in mind that a theory isn't evidence, no matter how much sense it makes or how useful we find it, and as you've seen in the book, our genetics can be used against us, too. The slide into eugenics is far easier than we like to imagine.)

We blame our genes because it suits us. Doing so takes away responsibility. If it's something inside you, something you can't do anything about, then it's not your fault. No one can criticize you for it. I think this is one of the reasons we like the idea so much. But genetics aren't everything. Mozart wouldn't have become a world-class composer if he hadn't been given a piano and encouraged to play it. Usain Bolt wouldn't have become the fastest human on the planet if he'd spent all his time sitting on the sofa, eating ice cream and watching soap operas. Our environment is important, too.

The three boys in the book—Simon, Jack, and Malcolm—have very different upbringings, and their lives diverge down very different paths as a result. Their parents have their own beliefs and agendas, which they stamp onto their sons as indelibly as if they were part of their DNA. Take Jack, for example, who was given the best of everything, told that he deserved all of it and more. Or Malcolm, written off at birth and treated as less than as a result. Would he have been the same person if he'd been given the chance to decide for himself who he was?

And then there's Simon. I have to wonder how his life would have turned out if he'd had Jack's opportunities. Would he, too, have become spoiled and entitled? Or, with his fundamentally different nature, would he have fulfilled his promise and become a good man?

Although I don't believe that biology is destiny, I don't think that we are born as the tabula rasa—the blank slate—either. We come into the world with certain genetic predispositions, inherited from our parents and their parents, and all the generations prior to that.

How we nurture that nature—how we raise our children, what we show them of the world, and what we teach them about their place in it—matters.

Jayne Cowie

ON MY BEDSIDE TABLE

A Dark-Adapted Eye by Barbara Vine

The Wild Silence by Raynor Winn

Targeted by Brittany Kaiser

The Thorn Birds by Colleen McCullough

Verity by Colleen Hoover

Dopesick by Beth Macy

Photo © Derek George

An avid reader and lifelong writer, **Jayne Cowie** also enjoys digging in her garden and making an excellent devil's food cake. She lives near London with her family.

Ready to find
your next great read?

Let us help.

Visit prh.com/nextread